I0766950

ELVERIAN

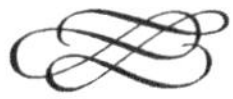

KAYDRIE TOLBERT

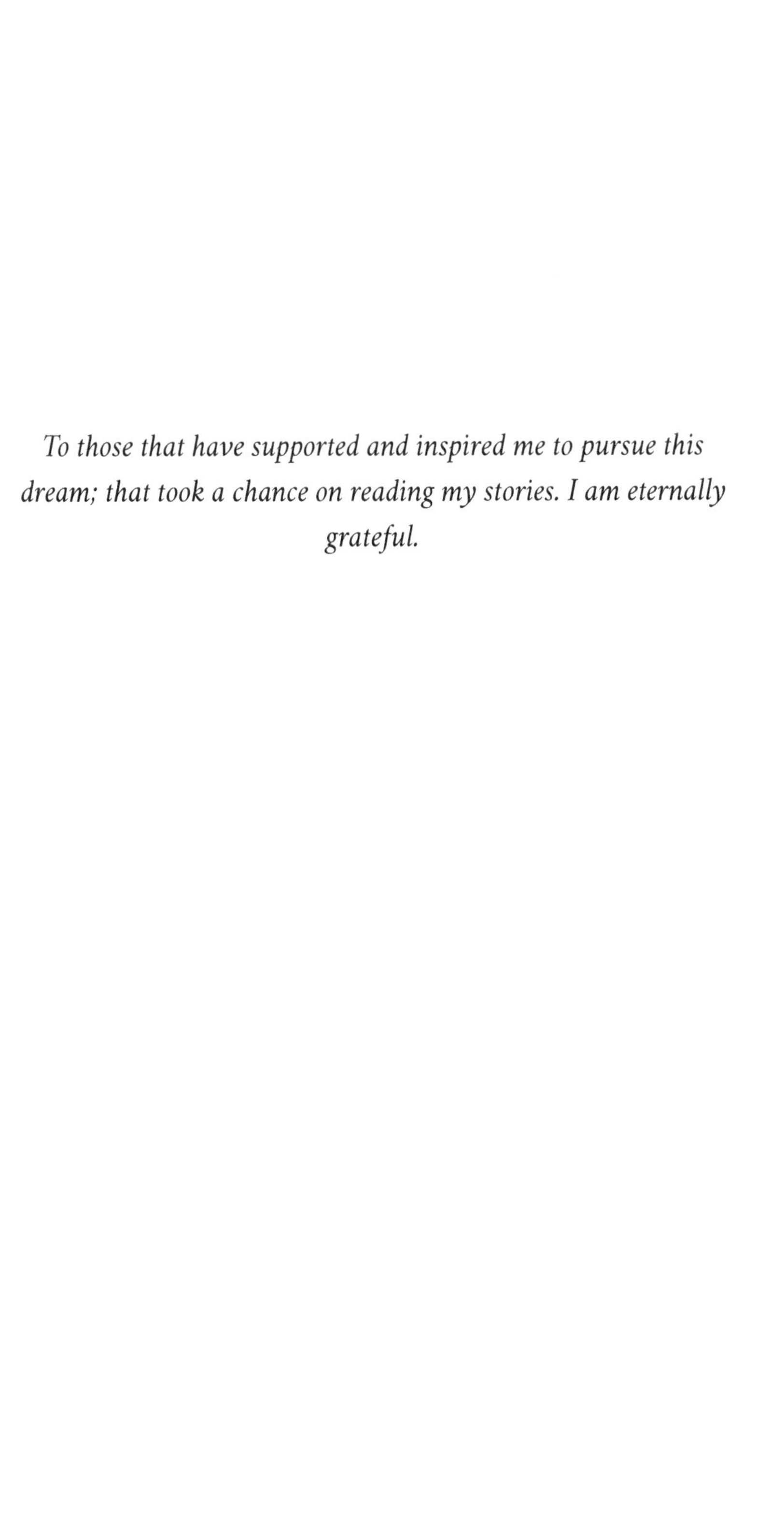

To those that have supported and inspired me to pursue this dream; that took a chance on reading my stories. I am eternally grateful.

Kaydrie Tolbert Books
ISBN: 978-1-7350974-6-6 Elverian Hardback
ISBN: 978-1-7350974-7-3 Elverian Paperback
ISBN: 978-1-7350974-8-0 Elverian Ebook

❋ Created with Vellum

ALERON

Thick snowflakes rushed past the large windows, their urgency increasing every minute. The granite walls let no sound penetrate the large room, but I could imagine the screeching cries of the wind as I watched the broad trees outside the castle struggle against its mighty force.

My limbs felt stiff, unable to move since dinner. There was nothing to do but wait, and I was growing impatient. They should have been here yesterday. If they were only a day behind, they could be caught in the storm, completely unprepared. They could have been attacked. They could have been lost. Killian could have betrayed us. The possibilities were too many, and they were all equally bleak.

I shouldn't have let her go. I should have insisted she come with me. I should have been there to protect her. I wanted to allow her space, give her time, and show I trusted her, but was that all worth it if she was dead?

If her faith in me hadn't shattered only days before our worlds turned upside down, I know things would have been different. I destroyed us, and that was my portentous reality. If something happened to her, I would be to blame.

I already had the weight of possibly losing her confidence in me, fully realizing I may never be able to recover what we lost — but the thought of losing *her* forever? I thought I had faced a dark amount of devastation after leaving Praseria, but if I lost Lia — *Allene* — it would shatter me.

The chatter behind me was a hum in the background of my thoughts. Each pointless conversation, each light-hearted laugh, each bite of food since we arrived, had made my skin crawl. Allene, Hassan, and Killian — they were out there, and I seemed to be the only one who was worried. It was Risa's sister, and it was Damien's brother — even my brother with all his faults — we should be searching for them. How could they be stuffing their faces with dessert with the uncertainty of where they were and what condition they were in?

Risa told me I was being overly anxious, Marshal continually supported Risa's opinions, and Damien said I was fretting over a day difference. During our journey, I was the outlier. I was the Praserian. They didn't trust me. They wouldn't listen to me. Risa was the only one who had made an effort to be polite, but that is as far as her kindness went.

I studied the bone-chilling storm and couldn't shake the feeling that the other group was in the middle of it —

that they were out there, that they were close. But if they were, they wouldn't make it through the night if we didn't do something.

This wasn't my kingdom. I was merely a temporary, unannounced guest, traveling with a group of people that hardly tolerated me. Making requests or demands was not the diplomatic way. Risa would scold me if I jeopardized anything, considering the contentious welcoming we had upon arriving at Cenan. But if Allene was out there, I couldn't sit and wait.

I turned on my heels and moved towards the door, not paying attention to the halt in conversation as I stole a fur coat off the coat rack and let myself out of the room.

Footsteps followed behind me, Damien's voice echoing in the stone halls.

"What are you doing?" Damien yelled after me.

I didn't falter or give him an answer. The exit was set in front of me, and I wouldn't debate, explain, or apologize for what I was about to do.

Damien's steps turned into a panicked run as he rushed to catch up. I took a deep breath as my hand now rested on the handle. I had to trust my gut.

"Aleron! Stop! Where are you going?" Damien questioned, urgency and alarm flooding his voice.

"To find them."

ALLENE

The fluffy white cloud that swirled above us deceitfully seemed innocent and beautiful. Assuming we'd be met with an endearing, gentle snowfall was quickly squashed by a vicious touch of pelting flurries.

The piercing wind lashed at my raw skin, mercilessly proving its strength. My body was past the point of numbness. I could no longer register if I was unbearably cold, consumed by pain, or possibly both.

There wasn't a great spot to shelter in place or retreat to. When the storm began, we had traveled for three days, and the snow was light. We only had one more day to go, and we would arrive in Cenan. We had made it far enough that it would've taken longer to turn back. Hassan said the only option was to keep going, but I knew we all regretted the decision.

The unexpected storm drowned out my senses. I had

no sense of how long we had been traveling or what time of day it was. I could only hear the howling of the wind, and see the faintest outline of Hassan in front of me. I prayed Hassan knew the direction of where to go through the abrasive storm as I blindly dragged my feet in the imprints Hassan had stepped before me. None of us had been to Cenan, we didn't know how far we had to go, and I knew we could easily be lost, especially in the storm.

This was my first encounter with weather like this, so it could be a fluke that the first snowfall I would experience was a blizzard, but either way, the experience led me to one strong feeling. I *hated* the snow. I never wanted to see another snowflake again. My preconceived dreamy notions about magical, peaceful winters had been entirely misled.

I envisioned the hot beaches of Praseria to displace my misery, pretending the sinking feeling as I trudged through the snow was actually wet sand consuming my feet. I focused on the memory of the burning sun and the way it tingled against my skin as it sent fiery warmth to the very marrow in my bones. I shivered at the thought and did my best not to acknowledge that the feeling may have been the start of frostbite.

Till warned us about the weather we could encounter going to Cenan, but none of us were prepared for this drastic weather shift. We each needed different shoes, more layers, thicker cloaks, and furs to keep us comfortable.

After a lengthy discussion with Killian and a fair

amount of begging and persuasion, I convinced him not to follow the Red Crows that were headed in the direction of Gelva. Killian agreed to go to Cenan, regroup, and get more men to pursue finding his mother.

As we faced the possibility of freezing to death, part of me wished I would have supported Killian's idea of going to Gelva. There was a chance we would have been killed by the Red Crows, but that somehow seemed a less painful and tragic way to die than the reality we were being faced with now.

I continued to daydream and tried to hum a song to distract myself a little longer, but the cold was too much. I couldn't register how exhausted my legs were until my knees buckled. My hands met the wet snow, and I didn't even cry out. All I wanted was to lay down and sleep.

Killian crouched beside me, his right arm holding himself upright as he reached down for me.

Calm blue eyes shone through the storm, illuminating his snow-plastered eyebrows and shaking jaw as the snow storm whited out the rest of his body. If I had the energy to smile at his angelic appearance, I would've.

"Allene, we are close; you have to stay awake. Look at me, don't close your eyes," Killian's voice was muffled through the wind, his plea barely reaching my ringing ears. His hand cupped my face, forcing me to look at him. My chin was so cold that I couldn't sense the heat of his hand, only the pressure on my skin.

I did my best to do as Killian requested. I wanted to

look at him. I wanted the distraction. I wanted the reminder that I wasn't alone.

Killian's collected demeanor eased some of my fear. The numbness taking over me was comforting in a way, and the moment felt very serene. I changed my mind. If I was going to die, this was better than the alternative in Gelva.

Killian's eyes stayed locked on mine, his body shaking as he held me in his arms, trying to keep me out of the snow. He continued to mumble words to me, but I didn't have the energy to reply. I stared at him, giving all my power to focus on his first request of keeping my eyes open.

As I stared back at Killian, the sounds of the storm began to change. The wind shifted to a new sound, or so I thought it was the wind. I felt my heart rate increase as I saw Killian's eyes peel away from mine and relief flash across his face.

His next words were a mixture of a shout and a sob. "Allene, help is coming."

KILLIAN

I stood by the roaring fire crackling and lighting the bare marble room. The heat of the flames made my body shake out the cold as the warmth penetrated my skin. I hadn't noticed much since arriving in Cenan — the unique castle, the stern faces of new people, the politics that weren't addressed upon arriving — none of it mattered to me. My only concern was Allene.

I helplessly watched as strangers wrapped Allene's delicate frozen body in warm clothes. The snow on her face and hair had melted, leaving her hair wet and cold as it clung to her pale skin. I pointed it out to the ladies helping her, and they all returned my observation with piercing glares, but it didn't faze me. When it came to protecting Allene, I wasn't going to be intimidated by anyone.

I turned around to face the door as the ladies silently peeled off Allene's sopping dress, placing her in dry, warm clothes and furs. They did their best to gather all the moisture in Allene's hair with towels, wringing out the water until her head was dry. Off and on the ladies would exchange irritated glances as their eyes flitted towards me, and they quickly realized I wasn't going anywhere, no matter how rude they tried to be. They had successfully shooed away Risa and Damien, but I wouldn't be swayed.

They soon began to assure me that Allene would be all right and that they would take care of her through the night to make sure her body temperature continued to rise. They insisted I needed to have my own needs tended to, while I insisted I was comfortable and fine where I was.

There was no other seating in the room, the only pieces of furniture being the large wood bed Allene lay on, drowning in furs and pillows, and a few footstools and side tables the ladies had brought in with them, along with their supplies. After they complained to me about how it wasn't good for me to be standing after such a long journey, I nodded and sat down on the chilling marble floor, the fire my only source of comfort.

I sat waiting and watching for a sign of life from Allene for what felt like hours. I was unaware of what time it was. I set my eyes on Allene, but I had caught glimpses in the window behind her bed of the storm that still raged on and drowned out any signs of time from the sky.

The lady's maids would occasionally switch out for someone else, bringing with the newcomer fresh supplies and hot drinks to spoon-feed Allene. They would some-times bring a bowl of soup or hot drink to me as well, with a look of annoyance in their eyes as they silently offered them to me.

Allene's body eventually stopped shaking, and her blue lips slowly began returning to a soft pink. I felt the same exciting relief as I did seeing Aleron, Damien, and the group of men that had come to find us. It had been a miracle we made it through that storm. It was a miracle I wouldn't take for granted.

I heard heavy footsteps enter the room and the clearing of a throat I knew all too well.

"Killian," Aleron's tone was more of an acknowledg-ment than a greeting, and I could feel his eyes had already moved from scrutinizing me, to studying Allene.

"Aleron," I nodded back.

"I expected you to still be sleeping; it's barely morn-ing," Aleron observed.

"I haven't slept," I replied flatly.

"You've been in here all night?" I could hear the confu-sion in Aleron's voice, envision the shock displayed on his face, and I could hear the real question he was asking. *Why would you care enough to watch over Allene? Why are you putting her needs before your own?*

That is what he actually wanted to ask. But he didn't, because to Aleron, he probably wanted to believe it meant nothing, that my gesture was somehow under selfish pretenses, likely assuming it was me being politically cautious about making sure nothing happened to her. I'd let him think of any reason he wanted to; I knew he wouldn't be able to see the true motive behind it.

I didn't have any energy to spare to go into the details of my new feelings for Allene. I could tell Aleron was protective of her, I knew he loved her, and this was not the time to tell him I did too. So much had happened since we saw each other last, and that was Allene's right to share when she wanted to, not mine. So I let silence be my answer to his question.

Aleron sighed. "You should really get some rest before we meet with the king. He was gracious enough to trust us to have time together before meeting with them as a group, but I'm uncertain how long they'll let us utilize their resources before they start to lose patience with our lack of diplomacy. We have a lot to discuss and not much time. I will stay with Allene," Aleron declared, leaving no opportunity to debate or argue.

I felt frustration and anger flare in my chest as I processed the situation and Aleron's words. As much as I loathed to admit it, I knew he was right. I needed rest, and I knew he would take care of her while I did, but it bothered me more than it should — the thought of Allene waking up in an unfamiliar place and the first person she saw being Aleron. But I couldn't insist on staying, Aleron would be suspicious, and I needed to do what was best for Allene. Besides, Aleron was not *offering* to stay with Allene; he was insisting.

I felt my jaw clench in protest as I swallowed my pride and nodded in reply. I could see a smirk on one of the lady's maid's faces, and I tried not to seem sour at their evident joy to have me gone.

I stood from my place on the floor, my bones and muscles protestingly sore from the journey and the poor choice of sitting on a marble surface for hours. As I made my way out of the room, I stopped by Aleron, our gazes both on Allene.

"In case I didn't say it earlier, thank you for finding us." The words came out hushed and low, barely audible, but I knew I needed to say them; to address the great service and courage Aleron had taken in ensuring our safe arrival when his gut told him something was amiss.

Aleron's eyes widened at the expression of gratitude, and he gave an unexpected short smile. "You're welcome. In case I didn't say it earlier, thank you for keeping Allene safe on the journey."

I felt my stomach drop at his warm sentiments. Aleron had always been more tender-hearted, sensitive, and trusting; making him the optimist when it came to people. It was the exact reason I was forced to become the opposite. As his older brother, it was my duty to protect him from the harsh reality of what really entailed being a member of the Hadway family.

The years I had spent protecting my brother only festered into Aleron misunderstanding my intentions and actions. Aleron had developed expectations and standards of me that my father had set, but there was so much he didn't know — so much that I had shielded him from.

I didn't mind that Aleron had misconceptions of me; I

had kept him safe. That is what mattered. But I would be lying to myself if I said it didn't hurt to know how little he thought of me. And now with everything that happened with Allene, I was afraid I would never find redemption with my little brother. I knew Aleron wouldn't be expecting what happened between Allene and me, and I knew it would likely shatter any kindness he had left to offer me — and I couldn't blame him if it did.

ALLENE

I had to be hallucinating. I felt warm. So warm I had to be sweating. I didn't know if hallucinations were a side effect of hypothermia, but I welcomed it. I didn't want to open my eyes; I wanted this feeling to never go away. The feeling of my toes, my fingers, the blood pulsing through my veins, I didn't want to lose any of it.

"Allene?" I could hear the hopeful chirp of Risa's voice, and my eyes willed themselves open.

"Risa?" my voice cracked, the words painfully escaping my windpipe as I frantically looked for the source of her heavenly voice.

My gaze fell on her round chocolate eyes, her smile as comforting as I remembered. Risa immediately embraced me, gripping me tightly.

"Thank heavens you are all right! You had us all

worried to death!" Risa exclaimed, soft cries of relief escaping her as she stroked my hair back from my face.

My heart felt like it was about to burst. I clung to Risa, realizing she was alive and well, suddenly boosting what little energy was inside me.

"You've been worried about me? I was worried about you!" I pulled away and held her pink cheeks in my hands, checking for any signs of injury, but Risa only radiated health and perfection. "It feels like it's been weeks since I saw you," I said with an exasperated breath.

Risa reached for my hands as she casually sat on my bed. Her blonde hair was beautifully braided on each side of her head, clinging tightly to her scalp and creating an elegant pattern. She wore one of her favorite blue dresses that she had brought with her when we left Valteria, but she had added a brown fur shawl that I didn't recognize, the additional piece drowning her slender figure.

"I wasn't the one who traveled through the worst blizzard Cenan has had in years," Risa shyly smiled, worry creasing in the corner of her eyes.

The memory came back too quickly, making me shiver at the mention of it. *Worst in years?* I would believe it; it had been a storm that I only thought could be imagined, not real. Then the last part of her sentence settled in. *Cenan.* We had made it to Cenan.

The kingdom that would be the hardest to win over, according to Aleron, Killian, and Hassan. I didn't know what to expect; I hadn't even seen the castle or met any of the people. I didn't know how Risa's meeting had gone upon their arrival or how our sudden appearance had been received. I hadn't witnessed any of the reunions. There was so much to be caught up on, so much still to do. The reality of what was required of me sunk in, and I could feel my mind begin to race as I processed my surroundings.

I slowly gazed around the room encapsulated in white and gray marble. The shiny, gleaming stone material covered everything, leaving a chill hollowness to the space. The room was bare, the only noticeable piece of furniture being the large bed I was lying in. Various animal furs made up the pillows and blankets, each feeling luxurious, warm, and soft as I settled into the unfamiliar materials. I now had a guess as to where Risa's shawl came from. A large fireplace burned the remaining embers of the fire from the night before, and it popped quietly at us, echoing off the walls as it died out.

I shook my head, my hand rubbing against my temple as I tried to pull the events of yesterday to the forefront of my mind. "I remember Killian telling me not to close my eyes. . . but I must've fallen asleep. I don't recall how we arrived here," I informed Risa, trying to piece together the failing memory bit by bit.

Risa gulped, her face flashing with discomfort as she squeezed her eyes tightly shut. "Aleron and Damien formed a search party for you all. They found you just in time," Risa exhaled, shaking on the last word.

"How did they know to come to look for us?" I asked, confusion lacing my voice.

Risa nervously shifted, fiddling with her hands as her eyes darted away from mine, unable to look at me as she answered.

"Aleron insisted. He kept saying he had a feeling. I wish I hadn't questioned him so much, but I'm glad he persevered even when Damien and I didn't support him. You were a day late, but we didn't think it was anything to be worried about. I shouldn't have dismissed it so easily," Risa reprimanded herself, the weight of her doubt showing visibly on her sunken shoulders.

I reached out to take Risa's hand once again, clasping it in mine, the warmth of her fingertips making me shiver. "It's all right, Risa; you couldn't have known. I would have likely thought the same if the roles had been reversed," I tried to reassure her.

Risa apprehensively nodded, her face bleak. "Perhaps, but it doesn't make me feel much better that Aleron was the only one advocating for you all. I'm truly sorry. I am happy you are here now, safe and well." Risa squeezed my hand tightly back, the sign of warm blood flooding to the tips of my fingers, a sight I was worried I wouldn't live to see again.

"As am I," I replied softly, exhaling in relief. "I am sure you have a lot to share," I added, raising an inquisitive eyebrow in her direction.

Risa gave a short, burdened smile. "You're right, much has happened since we were last together. The king has been kind enough to allow you time to heal before meeting him, but we don't want to be inconsiderate and impose on his offer."

I nodded at Risa, agreeing with her concern, and with unsteady arms, I pushed myself off the bed, letting my feet greet the frigid marble. "I agree, we need to meet with him. I don't want to delay our purpose here, more than I already have. Fill me in," I encouraged, trying to firmly stand before her.

Risa shook her head and pulled at my arm, forcing me back on the bed. "Don't rush yourself, Allene. Damien and Aleron would want all of us to discuss things together first anyway."

"You should send for them; we can all meet right now," I continued, sitting up tall in an attempt to convince her of my readiness.

Risa winced, her eyes full of pity, and not persuaded in the slightest. "We may want to wait a bit. Aleron just left; maybe we can all meet after breakfast," she suggested, rubbing a soothing hand up and down my back.

My eyes widened in surprise, my thoughts diverting from their original intentions. "Left? As in left *here?*" I asked Risa to clarify.

She nodded and almost hesitated to reply, but I could sense a prominent curiosity in her eyes that I wrongly assumed was tied to Aleron.

"Yes, Aleron insisted on watching over you after Killian was with you all night." The novelty I saw suddenly flared, and the unasked questions danced around her face.

I felt my stomach become mixed with sickness and excitement at the mention of Aleron and Killian. I knew where the excitement was coming from. *Killian had stayed with me all night.* I could hardly process how happy that made me as I became sick, thinking Aleron did not know about what had happened between Killian and I yet, and Aleron had already come to visit me.

I assumed Aleron and Killian had crossed paths in my room, and I could only guess how their interaction went. I could only imagine the worst in my mind. I had no idea how much Aleron knew, or if Killian had said anything, or if Aleron was jumping to his own conclusions and questions, as Risa seemed to be doing. Or maybe Aleron's feelings would make it impossible for him to see.

I knew I had to face telling the truth soon, but I hadn't had much time to consider how I would share it. Killian and I admitted how we felt only a few days ago. We hadn't had time alone since our confessions. We were still in the process of clarifying things ourselves. How could I explain it to others when I still had things to work out for myself?

I buried my worries and remained composed as Risa's prying eyes tried to tear away what I was hiding and thinking. I hoped I was convincing enough for her interest to fade, at least for now. But she could sense my anxiousness and addressed it.

"Are you sure you're feeling well enough to meet with everyone?" she asked, the prospect of doubt evident in her question.

I swallowed back my fear and apprehension and

managed to let out a small laugh, twirling my ruby ring that had become loose on my finger since our journey. "Even if I wasn't, I'm aware that we have already wasted more time than we should've because of me, and I won't let us waste anymore."

ALERON

I had hardly slept before I got the news that Allene was awake. I was famished, exhausted, and desperately needed a change of clothes, as I was still wearing the outfit I had on the day before, but none of that mattered. Allene was awake, and I had to see her — I had to speak to her — before the onslaught of politics and duties settled in.

I selfishly wanted to be the first person to see her. I had waited as long as I could by her bedside before Risa insisted I get some rest. The exhaustion didn't bother me; it truly meant more to me to stay, but I could sense Risa wanted to be with her sister, and I didn't want to make her uncomfortable, so I gave them space.

Gratefully, I wasn't far from Allene's room, but it felt like time was attempting to slow down my hurried pace. I paused to knock on the door when I could hear laughter coming from the room. I was too late.

I cracked open the door to see Damien and Risa sitting on the edge of Allene's bed. Damien let out another laugh as he playfully mocked Risa. I knew what he was going on about; he had been jeering at Marshal and Risa's awkward, lovey exchanges since we left Valteria, and it seemed he was filling Allene in on all of it.

Allene was sitting up, her silky black hair flowing across the fur pillows that supported her tired frame. Her cheeks had more color since I saw her a few hours ago, their pink shade returning. Her eyes seemed weary but determined as she listened and watched Damien's spectacle. It was the same stubbornness I caught in her eyes the first day I met her, and she was just as beautiful too.

Despite how worn out I knew she was, she still managed to appear graceful and present, sharp and prepared. I felt my heart ache as I watched her — *as I admired her* — and realized I wanted to be the one to make her smile like Damien was right now. I could see the true joy and happiness on her face as she watched her best friend, and I envied her attention.

I never imagined I would be in this position — that *we* would be in this position. I wasn't the first person she requested to see. I hadn't been significant enough, and that realization cut me like a knife. I was only here because I had asked the lady's maids to inform me when Allene awoke. It hadn't even passed through my mind that Allene might not want to see me, despite how much I wanted to see her, and my heart ached even more at the thought.

I attempted to turn away, but Allene noticed me lingering at the door.

"Aleron?" her delicate, sweet voice echoed in the spacious room. My cheeks blushed simply from the sound of my name leaving her lips, my lungs threatening to suffocate me as the interaction stole my breath.

I calmly opened the door to reveal my hiding place, and Damien and Risa slumped at the sight of me.

I cleared my throat and slowly approached them, mustering my confidence and conviction as I stopped a safe distance from the bed.

"I apologize for interrupting. I heard you were awake, and I had to see it for myself."

Allene's eyes softened as she stared at me, their cerulean blue color brightening the room and my soul. I had truly missed her. Seeing her look at me was what I missed the most — the feeling she lit deep within me just from being recognized by her; there was not another feeling like it.

Allene offered a shy smile as she tucked a piece of her hair behind her ear, a subconscious reaction to things that made her nervous. My heart leapt out of my chest realizing it had been my presence that made her nervous, a realization I didn't want going to my head too soon.

"I am, and from what Damien and Risa have told me, I have you to thank for my safe arrival to Cenan. We wouldn't have made it if you hadn't come to search for us when you did. Thank you, Aleron," Allene expressed her gratitude and shifted her gaze between Damien and Risa.

Risa straightened her back, making herself tall and proper as she offered me a curt nod. "Yes, thank you Aleron for your bravery and swift action," she said in her quiet voice.

Damien passed his hand through his hair that was clumped in awkward tangles all over his head. It stuck straight up from the length it acquired on the journey. Damien let out a hesitant sigh before mumbling his next words. "As much as it hurts to admit it, Allene is right. Thanks to you, I still have my brother and my best friend."

I offered them both a respectful nod. "Is Hassan recovering all right?" I didn't want to draw any additional praise for doing what I did, so I appreciated the opportunity to shift the conversation.

Damien nodded. "He's fine, he's just grumpy, hungry, and wants to sleep. I understand, I feel that way on a good day," Damien chuckled at his own comment, and Allene did too, bringing my attention back to her captivating presence.

The room briefly paused as we all seemed to debate if more pleasantries would be exchanged. I was the uninvited guest, and as much as I wanted to have any and every excuse to stay with Allene, I respected her need for distance. If she wanted me present, all she would have to do was ask.

I couldn't help but smile as I looked at Allene one more time, her deep sea-like eyes meeting mine, sending a jolt through my entire system.

"I'm relieved that you're doing well, Allene. I will be

going. Please let me know if you need anything, and once everyone is feeling well enough we can —"

"I want to meet with everyone today, over lunch," Allene interrupted me, her attractive determination and stubbornness shining through with the simple sentence. I knew better than to question her when she made such definitive statements. I was not going to argue or try to persuade her to rest. I selfishly wanted an excuse to see her again so soon, and I wasn't going to let that chance slip away.

I nodded as I turned toward the door, trying to suppress the happiness in my voice.

"Very well then. I will see you all at lunch."

ALLENE

My conversation with Damien and Risa had been casual and light. I needed a conversation like that before undertaking the one I was about to enter. I knew my time here in Cenan would be heavy, and the moment of lightheartedness, even as short as it was, was exactly what I needed.

None of us had a relationship with the kingdom of Cenan. They did not negotiate trade with other kingdoms, much less talk to them. Very little was known about Cenan, aside from its lack of hospitality and preference for being left alone, which left all of us dreading this final stop on our journey, because it was the most unknown. The most unpredictable.

Damien ensured everyone received the message of when we would be meeting. I waited next to him in the small, improvised dining room graciously arranged for our privacy.

The room had floors and walls made out of the same marble as the rest of the castle, with a round window that let in some natural light, resembling a glamorous cave. A thick wood table was placed in the center of the small room, with two large benches on each side. Three platters were on the table with offerings of various cheeses, meats, and fermented vegetables. Two pitchers of water were placed on each end of the table, with a pewter mug for each person.

Damien sat down and slid to the end of one of the benches, helping himself to the food in front of him as we waited. I decided to stand, hoping to take charge of the conversation once everyone arrived, and standing seemed the best chance to do that. Besides, I hadn't had a large appetite since arriving. Between the anxiety of seeing everyone all together again, hearing the experience of the other group, and hopefully forming a new alliance, I had much more on my mind than food.

Marshal and Risa arrived together, both of them beaming as they sat next to each other and remaining engrossed in their conversation. Damien rolled his eyes as he shot me a look, the silent communication that this had happened many times on their journey together. *Poor Damien.* But I was still overjoyed for Risa. If there was one person in this world that deserved unbridled happiness, it was my sister. Seeing her make a claim to that, even in our bleak circumstances, was comforting to me.

Hassan arrived a moment later, his face rugged and worn, dark circles framing his eyes as he took a seat next to Damien. He was wearing new clothes that had been provided to him by our hosts, his shirt and pants different shades of gray. Hassan cleared his throat as he looked at me and I could see the apology in his eyes. Getting caught in the storm wasn't his fault, but I could see his pain as he stared at my tired face.

I managed a small smile as I looked back at Hassan. "We made it to Cenan thanks to you."

Hassan grimaced. "I hoped it would've been a bit warmer and less life-threatening. I don't think I deserve much gratitude considering the condition we all arrived in."

"We are all okay, and I don't think we would have made it at all if you hadn't been with us," I added.

Hassan gave a humble nod. I could see he was still upset, and I couldn't think of anything else to say that might alleviate his guilt. In time I was sure he, and all of us, would move on from the memories of the storm.

Aleron and Killian were the last to arrive. They entered the room together, an unusual energy of civility clearly between the two of them.

Aleron smiled at me as he took a seat by Marshal. I noticed his hair was longer again, its length brushing past the tips of his ears and managing to curl just at the ends. He wore a similar outfit as the rest of the men, displaying various shades of gray between all of them.

Killian paused to look at me before taking his seat, his eyes a darker blue in the dim room. His hair was brushed back and his curls were laid against his neck. If he was weary from the journey, he did an excellent job of hiding it. He looked refreshed and alert, and my anxiety seemed to reduce simply by observing his equanimity.

I hadn't seen Killian since arriving in Cenan. I wished we had time together before this meeting. I had so much I wanted to say and ask Killian. I wanted to thank him for watching over me when we first arrived. I wanted to thank him for not letting me go when I felt myself slipping away into the storm's embrace. I wanted to know how his first interaction back with Aleron went, and I wanted to know if he was okay.

As if understanding my thoughts and questions, Killian eased my mind with a quick hidden wink and a fast smirk that only my eyes could see. I could feel my heart beat a bit faster at his attention and observance of me, and I did my best to shift my eyes away from him and hope to not draw the other's curiosity.

Killian sat next to Damien and casually waited for me to begin. I took a deep breath and hugged the fur shawl around my shoulders a little tighter, drawing courage and warmth from its encapsulating embrace.

"It's a relief to see everyone here, all of us in one piece," I sighed, trying to open with a somewhat heartfelt sentiment. "I don't mean to pass over pleasantries but time isn't on our side. Risa, I was hoping you could share everything from your journey to give us a full perspective on where we stand with Lokali, Gree, and Cenan."

I gestured toward Risa, and she immediately accepted my invitation to speak, her posture straightening as she leaned away from Marshal and placed her hands properly in her lap.

"Yes, well, to be brief, the King and Queen of Lokali, the Oswinns, were already aware of the situation. Nycolas was a disguised advisor in Lokali; he facilitated the attack on Valteria. After the attack was a success, Lokali officials quickly had their suspicions of who he was, as Nycolas disappeared suddenly and without a trace. They were hesitant to agree to an alliance with us; they almost refused. They don't trust Valteria, and Aleron's current standing with Praseria made them leery. Aleron managed to get them to agree to an alliance after sharing the news of his mother's capture." Risa's lips pursed together in a straight line as she mentioned the sensitive topic.

My eyes subconsciously looked to Aleron, his face hardened, then to Killian, his expression the same as when he initially sat down. *How could he always be so passive in his reactions?* It was a skill I aimed to master better eventually.

Risa continued, brushing her braids casually off her shoulders so they laid against her back. "In the end, King and Queen Oswinn agreed to help us fight against the Red Crows, if necessary." Risa paused for a moment, catching her breath as she took a long sip of water from her pewter mug.

"And Gree?" I asked, trying to move on from the awkward tension now clinging to the room.

"King and Queen Rosen were quick to offer their help when they learned Lokali was on our side. It was a short visit," Marshal interjected this time, his words concise and to the point.

"How was your arrival here at Cenan?" I asked, my eyes shifting between Damien and Aleron, seeing if either of them wanted to share.

Damien hesitated, and Aleron took it as an opportunity to speak. "We ran into a slight misunderstanding with King Seger," Aleron shrugged casually.

"A misunderstanding?" I asked, waiting for clarification.

Aleron nodded, his eyes fixated on the pewter mug he was twirling on the table. "With his chief intelligence spy. Before we arrived at Cenan, she and a group of her spies found our camp a few miles away from the castle. She thought we were assassins, and we thought she was a member of the Red Crows. We sorted it out after a long interrogation," Aleron explained.

"How did King Seger take this news?" I asked them all.

"It's difficult to say. He's a bit. . . capricious," Damien seemed uncomfortable as he said the last word.

"And his wife?" I added.

"He's unmarried," Damien replied dryly.

"So you fear with his *capricious* personality, that his kindness to us may be short lived?" I was trying to understand Damien's indirect concerns.

Damien shrugged. "I don't know what to expect, and that makes me anxious. I cannot tell if he's playing us, if he's a friend, if he's genuine, or if he's slightly lost his mind. I feel like I've seen all of it. I know we shouldn't procrastinate our conversation with him, but I also don't know how he will behave now that all of us have arrived here," Damien shared his fears, and the tension of his words settled upon everyone in the small space.

I let out a short breath to collect the nerves Damien had placed in my head. "You haven't put my mind at ease, but there is only one way to find out how King Seger will approach our situation. We need to meet with him today," I insisted.

"After you tell us what happened on your visits," Aleron now interjected, his eyes full of curiosity and concern as he looked at me.

My gaze shifted to Hassan and Killian, urging one of them to respond to Aleron's question. We hadn't met before this meeting, and I didn't know how much they wanted to share, or where they wanted to begin.

Hassan huffed as he propped his elbows on the table, and took a fast sip of water before taking on Aleron's question.

"Veruje was a success, Queen Lidia is safe and agreed to help if needed. She will keep a watchful eye for any possible Red Crows activity in her kingdom. As we passed through Selvet, we were attacked by members of the Red Crows. We con—" Hassan was cut off as Aleron immediately interrogated.

"Wait — attacked?" Aleron's eyes squinted in confusion and alarm.

"A failed assassination attempt of Allene and I," Killian answered flatly.

"And you didn't think to mention this first?" Aleron's eyes narrowed in on Killian.

Killian waved a hand in the air. "We are fine, we are here, and we have mentioned it. Can we move on?" Killian's voice was stern as he cut a sharp look at his brother next to him.

Aleron dismissed Killian's attempt to end the conversation and pointed his finger at Hassan instead. "Where were you during this assassination attempt?"

"Getting supplies before leaving for Gelva," Hassan stated soberly.

Aleron scoffed. "You left Allene and Killian alone? The two royals who look like your *enemy*, and would stand out the most in Selvet — you left them alone?" Aleron ran a hand down his stubbled face in stunned disbelief from what he was hearing.

Hassan's jaw clenched, his nostrils delicately flared as he let out a sigh. "They were at my home, I thought they would be safe."

"The point of going as a group was to stick together," Aleron seethed.

I shook my head and threw up my hands, the tension already getting to me. There was likely a lot more to come at me later on. How was I supposed to handle more if I couldn't even tolerate this arguing?

"Stop blaming Hassan, it wasn't his fault. He couldn't have predicted the threat the Red Crows would be; none of us expected it. Arguing about what should or shouldn't have happened is getting us nowhere. Without Hassan, we wouldn't have made it to Cenan. Without Killian, we wouldn't have made it out of Selvet. Without me, we wouldn't have secured Veruje," I pointed out everyone's contribution, trying to solidify some harmony before we met with King Seger.

"And Gelva?" Risa intervened, doing her best to pull back from Aleron's interrogation too.

"We didn't make it to Gelva. Killian spotted a group of the Red Crows heading in that direction. We didn't want to risk following behind them," Hassan answered.

"How did you know they were members of the Red Crows?" Damien questioned Killian.

Killian remained composed as he looked back at Damien's inquiring face. "I had seen them before. They were the men that attacked my mother and I on our way to Valteria."

Aleron's face hardened, immediately turning flaming red in color as he gripped the table. "You saw them, *again*, and you let them get away, *again?*" Aleron's voice was a spine-chilling whisper filled with searing hatred that made me shiver.

I knew the kidnapping of his mother was unimaginably painful, but his addition of pure detestation for Killian amplified the intensity of his feelings and obstructed his ability to hear Killian's reasoning. It was identical to his reaction when Killian shared the news of his mother's kidnapping initially in Valteria.

Killian didn't writhe under Aleron's scrutinizing glare, and instead coolly stared back at Aleron, the ease of his emotions dissipating some of the tension. "Aleron, I am on your side. I don't expect you to give me the benefit of the doubt, but I do expect us to all focus on what we are here for. Your overreactions and quick assumptions are slowing us down. You and I can discuss this later, alone."

Aleron's lips twisted to the side and his arms folded tightly to his chest. He locked eyes with Killian to exchange a moment of charged, harsh silence. After a short staring contest between the two of them, Aleron broke his gaze, shifting his eyes to the floor.

Damien sighed and stood up, leaning forward on the table as he quickly caught everyone's eyes.

"Let's meet the king."

King Seger brought us to his vacant throne room — a commonality I saw in much of the castle. No valuables adorned the halls or the walls for display, there was hardly even furniture. Everything was bare, as if only the minimum was provided. The few notable features of the castle were the fur accents and the marble that the castle seemed carved out of entirely.

The seven of us waited in a semi-circle as we looked out toward a host of new faces. Soldiers dressed in thick brown wool, black leather, and iron armor centered in a perfect line behind their king. One of the soldiers stuck out, from more than just the obvious reason of being the only soldier out of line.

A young female soldier, in more armor and weaponry than the rest, stood closely on the right side of the king. Her dirty blonde hair was braided tightly to her head in four rows, her scalp revealing a line of tattooed symbols between each of the parts. Her gray eyes were piercing, her stance stealthy, and her expression lethal. The woman caught me staring at her sheathed sword and she loosely gripped it, her eyes challenging me. My bored gaze shifted away to observe the man beside her, and I heard a snarl escape her throat at the insult of my fleeting attention.

King Seger sat on his throne, his brooding figure enlarged by the piles of animal skins that blanketed his shoulders. His light blonde beard was oiled and slicked into a single thick braid that hit near the base of his throat. His hair was loose and long, barely past his shoulders, making him appear older than he was. He couldn't be more than ten years my senior based on his smooth skin and strong stature, but it was clear he was trying to appear experienced and aged. He didn't smile with his teeth, only with his large and proud closed mouth smirk. His green eyes were teasing and roguish as he methodically studied each of us before speaking.

"I am King Trevet Seger, welcome to Cenan." He held his arms out dramatically at his introduction like he commanded more than just Cenan, acting like he ruled the world. I tried to stifle a laugh as I began to understand the reason behind the lack of novelty items in his castle for guests to gawk and admire. King Seger didn't want anything distracting from his greatest masterpiece and pride — himself.

I immediately knew his personality would require a sycophant from our side equal in self-importance if we wanted to persuade him to do anything that wasn't originally his idea, and I was dreading what it may require of us to gain his trust. For men like this, it is best to let them take the lead, let them talk the most, and let them feel in control. I only hoped the rest of the group would catch the unsaid signs of his personality too.

"So you are the three late comers?" King Seger gestured towards Hassan, Allene, and me. I exchanged a fast glance with them both, Allene was right by my side in the center and Hassan was on the other end of the semi-circle. They exchanged glances and both silently nodded their heads.

I gently placed my hands behind my back, gripping my right hand over my left wrist. I locked eyes with King Seger, and chose a reverent approach in the words I would say next.

"Yes, we apologize for the stir our late arrival caused. We are grateful for the aid you sent our way, and the hospitality you have shown us," I gave a slight bow, trying to display humility as best I could.

King Seger's head nodded slowly in acknowledgment of my attempted diplomacy. His eyes narrowed as he studied me silently, his smirk unfaltering.

"I recognize your attempt at pleasantries, and that may have worked in other kingdoms but that isn't how we operate here in Cenan," King Seger declared, his smile turning to a wicked state of mischief.

My brows furrowed in genuine confusion, my nerves struck into overdrive as I processed the fast change in direction that King Seger was leading the conversation. "I apologize, I'm not sure what you are alluding to?"

King Seger waved his hand in the air, his lips twisting in displeasure. "The flattery, the nonsense conversation. Here in Cenan, we are frank. We speak plainly as a sign of respect. We alley ourselves with those that are forthright, those with nothing to hide." King Seger's tone turned accusatory. He was proving to be one of the most irritating royals I had the displeasure of meeting, but that didn't change the fact that he was the one who needed the most cajoling.

Despite the slew of witty and clever responses rushing through my mind, I resisted the urge to say anything that could be interpreted as offensive. We hadn't come this far to lose an opportunity to form an alliance with Cenan. I knew how to keep in step with negotiations. I wouldn't ruin this.

I offered a compliant smile. "Then we should be great friends, as I assure you, we have nothing to hide."

King Seger's eyes widened in pleasure as I fell into his well laid trap. "Ah, Prince Killian, that is a daring claim. You see, I'm still a bit shaken by Princess Amena hiding her identity after a gracious, extended stay in Praseria. It is hard not to fear that such audacious lies could still be a habit for the princess, given the recent events. And with you all trusting her within such a short passage of time? I'd consider all your characters to be questionable," he smugly stated, his knuckles flashing white as he gripped the arm rests of his marble throne.

I grabbed Allene's arm next to me, trying to take control before she intervened, but she ignored my touch, her body cringing in defense and sending a scowl in King Seger's direction.

"How did you know about that?" Allene's frantic words escaped too quickly, her reaction solidifying King Seger's trap.

King Seger shook his head, his expression unimpressed as he casually placed his elbows on his knees and leaned forward. "No one cares to know about us, so I ensure we know a great deal about them," King Seger tisked, a disapproving expression flashing across his face. "Although I know many things about you all, your arrival here was unforeseen; it caught me by surprise. And I don't like surprises, they tend to cause overreactions on my part." The woman next to King Seger straightened her shoulders to stand a bit taller, her gaze shifting to the soldiers behind her.

The situation was turning against us before we could share our reason for seeking out Cenan. I needed to pique King Seger's interest to hold his attention — and his limited patience — a little longer.

I sighed dramatically, slumping my shoulders in a look of defeat. "It was as much of a surprise to us, as it was to you."

King Seger's eyebrows went up, his curiosity clear. "I am intrigued. What would motivate the two greatest kingdoms to join their enemies on a hastily, unanticipated journey?"

"An even greater enemy perhaps?" The woman beside King Seger spoke for the first time, her question prodding and on point, as her deep, gruff voice penetrated the room.

I placed my hands in front of me now, ready to take control of the conversation and cease the opportunity to finally explain ourselves. "The Red Crows have infiltrated our kingdoms and Lokali's. It is likely they also have spies in considerable positions in the other surrounding kingdoms. We have journeyed here as witnesses of these crimes and to warn of the Red Crows' motivation to destroy each kingdoms' monarchy from within, to the point that our kingdoms can be taken over, one by one."

The room was silent for a moment as we all awaited King Seger's response.

King Seger placed his hand over his mouth, his chest shaking as tried to suppress a roaring laugh that he couldn't contain. "This is the pressing news you came to share with us?" Humored tears pricked the corner of his eyes, his attempt to stifle his laugh making them slightly bulge.

I looked at Aleron, his expression stiff as his jaw tightened in gall. He was visibly shaken and offended by King Seger's response and I knew he wouldn't remain silent. I was right.

Aleron glared at King Seger, frustration radiating off his skin and irritation rattling his voice. "How could you dismiss this so easily? None of the facts that Killian shared concern you?"

King Seger's face turned to sheer vexation at Aleron's question. King Seger stood from his throne, taking an aggressive step towards us. "It might be less dismissable if it came as a shock to hear, but my spies shared this news with me months ago. I can guarantee Cenan has not, and will not, be infiltrated by the Red Crows. As soon as we heard about what was happening, I sent spies to join them. I've been aware of their plans, and their structure, for weeks," King Seger practically hissed out his last word, his eyes enraged.

King Seger's response only antagonized Aleron more. Aleron shook his head in disbelief. "Weeks? And you didn't think it was ethical to share this knowledge with the other kingdoms?"

King Seger gave a bitter scoff. "What would that have benefited me? What would have changed here in Cenan? We are not friends with other kingdoms, we aren't even associates. If anything happened to Valteria, Praseria, or any of the other kingdoms, nothing would have changed here. It would be the same as it always has been. It *is* the same as it's always been, and I plan for it to stay that way."

King Seger folded his arms across his chest, his fur shawls wrapping around his thick forearms. "We look out for ourselves because others cannot be trusted. That is why your kingdoms are losing a fight against the Red Crows. You believe in good faith, you focus on other enemies, and let outsiders influence your judgments and decisions," he spat in displeasure.

I cleared my throat, stealing King Seger's attention

from Aleron and doing my best to place it back on myself. "You're correct, we were ill-prepared for an attack strategy like the Red Crows. It would have benefited us to have Cenan as a friend to be a guide to such unseen threats," I interjected before anyone else tried to agitate King Seger even more. In this battle of minds and negotiations, we were losing.

King Seger studied me, his tensed shoulders relaxing as his attention on my brother was removed. He sighed, his eyes reflecting pity. "I feel this is the greatest advice I can offer you with your short visit here." King Seger slowly got up from his throne, walking directly to me, and stopping a foot away. He leaned in, the smell of a strong drink lingering on his breath and overtaking my sense of my smell. I maintained my composure, not letting my nose wrinkle at the putrid scent. "Be diligent in your intel, if you want a chance at having the upper hand." King Seger gave his advice and pulled back, his dirty smile reappearing as he looked at us. "You may stay tonight, and I expect you will take the lesson you have learned today and be on your way in the morning."

King Seger turned away, and it was obvious he would not be negotiated with, but Allene stepped forward, unable to let it go. "We haven't discussed —" Allene began to speak, but she was immediately cut off by King Seger.

"You had more to say than your warning of the Red Crow's plans?" His eyes were full of surprise that Allene dared to continue, but by interjecting, he had fallen into *her* trap — the trap of keeping him talking — because he would always want the last word.

I couldn't help but admire Allene as she confidently moved towards him, commanding his time a little longer. "We have made alliances with Valteria, Praseria, Veruje, Lokali, and Gree, that together we would be watchful of the Red Crows and offer each other aid if the Red Crows attempt any physical attacks on another kingdom. We have come here not just to offer a word of warning, but in the hopes of forming an alliance."

King Seger chuckled. "An alliance? If I were to ever form an alliance, it would require those involved in the alliance to be stable and united. You — Praseria and Valteria — are far from what I would consider a stable alliance. You are an unreliable, forced, and meager friendship," King Seger spit out his last word, his face twisting in a look of disgust.

I could see Allene processing King Seger's argument and concern. As I looked at the rest of our group, it was obvious they all took his words more to heart than they should. I sensed their defeat, the words unspoken, and the opportunity we never had.

We had already lost a chance to work with Gelva. There was too much at stake; too many people at risk — my mother, Aleron, Allene, all of our kingdoms. We were raised to handle moments like this, moments that required improvisation, difficult and unpopular decisions, observation, and wit. It was how kingdoms survived, and I was prepared to do what needed to be done, as I had time and time again.

I knew I would regret it as soon as the words escaped my mouth, but I also knew it was the only thing that might make sense to a man like King Seger. We had come this far, we couldn't lose an opportunity for the help of the Cenanites.

I took a step forward to stand next to Allene once again. I confidently grasped Allene's hand, our fingers interlocking. I could feel her grip tighten — from shock or embarrassment, I didn't know — but I hoped King Seger would be convinced of my next words.

"My wife and I will try not to be insulted by your assumption of merely a business relationship, King Seger."

I looked at Allene, her eyes wide with confusion, and possibly frustration, as she returned my stare. I couldn't help but give a genuine, tender smile as I observed her panic — her reaction solidifying my decision of direction.

"Wife?" King Seger asked, eyebrows furrowed in equal confusion.

My next words were spoken naturally and with ease. "Yes, Allene and I are married."

ALLENE

I tried to contain my shock as I stared at Killian's hand that gently clasped mine. I couldn't meet the eyes of the others behind me; if Killian told King Seger we were married, we had to act like everyone already knew and that our relationship was open and known.

"I was aware of the relationship between the prince of Praseria and princess of Valteria; however, I was unaware the relationship had evolved. When did this take place?" King Seger replied, his interest piqued.

Killian was confident and smooth as he looked at King Seger. His eyes softly prodded mine in a longing way that almost convinced me that what he said was real.

"While we visited Veruje, Allene's cousin, Queen Lidia, helped us with a small ceremony."

King Seger raised an eyebrow, his suspicions melting

away. "You should've shared this information earlier; our conversation would have been much different."

"It wasn't an announcement we wanted to share quite yet. We were trying to avoid the eyes of the Red Crows. But since you have brought my wife's character and integrity under speculation, I felt it needed to be revealed so you can understand the extent of our commitment to one another," Killian queerly smiled and continued.

"I believe what Allene has achieved is a testament to how loyal and trustworthy she is. Yes, her initial encounter with me wasn't entirely truthful. However, if she had been truthful, I know I wouldn't have tried to understand her as a person, but rather as a Valterian. Her decision was not harmful; it was tactful. She taught me not to dismiss a relationship without knowing the individual. Because of her bravery in remaining in an enemy land and her optimism for the good of others, two kingdoms at odds with one another for far too long have finally found peace. Diplomacy and grace; it is those two qualities that Princess Amena possesses that have filled my heart with a new perspective. *That* is what Princess Amena's story should convey to you." Killian's words were compelling, the ease of their delivery shifting the energy in the petrified room.

King Seger raised his eyebrows as he observed Killian and me, a smirk forming on his face. "I am not a close-minded man. Perhaps my decision-making has been a bit rash."

King Seger turned to the woman beside him, waiting

to see if she had anything to add. She remained silent and still, her stone face concealing any of her thoughts, but King Seger must have interpreted her lack of reply differently, as he took it as a sign of her approval.

"Prince Hadway, do you hunt?" King Seger inquired.

Killian squeezed my hand, and I could not tell if it was genuine or part of the act.

"I do when circumstances permit it," Killian confirmed.

"Do the rest of you hunt as well?" King Seger asked, looking at our group.

Even if we didn't hunt, we all knew the foolishness of not saying yes. We all nodded silently in reply.

King Seger smiled, a plan dancing behind his eyes. "All of you will join me and my hunting party tomorrow morning. I will ensure you are provided with all the necessary materials and supplies. Get some rest. We will leave at dawn."

———————————

My mind was spinning. My anxiety was beyond comprehension. After the meeting with King Seger, we were all escorted back to our private rooms, and although it wasn't said out loud, it seemed he wanted us to stay in our rooms until the morning hunt. King Seger likely had eyes on all of us, and the conversation had set me on edge. We couldn't raise more suspicion, so staying in my room was what I planned to do.

Even if I felt comfortable leaving my room, I would still choose to stay. I wasn't overly eager to jump into another conversation with anyone. I needed time to prepare for the possibilities of tomorrow, so I was grateful for the mandatory alone time.

I wasn't worried that King Seger would find out our marriage was a hoax; I was worried about the repercussions it would cause with the others — Risa, Damien, and more particularly, Aleron.

It was obvious Killian's improvisation salvaged any chance of allying with King Seger, but I was terrified the others would find a way to disagree. I could see the justification in Killian's thinking and actions, but would the others consider it reckless?

During the final days of our journey here to Cenan — after the moment and confession between Killian and me — I had been trying to mentally prepare myself for defending our relationship, our interaction — or whatever it was. I was still processing it all and knew Killian and I had an unfinished conversation about what our moment meant for us going forward. This new role we had to play as husband and wife meant that discussion would be required much sooner than I had planned.

The most challenging part was knowing that to the others, if I had to play the role of Killian's wife, it would all be out of the desire to secure an alliance with Cenan. It wouldn't cross their mind that when Killian took my hand, the warmth of his fingers sent a chill down my back; when he smiled at me, my heart jumped in my chest, my stomach twisted with satisfaction and delight at his nearness, his very touch; that a glimpse of his piercing blue eyes challenged my ability to think clearly, and when he defended my character to King Seger, the feeling of security I oddly felt with Killian only intensified. They wouldn't think any of it could be real. That is what terrified me the most.

I had already been nervous about having the inevitable conversation with the others, but now I was at even more of a loss for where to start. I was uncertain of their possible reactions. They were likely troubled and worried about the state and pressures Killian had forced upon me with his unexpected announcement. I had been shocked, but I was also flattered. Something about Killian's declaration of our fake engagement had ignited inside of me more exhilaration than irritation, and despite how much I knew I should fear those feelings, I found myself yearning to discover more. All I wanted was to see Killian.

How many times would I be fooled by him? How many times would I stand by idly and watch as Killian destroyed my life? How many times would I let him take the things most precious to me? How many times would I allow him to make decisions that impacted so many other people's lives? How many times would I go along with his lies?

Maybe I was being emotional, melodramatic, possibly irrational from unjustified envy — but that still left me with a valid reason for my frustration. Killian had placed us in a fragile position. Yes, his fraudulent marriage was an acute tactic to gain King Seger's trust, but if King Seger discovered he was being deceived. . . I was confident none of us would be leaving Cenan.

Was Killian's strategy worth the risk? Had lying ever been the solution in our lives? When had it provided the results we had hoped for? I couldn't recall any, which only fueled my doubt and indignation.

I didn't want to change Killian, for it felt like a fool's errand to try. I didn't expect him to change for anyone; however, during this process, it was imprudent to consider that his decision-making would at least be more inclusive of Valteria and Praseria.

We had more than just the responsibility of protecting Valteria and Praseria now. We had Veruje, Gree and Lokali. We were the largest kingdoms of them all. What would become of us if we couldn't represent and facilitate the alliances and lead our kingdoms? What impact could this lie have on our alliances? All for one kingdom? It didn't seem worth the risk, but the decision had been made for all of us as soon as Killian began leading the conversation with King Seger — and I stood by and let it happen.

Worst of all, Killian put Allene at the forefront of his deception. If things ended poorly, it wouldn't be Killian alone facing the consequences; it would be Allene too. I couldn't comprehend the confusion and fear pressing upon her mind as tomorrow approached. I could say nothing to Allene without the risk of being overheard by a Cenanite and exposing the lie. The greatest way I could protect her was to go along with Killian's story and pray our acting would be enough to secure an alliance and get out of Cenan before anything else could go wrong.

KILLIAN

I confidently looked at each servant as I walked past the other's rooms. The servants clearly suspected me, and I was sure King Seger had warned them to be more vigilant than before as our stay had been extended. I ignored the speculative glances and discreet whispers, not hesitating as I knocked on Allene's door.

I composedly placed my hands behind my back and listened to her soft footfalls approach. The surprise that lit up on her face made me smile in sheer delight. She hugged the fur shawl she had been wearing tighter around her arms, and it snugly tucked away her silky black locks inside it. Allene's flushed cheeks gave away her nerves as her eyes drifted back and forth from the servants in the hallway and to me. Her sapphire eyes glowed brightly as she stared at me, her posture relaxing as she leaned against the doorway.

"You came," she whispered, her lips curving into a shy smile.

My eyebrows raised in reply. "Are you surprised?"

Allene shrugged and crossed her feet. "I figured you would be tired. It has been a long few days for all of us, and we have an early start to our day tomorrow."

A quiet chuckle escaped my lips as I studied her face. "It doesn't matter how early I have to wake up tomorrow; there was no probability of me achieving a peaceful night's sleep unless I knew you were alright. It's been an emotionally charged day, and I had to check on you myself."

"I am okay," she assured me. "My body is already feeling drastically different from this morning. I am sure another good night's rest will resolve any lingering exhaustion."

I nodded, the curls on my head falling into my eyes, my right hand smoothly pushing them back into place. "Is there anything I can do for you?"

In posing such a question, it may have seemed to her like I had no power to help in Cenan even if Allene did have a pressing need, but that didn't matter to me. If there was anything I could do, I would, no matter the cost. She would always come first, above all else.

Allene paused for a moment, her crystal blue eyes roaming over me, my mind becoming foggy at the close attention she was gifting my way. "You can tell me how you are holding up," she inquired shyly.

I didn't have to spend any time considering my

answer. "I have never been better." My words were said with a sincere smile, as I truly meant every word.

Despite all that was going on and how bleak our circumstances may have seemed, internally, I had never felt more hope for my future than I had in the last few days. Allene was proving to be an answer to years of insecurities and damage that I thought would never be repaired. Slowly, day by day — piece by piece — she was mending the wounds. She was erasing the scars. She lit a fire inside of me that I assumed had died out long ago. She was changing me. Fueling me. Enveloping me. Refining me. She was a burning flame I never wanted to quench.

Allene let out a relieved sigh. "Then I suppose we can both sleep soundly tonight."

"I'll count on it," I smiled, my hand finding its way to her cheek as I mindlessly ran my thumb along her smooth skin, the sensation drastically different from my rough fingertips. Allene shivered underneath my touch, the reaction pulling me closer to her, only a breath separating us.

We both paused, a moment of charged silence lingering between us. I could feel myself struggling to leave. There was more I wanted to say, more I wanted to do, and more I wanted to hear, but the open and exposed hallway was not the time or place for it. For the sake of protecting everyone — protecting *her* — I smothered the desire to stay where it was, barely hidden beneath the surface.

Allene looked down at the ground and back up at me, her eyes reflecting a new emotion — curiosity.

"I wanted to say thank you for staying with me last night. Risa told me you waited for me to wake for quite some time." Her words were surprising, and the notion that she expected me not to wait to see that she was all right cut me deeper than it should.

My face crumbled as I fervently looked at her, desperate to communicate the trust I selfishly wanted her to instill in me. "Allene, you don't ever need to thank me for the privilege of being near you." I reached out my right hand to free her beautiful hair from the constraining shawl, allowing her heavy locks to brush against my skin as I stroked it delicately. I stared into her wondering blue eyes, anxious to communicate how she made me feel. "There was no other place I wanted to be."

I held back a sigh as I knew it was time to depart, as the circumstances necessitated a short visit. "I won't keep you any longer. My princess needs her rest. Sweet dreams, love." I brushed a kiss on the top of her forehead, waited for her to close the door, and clung to the feelings she had ignited inside me until I would be graced with her presence again in my dreams.

I wasn't fond of hunting. My father had tried to take Risa and me a handful of times to hunt ducks and other waterfowl, but I found it painstakingly dull, and my body would ache for days after all the rigid sitting. Adding freshly fallen snow to soak my boots, and the frigid, crisp air to bite at the exposed skin on my face, I could safely say I was especially not fond of hunting in Cenan.

Time passed scrupulously slow as we trudged through the mountains of snow, the memory of the recent storm sending a shiver down my back, impulsively making me pull the fur shawl tighter around my shoulders. I doused the feelings of fear threatening to escape me and risk foiling my attempt at composure. I chose to distract myself by counting the number of footprints ahead of me, paying particular attention to the ones I knew had been made by Killian, who had been ahead of the group with King Seger at his side.

The hunting groups split up halfway through the hunt as they attempted to surround a ram herd that had been spotted. Damien, Hassan, and Marshal had joined one group, while Risa, Aleron, Killian, and I stayed with King Seger's group.

Killian and King Seger continued to keep to themselves as they led us in the proper direction. I watched in awe as Killian made King Seger belly laugh on more than one occasion. For a man who had been intent on sending us away, he sure had opened his mind to Killian rather quickly.

Risa interrupted my gawking as she shivered next to me. "Is it only me that has felt hostile signals from King Seger's second?" Risa's eyes darted to King Seger's shadow, the woman we saw yesterday in the throne room with the braided hair and prevalent tattoos.

"Who? The woman?" I asked cryptically.

Risa nodded her head, her mouth frowning at me as she shot the woman a scrutinizing glare. "I haven't been shivering from the cold, Allene. Her stare alone makes me feel like she will tear me apart and eat me for dinner."

I couldn't help but laugh at her dramatic assumption. I patted her shoulder softly, doing my best to reassure her running thoughts. "I am sure if we got to know her better, we would discover it is her personality; we have nothing to be afraid of."

"Risa's right, she is the most intimidating woman I

have ever seen, and I am also certain she has contemplated the best way to prepare us for her next meal," Aleron's voice approached quietly from behind us.

"You too?" I considered acknowledging his eavesdropping but decided against it. "You both have untethered imaginations. It is your nerves making you see things," I assured them.

Aleron sighed softly, his nose scrunching as he eyed the woman ahead of us. "I have been unsettled since we arrived here. I was almost grateful to be turned away by King Seger yesterday and start our journey back home. I hope Killian's push for an alliance proves to be the right decision."

"If you're nervous about how their conversation is going, you should join," I encouraged. I was curious to know what Killian and King Seger had been discussing. I knew he would tell me later on, but I was also nervous to see how today would unravel.

Aleron scoffed. "And miss out on the debate of how *blondie bear* might eat us? I think I'll stay right where I am."

I let out a quiet chuckle at Aleron's joke; however, Risa's face remained firm. Risa squinted her eyes as she looked at all three of them now: King Seger, Killian, and "blondie bear." The intensity of her expression was a sight I rarely saw and it left me troubled.

"You have that much faith in Killian?" Risa's voice was low and hardly discernible as she asked her question.

"I do," I replied, quickly. Perhaps too quickly.

My face turned red as I felt Risa and Aleron stare at

me. We all fell silent as I realized who the question was intended for, the embarrassment stinging. Risa was asking Aleron for his opinion, *not* mine.

I didn't need to look at their faces to understand their reactions, and Aleron's following words only solidified my assumption.

Aleron's jaw ticked with displeasure as his eyes cemented on Killian's back. "Risa, if he managed to convince Allene in such a short time to trust him, then I am sure he won't have any issues with King Seger." Aleron let the words hang heavily in the air, the oxygen around me feeling thinner by the minute.

My heart rate accelerated as I heard the bellow of a ram. Without a moment of hesitation, Aleron jogged away to see the kill, not glancing back at Risa and me. I didn't think the moment could get worse until Risa directed her interrogating whisper at me.

"What happened between you and Killian?"

ALERON

I wanted to ignore it — the gnawing realization that my fears had come to fruition. I knew the charming enticement of my older brother, but I also had blind faith in Allene's judgment of character.

I felt embarrassed by my snide reaction. If Allene had opened her heart to Killian, even a sliver, my hot-headedness wouldn't gain me any additional favors. The circumstance of Allene being with Killian the last few weeks was my fault in the first place. As infuriating as my brother was, I knew he wasn't to blame for the situation — which made it that much worse.

Being around Killian again and watching him conduct himself as the prince of Praseria brought back a flood of memories and emotions. Memories that made me see Killian as I assume Allene currently did and emotions that left my heart aching from the betrayal of the brother I thought I'd known. Those painful reminders made me determined to show Allene Killian's true self.

I needed the best for Allene. As we had our time apart, I realized that the best for her may not be me. Considering my rash and hurtful decisions, I could understand if Allene chose not to pursue a future together. However, I also needed her to see why a future with Killian would be detrimental to her happiness and well-being. I needed to know that whoever she was with would protect her. I needed to know that her heart and future would be safe.

I was determined to speak with Killian later concerning Allene, but I knew now was not the time. Killian was having success making friends with King Seger, and I wouldn't be the reason an alliance failed to happen.

I stayed a few steps behind King Seger and Killian and observed their conversation quietly as we returned to the castle. King Seger continuously praised Killian's achievement of getting the ram. It was clear that the Killian's hunting skills had gained him favor in King Seger's sight.

Killian's intentions and plan seemed to be working. I was confident we could appease any suspicion of King Seger's and secure the alliance we had come here seeking. It was now a matter of all the alliances keeping their word and hoping diplomacy, and strategic friendships would be enough to save our kingdoms.

"Will you answer me now?"

Killian and I were finally alone, and I had burning questions that needed to be addressed.

Killian hung up his hunting bow, not turning around as he spoke with his back to me.

"What do you want to know?" he asked dryly, boredly blinking.

"I want to know why you let the members of the Red Crows that kidnapped our mother out of your sight. It was a cowardly thing to do. Are you working with them?" I accused, my fingers tapping against my leg as I impatiently waited for Killian's smug reply.

Killian scoffed as he turned his head to the side. "How could you ask me such a thing?"

"The thought has crossed my mind more than once," I admitted. I wasn't ashamed to let him know my suspicions and to let him realize how little I trusted him.

Killian rolled his eyes, cutting me a sharp look. "I let them get away because I only had Hassan with me. I was outnumbered — *again.* What good is it that I found them if, by tracking them, I got caught and kidnapped myself? And it wouldn't have been just me; Allene would have been with me too. I made a difficult decision, but it wasn't wrong, and I would do the same thing again," Killian defended, turning to confront me now, his arms folding over his chest as he loomed over me. "It is easy for you to assume you would intervene if you were in the same situation, but don't speak of things you don't understand, brother. If the same situation ever befalls you — which I pray that it doesn't — and you find a better solution, then you can critize me. So to answer your ignorant question, no, I'm not working with the Red Crows."

"Prove it," I insisted, my eyes glazed over at his attempt of a logical response.

Logic wasn't going to be the answer in securing my trust. My focus was set on my emotions, the most dominant being disappointment and betrayal. I sunk back at the bitterness of them both, eager to feel them fade.

"How do you propose I do that?" Killian impatiently replied, but the annoyance in his voice didn't dissuade me — he wouldn't shame me into silence on the matter.

"Show me your shoulder," I suggested.

The Red Crows each had a crow tattoo on their left shoulder. If he were telling the truth, the absence of a tattoo would testify to it.

Killian offered an insincere half smile. "I am not going to take my shirt off for you. I'm sorry to disappoint you by not delivering a show."

"It is the easiest way to prove your innocence," I persisted.

Killian growled. "I don't need to prove my innocence. But if you truly need to know if there is a tattoo on my shoulder, you can speak with Allene. She can verify that nothing is there."

My knuckle joints echoed in the room as I cracked my fingers, the frustration from Killian's comment immediately taking effect as my hands balled into fists. The image of Killian shirtless in front of Allene. . .it was a scene I never wanted to imagine. My stomach turned at even the mention of it.

"Killian, how far will you go?" I prodded through clenched teeth.

Killian waved his hand in front of his chest, motioning me to continue. "I need you to elaborate."

I released my tight fists and stretched out my aching fingers. The hatred in my eyes was enough to communicate my anger. "How far will you go with pursuing Allene?"

Killian was silent, and my blood boiled while my mind spinned. His lack of response was more damning than any words he could mutter.

"I know I can't expect much from you, and I know I shouldn't ask, but when it comes to Allene, I can't stop myself from getting involved. If you have any respect for me, you will leave her *alone*. For once in your life, don't be selfish."

I cringed at how closely my words sounded like a plea, but when it came to protecting Allene, I was desperate. I would plead, beg, bribe, do whatever it took to change Killian's mind and intentions about her — do *anything* to set his sights somewhere else. I knew my brother too well. He was stubborn and insufferably selfish. If he wanted Allene, he wouldn't hold back from doing all he could to secure her. He could try, but I would make it as difficult as possible. I would be the thorn in his side, the whisper in her ear, the doubt in her heart, the reasoning in her mind, for as long as she would let me. And maybe even if she wouldn't.

Killian moved forward and paused just a few inches away from me. It never ceased to amaze me how identical we were physically. Our heights were nearly the same, our hair, our eyes. Standing in front of my brother was like looking in the mirror — except what was reflected in his eyes was far from anything like me. He was a stanger to be feared.

Killian's eyes narrowed at me, the challenge dancing behind them clear. "Brother, I would advise you not speak of things you don't understand. There is much you don't know about my relationship with Allene. I don't find it fair for you to judge me and her so quickly."

"I don't want to know about your relationship — I am asking you to ensure there *isn't* one," I clarified.

"I can't promise you that. My priority is what Allene wants," Killian insisted, his face relaxing at the sound of her name leaving his lips.

I shuddered as rage slowly began to crawl over my skin. "Allene knows what she wants. At least she did before you entered our lives. Inserting yourself won't give her clarity; it will only confuse her."

Killian was silent again. I could see him reflecting on my words, his eyebrows creased for a split second before he put back on his collected mask. I knew how self-centered he was, but for that brief moment I thought I could see him truly contemplating and considering what I said — that he felt the weight of it — and that was something I never thought I would live to see Killian do.

"You almost killed her, Killian — you imprisoned her in Praseria. What type of redemption do you truly think you can receive from her?" I added, hoping to deliver my point.

Killian's eyes reflected sorrow and pain as he glared at me. "You don't think I can be good enough for her?"

"Never," I snapped, genuinely shocked that he would even ask.

Killian's lips pressed into a rigid line. "Do you trust her?" he queried.

I let out a fast breath. "With my life."

Killian huffed as he straightened his posture and walked towards the door, a passive expression placed on his face. "If you trust her, then let Allene be the judge of me, and leave her to be the judge of *her* feelings. I'll be going now — my wife is waiting."

KILLIAN

Time was a concept set with restraints. It placed universal expectations of how people should live in specific periods of life and circumstances. There was a set time when you should be able to walk, get ready unassisted, leave your home alone, fall in love, be married, have children, and even to die.

But time also has an ego and wants to prove that it makes the rules. If it decides to change its standards, we have no choice but to adapt to its change. Time can be the hero, and it can be the villain.

Time had been both a villain and a hero in my life. I couldn't tell if it was working to unravel my story or stitch it together — if it set out to mislead my life or redirect it. This unexpected journey with Allene, the short amount of time I had known her, seemed to be a welcomed change of direction. It was unexpected, it was fast, and it was everything I desired.

I had hope in a fulfilling future for the first time in years. I had hope that someone would see me for who I truly was. I had hope I wouldn't have to pretend anymore to get through life. I had hope I would receive love, and was determined to give more love in return. These were thoughts I believed could come to fruition. Allene was a miracle, a manifestation of my greatest dream, that rapidly surprised me. My only fear was that time could stop it.

I hated that Aleron wasn't wrong. Showing up in Allene's life likely had been a source of confusion for her. What happened in the woods could have been a fleeting moment of misunderstanding. I had hurt her, the people she loved, and her kingdom. I was a villain in her story. Receiving favor from her, much less love, was not fated to be. Her patience, grace, forgiveness — none of it was owed to me, and it definitely wasn't deserved.

My feelings for Allene were nothing short of pure adoration. I felt lost in her. If she wouldn't be intimidated by the timing — *intimidated by me* — I would have run away with her the day we kissed. I didn't need more time to know what she meant to me and who she was to me. She was the anchor to my existence, the very air that I breathed. In such a short amount of time, she had managed to rewrite what made sense in my selfish world. She was everything.

Now that I had a taste of what life was like with her in it, I was terrified of letting her go. But I was equally terrified of what our life would be like if she stayed. Neither path was easy or perfectly right, but when it came to Allene, I willed myself to be vulnerable and to take the risks, because she was worth every bit of heart ache and suffering that loving her could bring. She was the only person capable of being my undoing, and even if it all came crashing down in the end, it would still be worth it for every feeling she elicited in my unguarded heart.

I knew she would be better off if I left her alone, but I wanted her to take control of my sense of reason. Despite knowing how wrong a relationship with her would be — for her sake, not mine — I couldn't help but savor the circumstance I had been placed in here in Cenan, even if it wasn't real.

Publicly holding Allene's hand at dinner was natural; her touch alone put me at ease. I was unbothered by the mental turmoil it may have put our traveling companions through to remain composed and supportive as they watched us together. We had a stubborn and narcissistic King to convince of our authenticity, and it brought me joy knowing it wasn't entirely a lie.

The evening had been pleasant and casual. Small talk continued throughout most of the dinner, with lingering moments of silence in-between courses. The tension had slightly lifted since yesterday, but many things remained unspoken.

The last course had arrived, and everyone seemed to slow down eating as they waited to see where the conversation would go. King Seger had delightfully bit into his warm pudding as he looked at Allene.

"Princess Amena," he drawled, "I wanted to apologize for my harsh judgment of you yesterday. It was my mistake to be so critical of you and your traveling party without knowing all the facts. I hope you will forgive my rudeness and know I did not want to offend you." King Seger looked expectanctly at Allene, waiting for her reply — as did the rest of the room. The shift in conversation had been initiated, and Allene's hand gripped mine tightly as she had been singled out for the first time this evening.

Her timidness disappeared as soon as she began speaking, her eyes fully alert as she thought through her response. "I appreciate your apology," she began, "We equally regret the confusion our arrival must have caused. We know it was unexpected and unprecedented. I am not offended, nor would I hold a grudge against you. We arrived here with the intention of forming more than an alliance — we were looking to find friendship and common ground. Those intentions remain," she said, amplifying her tone with respect.

"I believe we are well on our way to friendship." King Seger offered a smug smile as he raised his glass towards me.

I raised the full glass in front of me with my free hand, motioning back to him. "Cheers to putting the past behind us and to a more unified future."

We all took a sip of our crimson drinks, shoulders visibly relaxing and deep exhales heard as the glasses fell back on the table. King Seger gulped his drink down the quickest while finishing with an exaggerated breath.

"Speaking of the future, when is the date?" King Seger inquired.

"What date?" I asked.

"The date of your honeymoon," King Seger replied plainly.

I tried not to hesitate to answer, even though King Seger's particular interest in Allene and I's relationship was beginning to be unnerving. I was still trying to peg his source of intrigue, but felt compelled to answer any of his questions to avoid being incredulous. "We haven't determined one; the current circumstances haven't allowed us to," I answered shortly.

Allene's hand became stiff in mine as she chimed in. "Killian's right; there are many details to sort through and too many uncertainties right now. Our focus is on the Red Crows. Once we have that under control, we can think about our personal matters."

King Seger grunted in aggravation, waving a dismissive hand at our words. "What is the fun of being royalty if you can't indulge in personal matters even at the worst times?"

"I would rarely ever say that being royalty is fun," Allene replied tensely. I could hear her holding back the irritation in her voice at King Seger's persistence and comment.

King Seger shook another hand in the air, clearly unaffected by Allene's disgust. "Then you aren't doing it right. Killian, please tell me you have a different opinion than your wife — please tell me you understand how to find joy in our role as royalty?" he crooned.

I paused for a moment before answering, observing the fine line we were walking and the chance of irritating him. "I have seen both. The key is finding a balance," I said flatly, hoping to not give him too much to ponder on.

King Seger slapped the table excitedly as if I had given him the most excellent answer.

"Exactly! A balance. The balance I have found is this — you take what you can when you can, if you want it, because you are never guaranteed a second opportunity. It is the key to longevity."

I offered King Seger a pained smile, doing my best to match his enthusiasm. "That is something I will keep in mind."

King Seger took a long sip of his drink, and his eyes focused on Allene and me. After setting his glass down, he paused and let out another exaggerated sigh. "If we are truly friends, and you appreciate my advice, then let me show you what I mean," King Seger goaded.

I could feel Allene's grip tighten on mine as if she were warning me to heavily consider all responses moving forward. I could already tell, however, that King Seger wouldn't back down from whatever he had in mind and that compliance was likely a better option than opposition.

"What do you have in mind?" I inquired.

"You can have your honeymoon here before you return to Valteria." The words fell out of his mouth so casually, like it was something he offered to all of his guests — like it wasn't an odd and offputting thing to do.

I could feel the bodies in the room tense up at King Seger's suggestion without even looking at everyone's physical reaction. Allene must've been the most bewildered, as she didn't tense at all, but quite the opposite; her hand had become so limp it nearly slipped out of my grip.

I had gathered King Seger as an eccentric man, but this was a different. I couldn't tell if he was being serious. The prospect of a honeymoon was such an intimate, special moment for a couple, and King Seger knew that. He was either trying to put uncomfortable pressure on us, call our bluff, or truly was the most idiosyncratic man I had ever met.

I didn't expect Allene to give a reply — I don't think she could have even if she wanted to — and the silence would be suspicious.

Aleron joined in on the conversation, clearly upset at the proposition. "As generous as your offer is, we unfortunately have to return right away to Valteria," Aleron interjected.

King Seger shook his head. "Is that the true reason for declining my offer? Or are you worried Cenan can't deliver a honeymoon worthy of two royals? Is my taste and kingdom not suitable enough for you?" King Seger's reply had confirmed my fear; he was being serious. He was absolutely insane, which also made him entirely unpredictable. As strange and off-putting as his offer was, we were not in a position to openly decline it.

"Of course not," I interjected this time.

King Seger's eyes lit up. "Then I insist. Consider it a wedding present while also honoring my new alliances for war — and as a token of our new friendship."

"As much as we appreciate the sincerity of your offer, we don't want to be a drain on your resources any more than we already have. Additionally, we aren't planning on needing Cenan to be involved in any battle. We truly hope this will all be settled soon and that you won't have to step foot out of Cenan," I assured him.

King Seger scoffed. "I have an abundance of resources, but I don't have an abundance of patience, neither do I ask others for permission. We will have all the preparations for your honeymoon within a day or two. All you need to worry about is resting and looking forward to a brief moment to celebrate your marriage — because I don't know how many more days of rest any of us will have, or days of enjoyment for that matter, in the near future." King Seger leaned forward on the table, inclining his head in my direction.

"You may not want this situation with the Red Crows to end in a battle, but I can guarantee it will. We are only borrowing time," his last words huffed out as a whisper, leaving a firm knot in my stomach. King Seger plastered on a twisted smile as he leaned back against his chair, threatening to tip it to the floor as he shouted loudly over the table. "So eat, drink, and rest! We have a whirlwind of changes ahead of us, my friend. I hope to see us all hold on!"

Killian didn't have another choice. That is what I told myself as I stared at the ceiling in my room in the middle of the night as sleep evaded me.

The events that transpired at dinner had been entirely unexpected. I was already anxious and in shock from the surprise of our fake marriage — now, in a few days, I would embark on a honeymoon. Things had escalated and gotten out of hand too quickly. Yes, we were desperate for an alliance, but I never imagined things would go this far or turn in this direction.

I was more concerned about how everyone else was processing the false marriage and arranged honeymoon that I didn't dare take the time to understand my thoughts and feelings on the matter. While hunting earlier with Risa, I convinced her that the relationship between Killian and I had merely developed into friendship. However, I could see she wasn't entirely convinced, and I wasn't sure how long it would be until she prodded me again on the subject.

I wanted to talk to the others, hoping their thoughts and reactions to Killian's decisions would help shape my own opinions, however, speaking to the others about this subject wasn't an option. We were in another kingdom, an unfamiliar one, with eyes and ears everywhere. If King Seger found out that we were lying about our marriage and that we had agreed to his terms of having a honeymoon here for the sake of forming an alliance — an alliance he insisted be based on trust and honesty — well, we likely wouldn't be leaving on pleasant terms. We didn't need another enemy. The Red Crows were enough of a worry.

It was my duty to see this alliance through. If what King Seger said at dinner was true, if we were going to end up at war, Cenan could be the difference in us winning or losing in the fight. We needed them on our side, not against us. There wasn't a reason to even consider how I felt about the impending honeymoon taking place. There wasn't another choice. It had to happen, but nothing had to *actually* happen — we just had to play the part, so I wouldn't allow myself to consider anything else.

I was startled from my thoughts when I heard my door crack open. Sitting up in a flurry, my heart racing, I clamored off the bed and made my way to the only other option of escape — the window.

"Calm down, Allene. It's me."

The voice sounded gruff through it's hushed tone, but it was all too familiar, however, it didn't leave me with any comfort. I gripped the edge of the window, my heart still racing at the discovery of who had entered.

"What are you doing here at this hour? You cannot be here! You need to leave. Now!" I hissed under my breath.

Aleron took his hand out from behind his back, the least bit fazed by my quick heated reaction, and placed a plate on the table near my bed.

"You hardly ate at dinner, I assumed you might get hungry tonight so I convinced the servants in the kitchen to make up an extra plate of food."

I instantly regretted my harsh response. My eyes flitted to Aleron's, his expression sullen and stern.

"Thank you," I croaked out my gratitude for his attentiveness. I hadn't eaten at dinner; I hadn't had much of an appetite the last few days. "I'm sorry for overreacting, but you shouldn't be here," I reiterated.

A muscle flared in his jaw. "I wasn't followed," Aleron assured me.

The nerves tangled in my stomach at the thought of a servant or passerby somehow noticing Aleron's disappearance into my room. I was already on edge; this was pushing me past it.

"If someone catches you, they'll get the wrong idea," I

explained.

I cautiously approached Aleron, my hands tugging on his arms to move him to the door. Aleron's feet remain planted in place with no signs of budging despite pushing on him with all my weight. Aleron firmly gripped my shoulders, holding me back.

"What will they get wrong?" Aleron scoffed, his hands tensing at his sides. " That I am upset the love of my life is shamelessly married to my older brother, having a honeymoon in a foreign kingdom without giving any thought to herself or me, and that I had to sneak into her room to talk her out of it? They'd be right," he said sharply, his glimmering blue eyes shrouded in the darkness of the room.

I held back a sigh, the pain of it nipping in my throat. "Aleron . . ."

"It isn't real," Aleron interrupted.

I couldn't tell if Aleron was making a statement or asking a question. "Aleron, we can't discuss this. Someone could be listening."

Aleron became flustered as he got out his following words. "Let them listen. I don't care if you are *"married"* to Killian; none of it matters if it isn't *real*," he exaggerated the last word, the weight of it sinking in my stomach.

"Then why are you here if it doesn't matter?" I spat back.

Aleron's expression became hollow. "Because there are feelings between you two, aren't there?"

Aleron's question surprised me. I hadn't expected him

to be so forward in his prodding, and my tongue felt tied as I searched for an answer that I didn't have the courage to give to him — it was an answer I still hadn't had the full courage to give myself.

I let out a tired sigh, my eyes blinking away the stress of the day as I exchanged with Aleron an unyielding stare. "It's been a long day, with many things to process. Can we discuss this at a different time, in a safer setting, please?" I pulled on Aleron's arms, trying to tug him to the door, but was met with his resistance once again.

Aleron's face crumbled as he looked at me, regret appearing in his eyes. "This isn't how I wanted this conversation to be — this isn't how I wanted things to unfold for us. I planned to reignite things slowly."

I gripped his arms tighter. "Aleron, stop," I hissed in warning.

Aleron's eyes reflected desperation as he shifted his hands to grip my forearms, pulling me to him. "I can't. I can't let you be alone with him. I know I hurt you, and I didn't want to overwhelm you by pursuing you again too quickly, but it seems fate has a much different idea of my timetable, and its scheming has pushed me to have this conversation with you."

I could feel myself begin to panic, the fear of being heard overwhelming me, my mind spinning. "There isn't an option to have this conversation. As twisted and fast as this has happened, it can't be changed. This discussion has to end." My words were no longer pleading; they were demanding.

Aleron loosened his grip and stepped back, creating a gap between us as his gaze roamed over me. "Fine, this discussion can end. I don't have to use words to prove my point."

"What point is that?" I felt my throat go dry as I croaked out my foolish response.

Aleron's eyes were delicate and piercing. He ran his hand down the length of my face like he was trying to memorize every pore. I could feel knots forming in my stomach as he wrapped me in his arms, cradling me into his chest. Aleron rested his chin on my head, his hands on the small of my back.

My muscles became rigid as Aleron leaned back, his gaze determined and tender.

"That despite whatever feelings you are experiencing with Killian, you still have feelings for me too."

Aleron didn't hesitate as he leaned in, and his lips softly pressed against mine. I knew I should've pulled away and scolded him immediately, but I was frozen. The memory of Aleron's touch came rushing back as his hands held me dearly. He tenderly kissed me — like it may be his last opportunity, making my heart ache. I hadn't been this close to Aleron since we left Valteria, and being this close to him — breathing in his permanent clove scent and feeling the comfort of his familiar embrace, the warmth of his lips, the pureness of his heart — it was a reminder of everything I had decided to let go when I chose to pursue Killian.

Aleron only kissed me once; it was all he had to do to

leave my emotions and thoughts in a jumbled mess. As he pulled away, I struggled to formulate a reply, and Aleron took the opportunity only to make me more confused and speechless.

"Being like this, being close to you," his hand trailed softly down my cheek, "it comes naturally when I am with you. Pushing you away as I did. . . it actively took my every effort to do that, and the only reason I could succeed was because I thought I was doing the right thing — I thought I was protecting you." Aleron's eyes were desperate as he seemed to cherish me being cradled closely in his arms.

"It was wrong of me to make such a rash, unilateral decision. I have a lot to mend between us. I will be patient, Allene; I am willing to wait. But don't take that as me being passive. I know what I want." Aleron's words were certain, his intentions straightforward. There was no questioning where his mind was at — or where his heart lay. His certainty left me panicked, and envious, that he could be so sure of his feelings; that he could be this consistent and dependable despite all we had been through.

Aleron's body tensed around me, and I could see how difficult it was for him to let me go. He cautiously stepped back, the room quiet as he approached the door.

"Allene, I don't expect you to make a decision right now or to have an answer for me. I only ask that you don't shut me out — keep a small piece of your heart open to me," Aleron let out a shaky breath, his hand cupping my chin as he tilted my gaze to his. "Allow me to make things right."

Aleron's plea was heartfelt and genuine. I could see how deeply he wanted to change things. His words of commitment and determination left me feeling conflicted. *Had I made a rash choice with Killian? Could I trust my feelings for him? Could I still have feelings for Aleron, or were the fond memories we shared the source of my confusion? Would abiding by Aleron's request falter the start of a relationship with Killian, or give me more clarity on the matter?*

I still wasn't sure where Killian and I stood regarding a relationship. There was too much to sort out with my thoughts and feelings; I couldn't produce a certain answer.

You don't have to make a decision right now. Aleron's words echoed in my head. All he wanted was for me to be open-minded. I owed Aleron that much. I owed him another chance, just as he graciously gave me.

I fought back the muscles in my forehead from turning down in worry and stress. I felt my face relax as I let out sigh. "I need time," I whispered, the only response I could safely give.

Aleron's posture relaxed at the sound of my reply, his eyes beaming with the sliver of hope it allotted him. "Take all the time you need." Aleron's hand dropped from my face and bowed his head as he quietly shut the door, leaving me to a restless night of little sleep and insurmountable questions.

Finding means of distraction had been challenging in the last few weeks. Today was no different. In fact, it was worse. At least while traveling, the monotony of each step, combined with the option to eavesdrop on others' conversations, numbed some of my own thoughts. But not today. I had to face the reality that today could change things between Allene and me, and I had no way of knowing if it would change things positively or negatively. I yearned for a distraction until I knew the answer.

Allene hadn't entirely turned me away. During our time apart, I had convinced myself that we had was stronger than anything she may feel towards Killian. Her time with Killian, it was just for today — and it wasn't real. They weren't actually on a honeymoon. Today could give Allene the clarity she needs. I wouldn't lose hope yet. Until there was a ring on her finger and vows exchanged,

I would still take all the chances I could to gain back her heart, because I couldn't begin to fathom what life would feel like without it.

I tried to suppress my worries, especially since any events that transpired today were entirely out of my control. It wasn't much, but I had found some relief in my spare time as Marshal and I played chess. I watched the snow lightly fall outside until Marshal's voice drew back my attention.

"Your move," Marshal said, his tone lingering in lethargy.

I glanced at the board momentarily, moved my knight, and looked out the window again.

"Are you all right?" Marshal asked, removing another of my pawns from the board.

Marshal and I had gotten along decently on our journey, but his inquiry into my feelings still surprised me.

"I'm fine," I replied flatly, taking out one of Marshal's bishops.

"So your conversation went well last night?" Marshal's eyes remained fixated on the chessboard, clearly uninterested in my reaction to his comment.

My eyebrows raised in alarm at the question, my eyelids blinking slowly. "How did you. . ."

Marshal raised his hand to stop me. "I am still a Valterian guard. It is my responsibility to ensure Risa and Allene are safe, which includes checking on them." Marshal looked up at me and shrugged like it should have been obvious. "I followed you to Allene's room last night."

I sighed, sinking deeper into the chair. "I thought I had been careful."

Marshal shook his head in disapproval. "You're fortunate I caught you and not one of the guards. You would have jeopardized everything."

"Why didn't you stop me?" I asked, leaning forward now to watch Marshal move a pawn almost to the end of the board.

Marshal's eyes narrowed as he displayed a new emotion I hadn't seen before — *pity*.

"Because I would've done the same if it was Risa. I don't envy you in the slightest," Marshal stated, any judgment in his tone doused from the sympathy he felt towards my situation.

"How comforting," I muttered, moving my rook to remove one of Marshal's pawn.

Marshal winced, letting out a sigh. "What I'm trying to say is I know what Allene means to you, and I empathize with your situation," Marshal clarified.

"I don't need your pity, Marshal," I assured him, flashing him a half-hearted smile.

"I'm not offering pity; I'm offering you a friend." Marshal looked up at me now, his expression as sincere as his voice.

I could feel my eyebrows furrowed in confusion as I leaned in closer to the board and to Marshal as I studied his expression. "Why would you want to be my friend?"

Marshal raised his shoulders, running his calloused hands through his straight sandy hair. "I'm not ashamed to acknowledge that you are a good person, which is enough of a reason, but I also don't see anyone else lining up to offer a listening ear, and I think you could use one right now."

I did not expect his offer to result in a close friendship, but I still appreciated the sentiment. "Thank you, Marshal," I managed to say, his sincerity a welcome contrast to what the last few weeks had been.

"You're welcome," he said simply. Marshal offered a coy smile as he made his next move. "Checkmate."

KILLIAN

The frost in the corner of the windows made the cozy room feel warmer. The firepit had burned down and let off an intense deep glow that enveloped my skin. The ambiance of the cottage was a stark contrast to the cold, granite castle. The room displayed mahogany wood furniture with dark upholstery, thick animal skins lined the rustic stone floor, and lanterns with lit candles left a low light that gave the entire room a mellow mood.

Allene's habit of rubbing her ruby ring when she was nervous had given away her feelings throughout the evening. I observed her, studied her, trying to silently communicate how much I wanted her to open up to me. I didn't want to appear desperate, and I didn't want to pressure her to speak to me if she didn't want to. We had engaged in light, easygoing conversation throughout our dinner, but it hadn't progressed past that.

By the time we had dessert, I had memorized every button on Allene's newly gifted golden dress, along with each seam and crease. Her long lashes masked her worried eyes that shied away from maintaining eye contact for too long. Her water glass became empty after each long gulp she used to delay the conversation. She tucked her silky hair behind her right ear, her beautiful long fingers fidgeting with a small escaped strand.

I knew that not discussing what was bothering her would only continue to make her uncomfortable. As we quietly sat side by side on the fur-adorned settee, I intuitively found myself reaching for Allene's anxious hand, firmly clasping it in mine.

Allene's doe-like eyes fluttered in surprise at the sudden gesture, her delicate pink lips finally moving to address me first that evening.

"You aren't obligated to do that," Allene whispered, her words not intended to cause harm, but each one cut sharply through me.

"Obligated?" I couldn't bury the disappointment in my voice from her reaction, and Allene's posture sunk in reply.

"We are alone, and I don't want you to feel pressured to continue the act of being my. . ." Allene practically choked on her words, unable to get out the title.

"Your husband?" I filled in her sentence for her.

She nodded shyly, the innocence in her expression made my stomach tighten in knots.

I felt my eyebrows raise in surprise. "Is this why you

have been uneasy all evening? Have you been worried that I am uncomfortable with the position and title of being your husband?"

Allene's silence was enough of a response as she stared at our hands that lightly grasped one another.

I casually leaned back, my elbow falling against the armrest, creating distance as I studied Allene's troubled facial expression, trying to learn how she displayed every emotion with each little movement.

"Allene, I can assure you that you are the only one uncomfortable right now."

Allene sighed in adorable frustration, her words fast and flustered. "I don't mean to be, but a lot has happened in such a short amount of time. I'm unsure how to approach you or what our dynamic should be."

I smirked, barely managing to stifle the laugh that attempted to escape my throat. "We're married; it is a pretty straightforward dynamic."

Allene huffed in irritation, rolling her eyes at me. "I'm serious, Killian. I don't know what to perceive as real or an act, what I should allow myself to feel, or what I should suppress. Things between us feel ambiguous. We haven't gotten a chance to talk since our. . .moment." Allene's voice became hushed at the end, like she was concealing an enormous secret.

"You mean our very pleasant makeout?" I clarified, brushing my fingertips across her blushed face, her cheek becoming hot against my touch.

Allene's shoulders slouched again at my response, her

worries heavier than I thought, and I feared she would perceive me as insincere.

I cleared my throat, my voice grave as I tried to articulate my emotions. "I do not mean to brush away your feelings with jests. I thought I had spoken plainly about my intentions, Allene," I attempted to clarify.

Allene's innocent eyes sincerely looked into mine, her search for already answered questions persevering. "I don't want any chance of misunderstanding," she nervously added.

This time I leaned forward, challenging her to look deeply into my eyes to see the confidence and transparency in my response. "Allene, I want to be with you. I promise, it couldn't be more simple or genuine than that." I brushed my thumb over her cheek, methodically stroking her smooth skin. The words had come out slow and pure, my heart racing as I admitted them out loud.

There it is. The draw, the tug, the pull, whatever it was, the invisible stronghold she had over me was in full force as I faltered in resisting keeping my distance. I urged Allene's face towards mine, eager to communicate once again my feelings in a different way than words, but I forced myself to pause, our lips almost touching. Her body was tense with nerves, but I knew it wasn't due to the anticipation of a kiss. I could feel she was holding back something that was burdening her mind, and if it wasn't me, then there was only one other explanation.

"I sense your unease has less to do with how *I* feel and more to do with how you feel —

or how you may still feel towards my brother." I didn't hold back in my observation, and I didn't hold back Allene as she jerked away in surprise.

"Excuse me?" The words caught in Allene's throat, her crystal blue eyes embarrassed and flustered.

I sighed, her reaction confirming my suspicion. "I am not the only one who has been candid in sharing my feelings with you since arriving in Cenan, am I?"

Allene hid her eyes behind her shiny curtain of hair, apprehensive about replying.

"Allene, it seems you are the only one uncertain of your feelings," I addressed her once again, trying not to appear as desperate as I felt in hearing some reassurance, and doing my best to conceal the disappointment that threatened to weave into my tone.

Allene's head snapped up, her expression stern and scolding. "I'm not uncertain," Allene said firmly, reaching for my hand that she now held tightly. "I know my feelings for you are intense and real." The last word emerged as merely a whisper as if it was only allowed to be known by the two of us. I suppressed the urge to be bothered by it and focused on her words. Her feelings were real, and that would be enough, for as long as it needed to be.

"Allene, I would rather you be brutally honest with me than shelter your thoughts to spare my feelings. The topic of my brother is not banned to be discussed," I assured her.

Conflicting emotions erupted on Allene's face, her eyelids blinking fast as she tried to compose herself. "You want me to be honest, but I don't want to hurt you, and more importantly," Allene hesitated, slightly shivering, "I don't want you to doubt my feelings for you," Allene admitted her fears.

I rubbed my thumb against Allene's palm, trying not to let my confidence falter in her presence as I clung to her last words. "I'm not oblivious. The feelings and memories you shared with my brother are recent and sincere, but I know the same can be said of your feelings for me."

"And that doesn't bother you?" she inquired.

I scoffed. "Of course it does. It stirs me deep with envy to think you may yet choose my brother. However, I am vain and ambitious enough that it isn't a strike to my confidence or a deterrent in my pursuit of you. I want to be the one you choose, even if that takes time and patience on my part as you discover where your heart lies." I pulled Allene closer, encouraging her to rest her cheek on my shoulder. Allene reluctantly nodded, her expression apologetic as she gained the courage to look up at me.

"I will make a decision soon. I just need a little bit of time." Allene let out a long, drawn-out sigh, her body becoming less tense as she exhaled.

"Take as much time as you need. One's heart is not an object that can be controlled at will. But if there is anything I can do to make your decision faster, don't hesitate to tell me."

Allene peered up at me, my offer catching her attention — an offer I may come to regret.

"You want to ask me questions?" Killian cautiously repeated my request.

"There is very little that I know about you," I pointed out.

Killian pondered on the idea momentarily, his hand rubbing his chin as he considered his reply. When he finally did speak, his voice was barely discernible.

"And if there are things I can't tell you?" Killian asked.

"I am okay with waiting until you feel ready to tell me certain things," I hurriedly replied, eager to obtain at least some answers from him.

Killian sighed. "Even if I was ready to tell you certain things, it doesn't mean I should. There are many parts about my past that you don't want to hear, Allene." Killian's eyes grew cold, and his jaw clenched as he processed the memories of what he wanted to keep to himself; the shields and masks that he wanted to remain in place. "I've buried the parts of my life that no one else should have to bear knowing."

Killian's response made me want to retreat. Maybe I was getting into an intense conversation too soon. But I couldn't quench the desire to learn more about him, even if it meant daunting him to be vulnerable and for me to be uncomfortable.

I interlaced our fingers, trying to offer him empathy. "Killian, that is a heavy and lonely way to live."

The corners of his mouth turned down as he solemnly looked at me, his expression shrouded in secrets. "I never said I enjoyed it. But I don't see the reason for others to suffer with knowledge that isn't necessary for them to know."

"For the people that care about you, watching you wrestle with unspoken burdens on your own is even more heartbreaking," I faintly mumbled, letting my thoughts freely spew from my lips as I fought to break down the walls he wanted to remain.

"Which is why I don't let people care about me," Killian's response was short and quick, the rush of it leaving a stinging sensation in my ears and a heaviness in my heart.

I whispered as tenderly as possible, hoping he wouldn't close up on me now. "I care about you."

"And I fear you will regret it one day." The pain in Killian's eyes that he desperately tried to suppress remained at the surface. "I wanted you so badly that I couldn't put up the walls that I normally do. I let you in, I let you care, and in return, you gave me a small taste of life with you. And I am too selfish to let you go, even if it ruins you." Killian's eyes fell to his hands, his lips pressed into a fine line as his eyebrows creased in sudden worry.

"You may view yourself as selfish, but I don't," I said, my hands resting on top of his. "You are determined and you are not willing to resign from what you care about. That may be your most attractive quality yet." A smile tugged at my lips while admitting the characteristics of him that had caught my affection, and the confession seemed to relax Killian slightly, his gaze flitting from his hands to meet my eyes. I leaned in closely, securing his attention as I nearly distracted myself by inhaling his intoxicating scent, pushing through to communicate my thoughts. "So call it selfishness, say it'll ruin me, but that is one thing I never want to change about you."

Killian's eyes widened in surprise, a brightness and ferocity returning to them instantaneously. "You have left me speechless, love," Killian's smile grew, his teeth glistening as he took in my determination to connect with him.

I swept my legs underneath me, raising myself a bit taller as we sat side by side so I could be eye level with Killian. His blue eyes were like watching a storm, the message and emotion behind them wild and unpredictable. Maintaining eye contact for too long was difficult; the tingling it sent through my body made me weak, but it was even more impossible to look away. He observed me, waiting for me to speak again.

"If we want a proper chance at this, I need the opportunity to get to know all of you," I eventually managed to say.

Killian's stormy eyes settled, their direction set as they locked with mine. "If we have this conversation, I won't hold back. Are you truly prepared for that?" he whispered in warning.

I withheld the urge to gulp, realizing I was nervous about what I had been pleading for. I pushed through with confidence and nodded.

"I want to understand you completely, Killian. I want to hear everything."

KILLIAN

"OK," I said.

"OK. . .?" Allene's eyebrows furrowed in confusion.

"OK, I will tell you anything you want to know," I declared.

"Is it really that simple?" Allene asked in disbelief.

I flashed her a smug smile. "Yes, only because it's you asking."

"I can ask you anything?" She was still in shock.

I nodded. "I warned you that there are many parts about my past that you won't want to hear, but I don't want to hide my life from you, Allene. If you want to know something, I'll give you an answer." I exhaled, mentally preparing myself for what the rest of our conversation may bring. "What's the first thing you want to know?"

Allene was quiet as she looked at me, her forehead

creasing as she heavily weighed what question she wanted to ask first, but her seriousness subsided quickly and turned her questions to start out lighthearted and easy. The discussion led us to learn more about the small details and preferences we hadn't yet shared with one another.

I shared things about me that seemed irrelevant, but Allene seemed to hang onto every word, eager to hear it all. I told her my love for hunting and the outdoors, swimming, my preference of eating crab for every meal if I could, raspberries as the superior fruit in my eyes, chocolate as my primary dessert choice, dark green was my favorite color, being at the ocean at sunset was my favorite view in the entire world, my short lived passion and hobby of glass work that I promised to show her one day, as well as my love for archery, and my struggle to carry a tune.

I learned that Allene didn't enjoy seafood, she loved aged cheese, anything with sugar, fresh homemade bread, playing the piano, writing poems and songs, scalding hot baths, she didn't enjoy the tugging feeling on her scalp when her hair was pulled up too tightly, she loved the smell of the woods after a rainstorm, white was her favorite color — which we then debated if white we even allowed to be considered as a favorite — and she won the debate. Risa and her were close, and Damien was like a brother to her. The relationship with her mother had always been strained, but had slowly improved. She opened up more about the relationship with her father and the experience it had been of losing him unexpectedly.

The tone of the conversation had shifted to be more serious and heavy, and Allene's eyes flitted to mine as she nervously traced circles on the palm of my hand. I could feel her tremble slightly as she asked her next question.

"Why did you leave Praseria?" she softly whispered the question.

I knew I had warned her, and done all I could to restrain her from asking questions she wouldn't want to hear the answers to, but I still felt obligated to ask again.

"Are you sure you want to hear these answers?" I cautiously confirmed.

She shrugged her shoulders and folded her arms across her chest, sinking into the settee. "I'm not certain when you will give me an opportunity like this again; I need to be considering questions that have been unanswered."

I understood her perspective, but regretted the turn the conversation was about to take.

"I'm sure you've already heard Aleron's side as to why I left," I assumed.

She nodded. "I have, but I want to hear it from you."

"All right then, let's start from the beginning." I sighed, trying to remove all my learned inclinations to keep the difficult information close to me. She wanted me to be vulnerable. She wanted me to be honest. If that is what she needed to open her heart to me, then I would do exactly that.

"The first incident with my father happened on my seventh birthday. He gifted me my first horse and his eagerness for me to start learning to ride was evident. As a child, I developed a fear of horses. Their size, their unpredictableness, to my seven-year-old self, I was terrified, not empowered, at the idea of riding such a large animal. The instant my father gifted me that horse, he expected me to ride it. I protested and did my best to negotiate, taking a few weeks to train and learn. My father promised me he wouldn't make me ride it, but he at least wanted me to sit on the horse as a first step."

As I recollected the memory, I could feel my body shiver, but Allene's gentle touch urged me on. I cleared my throat, shoveling down my hesitation as her eyes prodded me to continue.

"I mustered all the courage I had to sit atop that horse, and within seconds, my father betrayed me. He hit the back of the horse, and it ran. I desperately held on, but with little to grasp and no experience riding, it didn't take long for me to take an intense blow straight into the ground." My neck ached at the mention of it, the sharpness of the pain cutting through my memory as I rubbed the muscles, letting out a shaky breath before I continued.

"I lay on the ground, filled with pain and shock, convinced I had broken something as I watched the horse run away. I waited, fearful to move or look at my body with the chance I would see blood trickling from the scrape I knew was on my leg. I remember smelling the blood and being nauseated and frightened at the scent of it. I could hear my father's footsteps as he approached me. When his eyes looked at mine, it was as if I was seeing an entirely new man. The rage, the dissatisfied glare, was not one the father I knew would give, and I cried at the sight of his face."

I paused. I hadn't shared the beginnings of my hurtful upbringing with anyone before. These stories, this memory, had been exclusively mine to shoulder. Even now, with my father in an entirely different kingdom, I could still feel myself fighting against the fear that he could hurt me if I told anyone — that he could hurt those I loved if the secrets of his abuse were shared.

Allene's tear-stricken eyes were attentive and saddened as she stroked my arm lightly.

"What happened?" she whispered solemnly.

I clenched my jaw in discomfort as the memory felt relived as I shared. "He watched me helplessly on the ground, and rather than offer me a helping hand, an apology, or a concerned expression, he kicked me in the stomach. When that didn't stop me from crying, he kicked my wounded leg. He didn't stop until my tears ceased because a future king doesn't cry, even after they have been hurt or betrayed by people they trust. That was the first lesson my father decided to teach me."

I'm sure Allene had previous assumptions about why I left Praseria, but her gaping and worried expression made me fear she didn't imagine it to the extent I shared. She did her best to hide her reactions. However, as I told her more of the grimacing details of my father's abuse and raging temper to explain every physical, mental, and emotional scar he inflicted upon me — from kicking me, hitting me, throwing objects at me, yelling at me, cutting me, and solitary punishment — it made her visibly upset and uncomfortable, just as I knew it would. I was broken, and she now saw the true mess of all my pieces.

I could see the pity in her eyes as I reflected on the harsh ridicule and punishment my father doled out in his efforts to make me strong-minded, uncompromising, and unbreakable to our enemies as the future king. His abuse was disguised as teaching me not to be weak, to ensure my loyalty, and to show my ability for discretion. In real-ity, he made me the scapegoat of his anger.

My father wanted me to be ruthless. He tried to control me. He wanted my submission.

I saw the surprise in her clear blue eyes as I told her Aleron and my mother never knew what my father did to me or his plans for me. I was honest and expressed my fear of my father's rage turning on them if he ever found out I had exposed what he did to me behind closed doors. I shared the fear of what he would one day ask me to do, the orders he may give me, and the threats he would make if I didn't comply with his demands.

Allene's tears continued to fall as I shared the moment that I decided to leave, the moment I decided I couldn't handle another encounter with my father because I feared that if I did, it would kill me.

"Killian. . ." Allene was speechless, and the air was heavy. I knew it would be, and I warned Allene that if she asked, there would be many things she didn't want to know, but it still didn't make it any easier to see her processing my past.

"Now you know why I left."

Allene wiped away her drying tears as she tried to swallow her emotions and maintain her composure. "Why do you still keep it a secret from Aleron? Why not tell him the truth?"

Her question was one I had asked myself more than a hundred times. I had dreamed about the difference the relationship with my brother may offer if I would only be honest with him. But I would rather him blame and hate me than blame and hate himself.

"Aleron is the most empathetic person I know, although he finds it hard to forgive himself. I worry he would find a way to feel responsible for not stopping my father or be consumed by guilt not knowing what had happened when I was in Praseria. I can't burden him that way."

"Doesn't it bother you that Aleron dislikes you so much when he doesn't truly understand the circumstances of you leaving?" she implored.

I shook my head. "I left in the hopes that Aleron and my mother wouldn't know the pain of what I had been through. Telling Aleron defeats that purpose. I would rather him dislike me and have myself be the only one to suffer the pain of what my father has done. I don't want to inflict that on Aleron too."

Allene was silent for a moment. I could see she was

considering if asking any more questions tonight was necessary. I believe she felt it as much as I did, that while the emotions were raw and dense, we may as well get it all out at once.

"Why did you go back to Praseria?" Allene asked hesitantly.

I stood from the settee and moved over to the frosted window, leaning against the wall as I stared at the tumbling snowfall. My legs had become restless as we continued the deep conversation, and I found myself slowly pacing the room as I spoke.

"When I left Praseria, my mindset shifted. I planned to instill fear in others, hoping to lessen my own. I thought if I could project myself as a person with no concerns, maybe I wouldn't actually care, and my life would hurt a bit less." A weak smile escaped my lips as I reflected on the stigma I tried to carry for so long — a persona that wasn't me. "While maintaining such an image, it allowed me to know things that I wouldn't have known in Praseria and speak to people my father would have likely killed me for speaking to. My life and associations had become unfiltered. One particular group I got information from disclosed rumors of my father's involvement with the Red Crows."

"Wait. . .what are you saying?" Allene said each word slowly as she tried to process my statement.

"I'm not saying anything. I am still uncertain. But I have my suspicions regarding my father." The words were dry in my throat, the admission subconsciously filling me with unnecessary guilt.

I could see Allene assessing my words, trying to calm herself down, but she became restless, standing up and walking over to me. "Explain," she demanded.

"It comes back to your original question — why did I return to Praseria? I had heard the rumors about my father's involvement with the Red Crows. I knew the only way to confirm it was by returning to my father and convincing him I wanted to participate in whatever he was planning.

My father had wanted me to be his right hand in everything. I knew he was desperate for one of his sons to follow in his footsteps, go wherever he wanted us to, and do whatever he asked us to do. I knew if he was involved with the Red Crows and I wasn't there to heed his demands, then Aleron would be subject to the same things I had suffered. And if anything happened to Aleron, my mother. . ." my voice trailed off as I considered how to say my thoughts delicately. I sighed. "My mother cared for me, of course, but Aleron was different. Aleron holds a special place in my mother's heart. Her happiness is very much tied to his. If he suffered, she would suffer too."

Allene's eyebrows creased as her frantic gaze roamed over me. "So you came back to Praseria to protect Aleron and your mother and to try and expose your father's involvement in the Red Crows?" Allene summarized my lengthy explanation.

I nodded. "When I came back, exiling Aleron. . .it was

my way of getting him away from my father and gaining my father's trust. I knew that my mother wouldn't be able to stand Aleron being away and that she would eventually go after him. So, when I approached my mother about going to Valteria to bring back Aleron, I knew she would agree. But going against my father's direct order, we both knew we'd have to leave secretly." I clenched my jaw as I tried to hold back the anger and guilt that boiled inside me as I thought about my mother. I closed my eyes and took a deep, shaky breath. I couldn't let my emotions get the better of me.

Allene's soft, delicate hands gently cupped my face. The frustration melted away as I opened my eyes to see her concerned and empathetic expression, quietly allowing me to feel safe. I didn't move. I didn't want to. I wanted her to stay close; I wanted her to quiet my worries, as she miraculously had the ability to do.

"I thought I had it all planned. Once we got to Valteria, I thought I could be honest about everything and escape to a safe place in Lokali with Aleron and my mother. I intended to get them away from my father permanently. I had been working towards it since I left, creating somewhere the three of us could flee to if necessary. But everything fell apart. My father got the best of me."

"What do you mean?" Allene's voice cracked under the pressure of the question.

"The Red Crows did attack us, and I have my suspicions that my father sent them. I don't know the extent of his involvement, he never did open up to me like I had hoped while I was in Praseria, but after the rumors in Lokali and the attack on my mother and me, it all feels like actions my father would take."

"You think your father would kidnap your mother?" Allene questioned in disbelief.

I pursed my lips. "I think he would do just about anything to instill fear into me and my brother."

Allene's hands dropped from my face and comfortably slid down my arms. She took my hands that she now firmly held.

"How did you leave Praseria with your mother in the first place?" she asked.

She really was asking everything. I hoped my transparency was building the trust and understanding she was seeking from me.

I continued answering without hesitation. "An old friend of mine in the castle helped arrange our secret passage out of Praseria."

She raised an expectant eyebrow. "Old friend?"

"The only one in the castle that ever knew the extent of my suffering. He tended to my wounds when they were too severe for me to manage independently. He was a physician at the castle."

Allene slowly blinked as she processed my response. "Ezra? Ezra helped you escape?"

I nodded. "He is the only loyal friend I have in Praseria. Do you know him?"

Allene sank to the ground, pulling me down with her as she sat on the plush rug underneath us. I couldn't tell if she was happy, angry, or sad. Her expression seemed to flicker between all three emotions. "He's my grandfather," she finally choked out.

I almost didn't contain my shock, but instead let out a shaky breath. It all made sense. I couldn't believe I had forgotten Ezra's past, and the connection he would have to Allene.

"He was the father of the previous king. I feel foolish for forgetting that it would mean he was related to you. I forget the connections our kingdoms have with one another."

Allene nodded quietly, her eyes welling up with tears again. The mention of her grandfather seemed to affect her greatly. The extent of their relationship while she was in Praseria hadn't been brought to my knowledge. Through this questioning of me, I was also discovering things about Allene.

"Ezra is a good man," I told her softly.

Allene shook her head quickly, stifling her soft sobs, and cleared her throat. "I apologize; I don't mean to be taken back by the mention of him. It is a lot to process. The reminder of him, the memories I have of your father while I was in Praseria as well. I am trying to connect everything together."

The length of our conversation had been driven deep into the night, and I could see Allene beginning to waiver with fatigue. I understood much would be pressing on her mind now, stringing together all the events and molding them with her own understanding of the same events.

Having a different perspective wasn't always clarifying; it often complicated things.

I wanted to give Allene time to comprehend everything I had added to her thoughts.

"The sun will be up soon, Allene. You should get some rest," I suggested.

"I have one more question," Allene quickly interjected.

I sighed in reluctant agreement. "One more."

Allene swept her legs to the side as she leaned in closer, her hair falling in front of her face.

"Why me? What is different this time that has made you want me?"

I felt the urge to change the topic, make humor of the inquiry, and run, as I had trained myself to do for years. It took my every effort to brush aside my natural self. *Don't put up your defenses now, Killian. She is the greatest thing to ever happen to you. Let her in.*

I tucked Allene's hair behind her ear, my hand resting on her cheek. "You're the first person to see me for who I am, even without me showing it to you. You're the only one who has dared to look past the superficial." I felt my lips part with anxiety as I shared more. "My father claimed all the things he did were out of care for me. I was conditioned to believe that caring for someone meant treating them like objects. I had taught myself to be distant and disengaged to protect myself from being unvalued and unloved. I was never anyone's first, nor was anyone's true priority or concern — until I met you."

We were silent for many moments, and I didn't mind. I

didn't expect Allene to respond to my heartfelt declaration, but the words needed to be shared. They needed to no longer be contained only in my thoughts. I had no way of knowing what Aleron may have said to Allene, and I knew he wore his heart on his sleeve. If I stood any chance of securing her heart, I had to be completely transparent, and not expect anything in return.

Allene rubbed her palms together and intently stared at her hands. Her eyes shifted as she cautiously looked at my chest. I felt nerves tingling in my stomach as her fingers apprehensively fumbled, slowly pulling up the hem of my shirt.

Without thought, I reacted. My hand shot to hers, stopping the movement. I could feel my eyes darken as Allene looked at me more closely. Her expression remained calm and still, her silence letting me process her intentions.

I was frozen in shock at the sudden change — it wasn't a gesture from Allene I expected. I knew by the look in her eyes that her motives were not suggestive. I could see she was trying to understand everything I had shared. She was trying to *see* me fully.

At that moment, I understood. I knew she was trying to look at my scars. That day in the spring, she saw my bare chest and arms, it only happened because it was an accident. For most of my life, I had trained myself to shield the physical signs of my hardships.

I hid them for many reasons. I didn't want people to be aware of what I had gone through, and I was worried that if someone did find out and the news got back to my father, I would suffer extreme repercussions. I was also embarrassed by them. I portrayed much self-confidence, but I knew where each scar lay and how long each was, and I remembered exactly how I got it. Seeing them made me uneasy. Certain scars were more sensitive than others, a few were still tender to touch even after all these years.

After reviewing my reasons for not letting Allene continue, I also considered why I should. The one answer I kept coming to was simple — I had nothing left to hide. Allene had asked the most difficult questions, reminding me she had already seen my actual scars. There was nothing I had withheld from her. I had succeeded in being vulnerable, and she somehow had managed to make me feel comfortable while doing so.

I slowly removed my hand from hers, placing it at my side, forcing myself to trust her. If she felt a need to see my scars, whatever her reason, I wouldn't stop her.

Allene's eyes remained firm on mine as she cautiously began to slip the fabric over my head and unapologetically studied my body. Her eyes were full of empathy as she spent many minutes digesting and looking at each scar on my chest, shoulders, and arms.

Just like in the cave, when the moon glaringly reflected each of my scars, the low light of the candles bounced off the rough edges of my old wounds. She tried her best to steady her hands as her fingertips brushed against the jagged memories that had been etched as a permanent reminder into my tan skin, the sensation leaving a burning in my stomach. Each scar left my heart heavier, and Allene's face was like stone as I patiently allowed her to take it all in.

I always put on a show for the others. My smile was never truly free; it was a mask for my deeper pains. If only others knew how much I hid, how much I was burdened with — people might see me differently. They would see me as Allene did. *Allene sees me.*

I caught my breath in awe, the heartache replaced with the purest form of admiration I had ever felt. I knew my feelings for this woman could only grow. I could not imagine ever letting her go.

"Killian. . ." Allene whispered as she placed her hand on my chest, leaning in gently as she pressed a single kiss to the scar on my collarbone.

I felt my body go numb just at the sound of my name leaving her lips, my throat going dry from the sensation she elicited inside of me. I closed my eyes tightly, trying to keep my emotions in check.

"Allene, you don't realize the effect you have on me when you do things like that." I wanted my words to come off as a warning to her, but deep down, I didn't want to warn her any longer. I didn't want her to run away. I wanted her to stay right where she was, I wanted her to stay with me and never let her go. I wanted to get lost in her. I wanted to be hers.

Allene nervously bit her lip, and it felt like I might go crazy holding myself back as she longingly looked at me.

"You mean, like this?" she sheepishly asked, her lips

now pressing against the base of my neck, her nose nuzzling into my collarbone, her body weight shifting into my lap.

I gripped Allene's waist, holding her tightly in place. "Careful, love, I wouldn't continue unless you are comfortable with the consequences it may elicit," I cautioned.

Allene's body shook at my comment, and my insides groaned in pain as I tried to hold myself back a bit longer.

Allene looked at me in a way that made me weak; she made me vulnerable, to the point that I didn't care to stop myself from being made a lovesick fool. The longing in her eyes, the smile on her pink lips after hanging on to each of my words. I would do anything, be anything, say anything to make her mine.

Allene's head turned to the side, her hands falling softly on my chest, her lips grazing against my ear as she whispered the words of my undoing. "Killian, you are stunningly beautiful."

I growled under my breath, this time not hesitating as I closed the distance between us and kissed her slowly, the heat from her lips tingling against mine. "Now you've done it," my lips hovered over hers as I spoke. "I want you." I kissed her again. "Every piece of you." And again. "I will challenge any person that gets in the way of that."

I kissed her again, gently and tender, not wanting to let the moment escape us, pressing her into my bare chest. I was surprised as Allene cupped my face and pulled me to her. As she kissed me, any reservation she had been holding was gone. The scent of her skin tingled in my nose, and her fingertips dug into my bare back, our bodies colliding even closer than before. The hunger I had for her was insatiable. I would never have enough. Allene tantalized all of my senses and the fire she had ignited inside of me was impossible to extinguish.

Through exasperated breath, I whispered against Allene's lips. "Allene, you have to say the words."

"What words?" she asked between a kiss.

I managed to pull myself far enough away that only our noses were touching, the pause allowing me to catch my breath, heart, and mind that I felt slipping from my command.

I shook my head, and Allene immediately laced her fingers through my haphazard curls, tugging on them gently, a satisfied groan escaping my chest.

"You have to tell me to stop. I won't have the strength to hold myself back otherwise," I admitted to my lack of self-control.

Allene didn't move after hearing my confession; her nose remained pressed against mine, and her eyes closed tightly.

"What happens if I don't say the words?" she asked the unraveling question.

My tone became severe as I admired her long eyelashes that concealed her piercing eyes.

She really is my undoing.

"I will do everything in my power to make you mine." I know she could hear the graveness in my voice.

Allene's eyes fluttered open, their blue intensity burning into mine. The sweet smell of lavender coming from her hair that brushed against my cheeks and chest was burning my nostrils in the most satisfying way.

A part of me hoped she would pull away and save herself from me. I knew this was a pivotal moment for our future. But another part of me hoped she would say the words, because I feared the suffering she would cause me if she didn't.

Allene's fingertips brushed against my lips. "Killian, I can't say the words." She stroked my cheek softly, her hand brushing back a curl of my hair that had fallen into my eyes. "Because I don't want you to stop."

Allene bit her lip as she held back a smile. I sighed, my heart aching and jumping simultaneously, but I did all I could not to let my emotions overshow.

"Allene, I hope you are aware, given full acknowledgment of my selfish tendencies, I make no promises of being fair or considerate when it comes to the affairs of securing your heart." My tone was serious, and I meant it entirely. "I'll anxiously await the day you tell me I'm yours."

The honeymoon hadn't been what I expected. I expected Killian to be angry or awkward with me. I expected him to excuse his actions that day in the forest. I expected the Killian I had become infatuated by to disappear, but he hadn't. His even temperament during our conversation, the transparency of his thoughts, the honesty regarding who he is, the light-hearted dinner topics, the romantic evening he managed to facilitate, the vulnerability of our conversation, the excitement he managed to evoke inside of me — Killian had become even more charming and desirable than before. My fondness for him was only growing.

You promised to give Aleron a chance, Allene. He is your first love. You have to give him another chance. But if I was being honest, I doubted that I could. My experience with Killian last night — *every night since I met him* — was drastically different. Aleron was a significant part of me, but

Killian *consumed me.* I had to consider what I was willing to let go, and the more time I considered it, and let myself feel what was in my heart — moving on from Killian became less and less of an option.

"Allene?" Risa's voice echoed throughout the room, her concerned eyes prodding me.

"I'm sorry; what did you say?" I asked, fumbling over my words as I tried to snap myself back from fleeting thoughts.

Risa and Damien had come to my room after break-fast, needing to coordinate our next move, but I knew that it wasn't their main priority for meeting together.

Risa huffed, pouting as she folded her arms. "Is something more important than the affairs of our kingdom? What is distracting you?" she tisked.

Damien patted Risa on the shoulder, shaking his head. "Risa, let's not be petty. We are all open and honest with each other here. We have supported each other through the years. Nothing can break our bond—" Damien had begun his exaggerated tone, and I knew what that meant.

"Out with it, Damien. What do you want to say?" I narrowed my eyes at him, bracing myself for a dramatic question based on his sizable preface.

"Did anything happen between you and Killian last night?" Risa blurted out the question, her foot tapping with anxiety.

"I don't know how to answer that. Killian is my husband—" I started, but Damien interrupted me, rolling his eyes.

"Spare us the theatrics, Allene," he huffed.

"That is entirely hypocritical coming from you," I snapped back at him, my lips in a thin line as I pouted at him.

"Ever since the hunt, we can sense something was going on between you two. How long do we have to pry until you open up?" Damien queried, eyeing me expectantly.

Risa sat down next to me, her face filled with concern. "Damien's right, we are trying to understand, but you haven't shared anything with us. We just want to talk about the situation," Risa explained.

My eyebrows raised towards my forehead, my gawking expression making them squirm. "Talk about it or talk me *out* of it? You both seem too ready for this conversation for it to be only casual," I pointed out.

Risa groaned in frustration, her hands pulling at her scalp. "Allene, it's *Killian*. The brazen, narcissistic, divisive evil brother of our enemy kingdom! You do remember all of that, right?" she asked with a shaky breath.

I scoffed. "Of course I do, but Killian isn't all that he seems. There is much more to Killian than the superficial exterior he hides behind."

Risa didn't even attempt to hide her frustration as her face turned a brighter shade of red as she spoke. "I feel like I am trapped in a recurring nightmare, Allene. I thought you falling in love with one enemy prince meant it couldn't get worse. Now you've fallen for another enemy prince; and this time, he is much more unfavorable than the first. Are you trying to set yourself up for ruin?" Risa interrogated, her voice exasperated as she rubbed her neck in worry.

I didn't know how to reply to Risa. In some ways, I saw what she was seeing. I had questioned myself on the matter of Killian and Aleron more than I had trusted it. I had the same reservations but also had a different perspective on who they both were, which complicated seeing things plainly and simply. I did my best to answer her question, a question I was still determining myself.

"I don't intend to set myself up for anything, especially not ruin; that is a substantial accusation," I said, sending a drawled glare at Risa. "Damien, you have spent time with Aleron the last few weeks. Have your impressions of him changed at all?" I asked, blindly hoping my best friend could be a source of help on the matter.

Damien shrugged, offering a lazy wave of his hand. "He isn't as bad as I thought he would be if that's what you're asking."

It wasn't much, but I would take it. "See? Risa, wouldn't you agree?" I directed the question to her.

Risa's face became sour, her lips twisting to the side as she answered. "Marshal did say he and Aleron have become friends."

I sighed, taking a seat in front of them both. "Months ago, we had this same judgemental conversation about Aleron, and look how time has changed your preconceptions. What if the same could be said about Killian?" I proposed the possibility.

"It won't," Risa stated matter-of-factly.

Damien nodded. "I agree with Risa. It doesn't seem possible."

I groaned as I thought of another way to approach the debate. Both Damien and Risa weren't going to surrender their opinions easily.

We sat in silence for a few moments before I settled on my next futile attempt of convincing them to consider things from my point of view. "You all saw how much I loathed Killian before we left Valteria. Do you think I would change my mind so positively about him unless I had a good reason?" I couldn't hold back the defeated sigh that escaped my lips as I gave them each a pleading stare, but all it managed to deliver was doubtful glances between Risa and Damien. It felt more difficult to convince them of my perspective when they were together as they fed on one another's comments and reactions.

Damien shrugged off my question. "I vote for Aleron," he said.

"I second that," Risa added, raising her hand in notion.

I held back my irritation a bit longer, trying to be patient with them both. *I know they're only being annoying out of their care and concern for me* — or so I told myself to keep my frustration suppressed.

"Can't you lay aside your enmity? My love life is not a democracy. I will determine who I want to choose on my own, and I expect both of you to support and trust me in my decision," I declared, giving them each a final earnest stare.

"Wait, are you saying you and Killian aren't a certainty yet? Is Aleron still a possible choice?" Risa pressed, the sudden light in her eyes snuffing out the light in mine.

I frowned at Risa's reaction. "I am figuring it out," I muttered.

Risa beamed in return. "Don't feel rushed to figure it out, Allene. You have months—"

"Years!" Damien chimed enthusiastically.

Risa rushed to nod in agreement. "Yes, years to figure it out if you need to!" Risa joyfully assured me.

"How about simply saying you both are happy to see me happy? No matter who I end up with?" I begged the question, my jaw tight as I frowned at the sight of their hopes.

"We just want to protect you," Damien solemnly said, sinking back into his chair..

I placed my hand on his broad shoulder, still uncertain when the boy I had known for so long had changed into the man before me. "Falling in love isn't something you need to protect me from," I sighed, stepping back from them both as I imploring looked between them. "If you care for me and want to see me happy, don't force me to defend my decision-making. I need you both to trust me."

Risa and Damien exchanged an unspoken conversation as they looked to one another, their eyes incrementally filling with mutual understanding.

Risa let out a soft sigh, her shoulders slumping as her

thoughts visibly weighed down her body. "We do care for you," Risa assured me.

"And trust you," Damien added, cocking his head in my direction.

Risa seemed pained as she forced each of her next words out, but she held a tight, fake smile anyway. "We will keep our opinions to ourselves and do our best to be enthusiastic with whatever decision you make."

"But if Killian or Aleron hurt you in any way. . ." Damien wagged his finger in warning. "Then all measures will be taken to ensure they face proper consequences."

I nodded in compliance, a smug smile gracing my lips at the loyalty and love they both displayed for my well being. "Fair enough," I said, agreeing to Damien's point.

"And you need to tell us when you do know how you're feeling. I don't prefer having to corner you for answers," Risa expressed.

"I understand," I acknowledged back, noting their patience with me as I sorted out my feelings.

"Can we discuss another important matter?" Risa pressed, adjusting her posture to be tall and proper as she batted her eyelashes my way.

I gulped, my throat dry at the sudden change. "Do I want to know?"

"Your birthday is in a few days," Risa beamed with excitement at the mention of it.

I couldn't hold back the smile that came to my lips. I had always loved birthdays and looked forward to mine more than any other day of the year. Risa and Damien knew that, and in the chaos of everything that had been going on, I had forgotten how soon my birthday actually was. It may not have been in circumstances I wished my birthday to fall upon, but I looked forward to it nonetheless.

My excitement was cut short as we all heard shouting echoing outside the room.

"Risa! Risa!" Marshal burst through the door, his panicked eyes immediately focused on my sister. He rushed to her side, kneeling down as he spoke through his troubled facial expression.

Risa reached out to cup Marshal's face, her concern quickly matching his. "Marshal, what's wrong?"

Marshal's face went pale as he gripped Risa's arms for support as he got out the words. "The kingdoms have been attacked."

We were all in disbelief. This was the second time we heard the retelling of the personal witness of the attack from King Seger's spy. It still didn't feel real. Praseria and Valteria both had been *attacked*. Risa, Allene, Killian, and myself were personally being sought after by the Red Crows. Our people that chose to flee were scattered and hiding. The queens — our mothers, were now both missing. The Red Crows had taken control of the castles in Valteria and Praseria, along with our resources. Our worst nightmare, the fallout we were trying to avoid, had become inevitable, and it had even exceeded our greatest fears because the person leading the attacks was someone who knew each of us — King Vincent, my father.

Risa was sobbing in Allene's arms, her distress rising by the minute. Allene sat down with her on the floor, doing all she could to calm her sister's troubled heart. Allene's porcelain face had become even whiter from shock as she processed the news. As Risa reacted by crying, Allene responded with silence, but it was apparent they were both afraid and in pain from the report.

I tore my eyes away from Allene, prepared to take out the frustrations of seeing the love of my life and her sister in such despair on the only possible culprit in all of this.

"Did you know?" I asked Killian through gritted teeth, hoping he would at least writhe under my glare, but he remained composed as usual.

Killian's eyes had also been fixated on Allene, his face obscure. He sat calmly in a chair, his body relaxed and casual as he looked at me.

"About the plan for the attacks?" Killian asked obliviously.

"No, about our father's involvement with the Red Crows," I pressed him. The thought continued to come to my mind; the possibility that Killian had preexisting knowledge of it all seemed feasible.

Killian's face was stern as he scowled at me across the vast room. "Our people are displaced and in chaos, and you're taking the time to interrogate me?"

I balked. "Who else is there to ask? Out of everyone in this room, you were the last to see our father. Did he give you any reason to be suspicious of him?" I inquired. Even if he did have preexisting knowledge, I doubt he would admit it.

Killian shifted in his chair, propping his elbow on the

armrest and resting his cheek in the palm of his hand. "I may have been with him last, but you were with him more than I ever was. Father has been suspicious his entire life. This news actually shocks you?" Killian jeered at me.

Damien waved his arms as he took to the center of the room. "You both need to stop; your family feud can wait. King Seger will be walking through that door at any moment, and we have to show a united front; otherwise, we stand no chance of receiving any of his help," Damien warned us in an even and irked tone.

"Damien's right. It does us no good to speculate if there were indications or signs that this would occur. We can't reverse what has taken place. All we can do now is react," Hassan added.

"King Seger will have questions and concerns. I am certain I can convince him to help us; however, I think it would be wise if I speak to him alone," Killian proposed, his arms folded tightly across his chest as he directed his input to Damien and Hassan, easily glazing over me.

"No, I will go with you," I insisted, not allowing him to dismiss me.

Killian groaned, his hand trailing the length of his face. "You still don't trust me, brother? Aren't we past this by now?" Killian's piercing eyes scolded mine, but I wouldn't bend at his attempt at intimidation.

"We won't ever be past this," I gave my short and honest reply. What Killian had done, the pain and hurt he had caused me and our family, was unable to be repaired.

The muscles in Killian's cheeks feathered in frustration. "Fine, if you are adamant I don't go alone, then I suppose it makes more sense to bring my wife, considering both our kingdoms were attacked," Killian snapped back, his tone sharper than his glare.

I immediately regretted my persistence, forgetting for a moment who else was in the room with us. Allene's glossed-over eyes fluttered back to reality as Killian stood up and paced to her side. Marshal had taken his chance of approaching Risa as well, trying to pull her away from Allene and into his embrace as her crying had started to subside.

I heard my blood pulsing in my ears as Killian scooped his arm around Allene's waist, hoisting her to a standing position nestled into his chest.

"We will be back," Killian declared, making his way to the door.

I tried to restrain myself, but I couldn't control my impulses. As Killian walked by, I reached for Allene's free hand, gripping it tightly as I pulled her in my direction. With Allene's hand in mine and before Killian could grasp the handle or react, the door swung open with brute force, taking everyone by surprise.

King Seger stood in the doorway, his expression wiley and exhilarated as his laugh bellowed in the intimate room. His eyes squinted as he looked directly at me, Killian, and Allene — like he was attempting to get a clearer view as he observed the scene before him. King Seger shook his head as he chuckled in amusement and addressed himself.

"How foolish was I to think today wouldn't be met with any other surprises." He cocked his eyebrow to the side and offered a sly smirk. "You all are full of constant entertainment and excitement."

KILLIAN

"**W**hat am I to do with all of you?" King Seger followed up after another laugh.

None of us knew how to react. Allene had sheepishly nestled deeper in my shoulder, folding her arms tightly around her chest. It wasn't clear if she was clinging closer to me out of fear, avoidance of speaking, for appearances' sake, or if she genuinely felt comfort in me. I didn't take the time to ponder on it. I needed to draw King Seger's attention away from the conspicuous expressions on everyone's faces.

Damien, clearly trying too hard to look natural, Risa and Marshal avoiding eye contact, Hassan smirking in the corner, and Aleron looking ashamed. I couldn't imagine King Seger's reaction if he put together that we had been dishonest regarding our relationship, and none of the others in our group seemed to be able to conceal their guilt.

"This situation isn't as it appears," I attempted to inter-ject, stepping forward to block his view of the others while pulling Allene behind my back, removing her from the middle.

King Seger waved his hand back and forth at Aleron and Allene. "Your brother isn't in love with your wife?" he chortled. The room fell into a tense silence, none of us knowing how to rebuttal.

King Seger grinned in obvious amusement at the situ-ation. Seeing his twisted joy in such a bitter circumstance made my stomach lurch. "No reason to hide it now," he drawled, his voice dripping with false security.

I couldn't muster enough enthusiasm to offer a fake smile, so I remained stern, standing still, collected, and quiet. I knew King Seger wouldn't endure the silence for long; he enjoyed hearing himself speak too much, and I was correct.

King Seger loudly clapped his hands together. I could feel Allene slightly jolt at the unexpected sound in the quiet room. "Well, as intriguing as this all is, and much as I would love to unravel your family drama some more, I believe we have more grave matters to discuss. Shall we?" King Seger pointedly locked his eyes on mine as he motioned me to the doorway, daring me to enter the conversation that would seal our kingdom's fate.

Two days. Since the news of the attacks and the start

of our trek back to Valteria, it had been two excruciatingly exhausting, demanding, long days.

King Seger had surprised us all. His willingness to help us was palpable. For being an unpredictable and ungovernable man, our situation fueled his greatest curiosities. I had become convinced he had some twisted, joyous reaction to unfortunate circumstances and craved the prospect of war. We offered him both, and he seemed happier now than before we arrived.

King Seger was quick to act. He organized his soldiers and weapons of war, sent his fastest messengers to Veruje, Gree, and Lokali on our behalf, and gathered all the provisions and supplies we would need for the dreaded journey to Valteria, where we could only imagine the chaos and ruin we would be returning to.

Perhaps it was my way of trying to find a positive side to all of this, but despite the dreadful situation, I couldn't help but feel a tinge of success. If we had stayed behind, although we would have been with our kingdoms, we would've likely been overtaken, in which circumstance our governance would be of no benefit to our kingdoms.

Although we were still far away from home, with a two-day journey ahead, we were alive and free. More importantly, we had achieved what we set out to do — we had successfully formed alliances. We had gathered strength in numbers. We had the tools to fight back properly, the possibility to reclaim our kingdoms, and liberate our people — none of which would have been options if we had stayed behind.

I found myself repeating the same points over and over to comfort myself but also to console Allene. Since the news of the attack, her anguish and frustration were tangible. I had accepted the separation and chance of losing my parents when I left Praseria all those years ago. However, Allene had only recently lost her father, and the fear of losing her mother too, so close to each other, was unmistakably causing her immense torment. Not only was she worried about her family, but she likely feared for herself, too.

We all had thought of it by now — Risa, Allene, Aleron, and myself — what did this attack on our kingdoms mean for our future as heirs to the throne for Valteria and Praseria? None of us wanted to consider it, but it was impossible to ignore — what if we didn't take back what was ours? What if we didn't win? Those hard questions were a reality. We could lose. We could lose everything. Then what? What would we do? What would our futures look like?

I didn't want to dwell on it. I had suffered my fair share; a little more wouldn't hurt me. My concern was Allene and the people she cared about. Seeing her suffer hurt me more than my own afflictions ever had, and there wasn't much solace I could offer as we awaited our unknown fates.

To my equal relief and displeasure, Allene, Risa, and Damien had been inseparable since leaving Cenan. They had been closed off to everyone else, leaving the remainder of us to watch them interact on our journey.

Allene viewed both Damien and Risa as siblings, and this created a special relationship between them. I was grateful Allene wasn't shutting herself off from sources of comfort, but I still envied the alleviation Damien and Risa seemed to offer Allene. I wasn't alone. Marshal, Aleron, Hassan, and I had no words to exchange with one another, even if we wanted to. This left all of us irked by the strong bond and connection between them that only years of history could forge.

Marshal was left to gaze desperately at Risa, while Aleron failed to divert his eyes from Allene for even a minute. Hassan constantly shot his brother annoyed looks for being left out. Our only company was King Seger and his intimidating second, the woman with the braids. I caught her name only once, and it was only because a soldier had addressed her. Kijana.

Kijana was a woman of few words or pleasantries. Her eyes seemed to never stop moving, shifting from one person to the next, always alert and ready for a fight. She was loyal to King Seger, never leaving his side and refusing to let her guard down. Maintaining her trust seemed more vital than even convincing King Seger. I didn't doubt the sway and influence she had over him. If she had any suspicion of us and she told King Seger, that would surely be the end of our alliance.

With that fact in mind, I tried to distract myself from the jealousy over Allene and give her space while lending my efforts and energy to keep our delicate new alliance from falling apart too soon.

ALLENE

etween the frigid air in our temporary shelters, the faint amount of light from the dwindled fire, and the various sounds of plants rustling from the wind or animals moving about in the woods, I had failed to find enough peace and quiet to fall into a deep sleep.

Every noise I heard at night in the vast woods made my stomach lurch with anxiety. My imagination took hold of any sense of reason and convinced me that creatures and enemies alike would take the opportunity to hide under the cover of moonlight to attack.

I knew it was a ridiculous fear. Surrounding my tent were over a hundred others, the camp filled with King Seger's soldiers. In all of our travels, I had never been safer. Even with that realization, I still couldn't suppress my worries. I wish I could've been exhausted enough to fall asleep despite the various distractions. Considering how much energy I had been exerting every day on our trek to Valteria, I was surprised I hadn't given in to sleep, but my anxiety proved to possess a stronger will.

I had patiently waited for the light to begin to increase, signaling the steady rise of dawn. I delicately made my way out of the tent to avoid stirring Risa. She had been emotionally drained the entire journey, her body unable to wait for the end of the day for us to make camp and allow her to rest. I glanced at her swollen eyes and cheeks, which were stained with tears. I prayed that her dreams would offer solace, as no efforts to lift her and help return her to her traditionally happy and positive self seemed to be working.

I let out a soft sigh, mentally preparing to face another day. I tightly wrapped my fur shawl around my torso and shoulders as I went to the fire that had burned out almost completely. I set my eyes on an ember at the edge that had almost solidified to its final white color, giving up its last bit of warmth. My gaze shifted away as I caught movement to the right of me, and my heart immediately froze in panic.

The thumping inside my chest settled when I observed my visitor. Kijana had made her way out of her tent, sitting down, coldly staring at me. She clearly had no desire to make small talk or offer a proper salutation.

"Are you actually a married woman?" Kijana barked, rolling back her shoulders as rolled out her neck, her hands rubbing the muscles that I imagined were as sore as mine from our current sleeping arrangements.

I felt my mouth gape at the unexpected question. "Why would you ask such a thing?"

Kijana's stare became even fiercer as she glared at me with suspicion. "You're never with your husband."

"I have been at his side for weeks," I corrected her.

Kijana scoffed, choking back a chortle. "Not in his general presence, I mean *with* him. As newlyweds, isn't it a general assumption that you can't stand being even a few feet away from each other? You have been sleeping in your sister's tent the last two nights and took your own room at the castle. I find it odd," she ground out the words, letting her sharp accusation make me squirm.

I cleared my throat while simultaneously trying to clear my head to not display how unsettled her accusation made me. "You find it odd that as the older sister, I am offering comfort to my younger sister?" I couldn't contain the shock on my face. Even if she was right about the situation with Killian, I still didn't feel my actions were odd, and I attempted to cling to that in order to portray a sense of innocence.

Kijana sat across from me, the burning in her eyes harsher than the actual fire in front of us. She was silent as she dismissed my question. She pulled out a dark red apple from her vest pocket, along with a small, sharp blade, and began peeling her breakfast precisely and quickly. She threw the peeled apple skins into the fire, not glancing at her hands once as she worked, clearly showing off her keen awareness of her surroundings. She delivered her message without saying a word. She was terrifying.

Who knew eating an apple could make such a strong point in a conversation?

I rolled my shoulders and straightened my back, elevating my posture as I tried to take my point in a different direction. I had to acknowledge her observations and reasoning — she wasn't wrong — but I had to convince her that my approach wasn't wrong either.

"Of course, the passion of being a newlywed is strong, but my duty — *our* duty — as representatives of our kingdoms, that responsibility comes first. As royals, we are expected to keep our emotions in line." I shifted, trying to bury the discomfort that speaking so casually about Killian — even if it wasn't a real scenario — caused inside of me. "Focusing on our lust while our kingdoms are in crisis would be inappropriate. Keeping our distance and separating our bed chambers makes the situation slightly more tolerable as we patiently remain professional and proper." I flashed her a tight grin and felt satisfied with my answer. I knew it made sense and hoped it would remove Kijana's suspicions.

I cleared my throat, trying to shake my nerves as Kijana mulled over and judged my every word.

She took a fierce bite of her apple, chewing it loudly, her teeth chomping together. She offered a satisfied smirk as she swallowed. "I couldn't say I would have the same willpower in your situation. Killian is. . ." Kijana's eyes and voice trailed off as she fixated on the fire, her smirk growing wider. She made no effort to hide her satisfaction as she daydreamed of Killian right in front of my eyes, exposing a side of her I never imagined I would see. I thought she was terrifying by hardly ever speaking, but now I realized I preferred the silent version of Kijana more.

I shuddered as I watched Kijana fantasize about my "husband" openly and disrespectfully. Although I wasn't married to Killian, watching Kijana desire him made my blood boil. I realized that even being "married" didn't stop other women from noticing Killian, and the growing pit in my stomach made me anxious.

Was this a taste of my future if a relationship with Killian came to fruition? Would I continually have to bolster my confidence to combat the wandering eyes of other women preying on and hoping to catch his attention? Would I ever feel secure enough that it wouldn't bother me when they did?

Kijana snapped back to the present and cocked her head to the side, her head shaking back and forth as she looked at me like a wounded animal.

"I do not mean to offend you, princess, but I do have eyes, and having to hold back from a man like that? I don't envy you in the slightest," Kijana finally said, taking another bite of her apple as she leaned back casually, like I shouldn't be bothered by her outburst.

I felt myself swallow the urge to reprimand her as I reverted back to silence, hoping our inappropriate conversation would fade out.

Kijana seemed to observe more than she spoke, and the need to be on guard in her presence was more apparent now. It only reiterated the need to focus on playing the role of Killian's wife. I had to do better. I couldn't allow any doubts or questions from King Seger or Kijana. I needed to do things differently to ensure our alliance and to remain convincing.

I knew the only way to properly deliver in my role was to commit to how I felt. My true feelings were behind all the barriers I had placed around my heart to protect myself from getting hurt again. They were emotions that would not require me to convince anyone of my sincerity because they would be authentic. But to do that meant I would have to let Killian in and release the hold on my heart. I had to be willing to let Killian ruin me. I had to have the resolve to pursue what my heart wanted, and it terrified me more than anything.

Kijana interrupted my thoughts as she threw the pit of her apple into the fire, letting it consume the remains. "I am curious to hear the story of how you also stole the heart of pretty prince number two, but we can save that conversation for another morning." Kijana gave a curt nod and short bow as she turned away, leaving me anxious for the rest of the sunrise.

"Good morning, love." Killian had slipped in beside me, walking in slow strides to match my pace, his hand reaching for mine.

I knew people were watching, and after the interaction

with Kijana, Killian's intuition for how to behave couldn't have occurred at a better time.

"Is it a good morning?" I quipped back, my mood still soured from Kijana.

Killian's eyebrows raised on his forehead. "Is there a reason it wouldn't be?" he pressed.

"Is that a rhetorical question? Or do you truly want me to list all the reasons?" The words felt like grit against my teeth, Kijana's smugness and overstepping leaving my blood simmering.

Killian let out a light-hearted chuckle, not taking the bait so easily. "I would rather focus on something exciting."

I cocked my head to the side, gauging his reason for changing the conversation's direction, my interest piqued. "Well, don't reserve all the excitement for yourself. What has caught you in such gripping anticipation?" I crooned.

Killian grinned widely, his tantalizing mischievousness shining through his eyes. "Your birthday."

The second mention of my birthday did bring a smile to my face, but it was short-lived. As much as I adored my birthday, I knew it was only two days away, and a lot could happen in that time. We were walking towards heartbreaking news, approaching the dark reality of the condition of our kingdoms — not even my birthday could drown out the heaviness of it, and celebrating something so trivial felt wrong in a time like this.

I shrugged off my disappointment and hoped my birthday next year would fall on much better circumstances. That was all I could hope for — peace and safety for our kingdoms.

"Who told?" I asked Killian. I hadn't mentioned my birthday to him before, so I knew someone had let it slip.

Killian's eyes squinted as he looked in the distance, avoiding my gaze. "I wasn't necessarily told directly, but I did overhear Damien and Risa discussing their plans to celebrate your birthday, and I assumed it was soon. When is it?"

"Two days," I huffed.

Killian rhythmically nodded, his expression set in hard contemplation. "That doesn't give me much time to get you a gift."

An embittered laugh escaped my lips. "I wasn't expecting one."

Killian squeezed my hand, which I had forgotten was even holding mine, the feeling of it completely natural. "It's the one day of the year that I get to celebrate the most beautiful woman to grace this universe — who happens to be my wife, and you weren't expecting a gift?" His eyes twinkled with amusement as he waited for me to digest his words.

Killian's compliment sent a tingling sensation through my body; his exaggeration of adoration made my heart race. I knew people were behind us, I knew they were close, I knew they could hear every word he said, and I knew it was likely his effort to solidify our appearance as a married couple — but I wanted it to be real. It *felt* real, and so were my blushing cheeks.

I patted my cheeks with my free hand and fanned my warming face. Killian kissed the top of my hand, his every movement and word so smooth and instinctive.

Killian continued. "Since I can't retrieve a monetary gift for your birthday this year, I hope you will accept an untraditional gift in its place."

I paused and turned my head to the side in curiosity. "What do you have in mind?"

"An asset for the future," he said casually, his arms wrapping behind his back now as he held his wrists innocently. "For your birthday, you can ask me for *one* thing, at the time of your choice. It can be tomorrow, or it can be years from now. It can be anything you want, and I can't say no. I won't protest, I won't ask questions, I will humbly accept and submit to one request," he leaned towards me, pressing a gentle kiss against my cheek, my skin heating from the attention he and the others gave to it. "That is my gift to you," he promised quietly against my burning face.

My eyebrows raised at the gracious offer of a free, untethered request from someone who wasn't keen on handouts — an offer I knew he held in high regard, and one I knew he'd only made for me. "That is a powerful gift," I faintly whispered.

Killian winked at me, his smile growing wide. "I don't mind you having power over me."

––––––––

I couldn't sleep again. The unfamiliar sounds caused my heart to jolt continuously, not ever allowing time to calm me down enough to feel drowsy.

Risa had no difficulty sleeping. She was asleep as soon as she laid her head on the thin cushion — that only provided a barrier between the dirt and her blonde hair. I had envied my sister about many things in the past — her positivity, her beauty, her childlike sweetness, but now I was experiencing jealousy of her heavy sleeping ability, something I never thought I would be jealous about.

I was past the point of being overly tired, and Risa's deep, rhythmic breathing only added to my frustration from lack of sleep. I didn't make a polite effort to be quiet as I rolled out of the tent and went to the fire outside, secretly hoping the movement would at least stir Risa, but she didn't even flinch.

Letting out a deep sigh, I silently approached the fire, and was met with the sound of shuffling behind me. *Maybe I had awakened Risa.* I turned around to take in her irritated expression from my disturbance yet found I was alone — but the sound of shuffling hadn't ceased. I squinted my eyes, my heart racing in alert to the unwelcome sound.

I could see from a distance that the noise was actually tree branches brushing against one another as a large silhouette moved them out of his path, clearly having exited from our camp. I tried not to panic as my eyes darted to each tent, and the pair of sleeping guards, trying to deduct the silhouette as someone from our group that slipped away to relieve themselves in the middle of the night.

Unable to fully convince myself that that was all the situation was, I made my way to the edge of the camp and crouched behind a large tree, my eyes focused on the direction in which the figure had disappeared. If they were part of our camp, they would be coming back soon, and my worry would be for nothing. *I hoped it was nothing.*

If it were someone to be worried about, I would be close enough to alert the guards, but if I stirred people too soon, it might put everyone at unnecessary risk.

Minutes passed, and no movement came. My breathing became shallow and quiet as I stared into the darkness, my eyes deceiving me the longer I waited — until I saw not one, but two figures in the distance.

I crouched even lower now, the voices barely audible. I tried to hear what was being said between the two men, and attempted to guess who from our camp was meeting with another person in the middle of the night. My heartbeat was pounding in my ears, the sound ringing through my temples as I concentrated intently on the voices as they slowly got closer.

"Go back," I heard a man hiss under his breath. "I told you I would let you know when the time is right." *That voice.* It sounded familiar, but being so far away and whispering, I struggled to determine who it belonged to.

"I will go back when we have finished our conversation! You've said that for far too long now — Nycolas is starting to have doubts, and I promised to return to him with answers," the other man growled in a low whisper.

My body froze. *Nycolas? As in the Nycolas? The involved with the Red Crows that disappeared from Valteria, Nycolas?* We were in trouble, and I didn't know what to do. I felt petrified from fear as I tried to get more information before acting. I patiently waited for a counter reply, but all became silent. Too silent, for too long.

A hand suddenly clamped over my mouth while a strong arm lurched into my stomach and dragged me into the forest.

"I don't know if I should say you have luck, stupidity, or wits. Out of everyone, I did not expect you to be the one to find me out."

Hassan studied me, his gaze making me shiver. *Stupidity, that was what it was.* I felt my body shaking and my stomach churning into knots as I looked betrayal straight in the eyes.

"Let me go," I weakly pleaded, trying to pull apart the ropes that bound my hands as I kneeled on the forest floor.

"I can't do that," Hassan firmly replied, his eyes glazed over with little emotion, his face a hard set mask for me to try and decipher under the fading moonlight.

My mind had been racing in a hundred different directions as I stared back into those empty eyes, trying to think rationally of what my next action would be, the weight of making the right decision heavy and obvious.

One wrong move, and I could be dead. I don't know if it was out of shock, but my brain was struggling to formulate a rational plan of action, and I could feel myself beginning to panic.

My eyes darted between Hassan and our camp that wasn't far off. He had dragged me out of direct sight of the camp, but I could still see the faint glow of the fire in the distance. Since my legs weren't tied and my mouth wasn't gagged, I could run or scream. I told myself I had a chance to make it to the camp before Hassan could catch me. Running. That was the only thought and plan I was managing to come up with, but Hassan seemed to read my thoughts as fast as I thought them.

I inhaled in preparation to shriek, as Hassan crushed his hand over my mouth, muffling the sound to a short heard cry, the tears stinging the corner of my eyes as they were tempted to fall.

"Scream, and you jeopardize the lives of everyone in that camp," Hassan hissed, "your sister and lovers included." Hassan's jaw was set rigid, his eyes intense and sincere in his threat. I held back the sound of a whimper as I stared back at the face of a man that I thought I knew.

My heart began to race so fast that my chest hurt, and the contents of my dinner flipped in my stomach. My face was hot as I tried to suppress the urge to vomit, but the rush to cry could not be stopped. Tears slid down my cheeks as I realized how foolish I had been in being so easily trusting. Shock numbed my body as I tried to make sense of the broken reality that now faced me.

"If you're going to kill me, why don't you get on with it," I cried out.

Hassan sighed, running an anxious hand through his hair. "I'm not going to kill you, Allene, but you spying on me. . ." his eyes darted down to the ground in what appeared to be disappointment, possibly even fear, but his mask was back on in an instant before I could read into it more. "I wasn't expecting that, and now I need to make a decision on how to proceed."

"What about your friend? Won't he be running back to tell the others I know your secret?" I seethed, my tone dripping in hatred from Hassan's outright betrayal of his princess, his brother, his friends, and his people.

Hassan glared at me, his voice in a low growl. "I assured him I would take care of it," he snipped.

My heart raced even faster as I tried to interpret what he meant by *taking care of it*. I felt the temptation to scream again, but I stifled the urge and chose to keep my mind occupied and focused on drawing out information instead.

"Have you been a part of the Red Crows this entire time?" I choked on the question, the taste of it bitter in my mouth.

Hassan's eyes glazed over, no trace of remorse or pity visible anywhere. Hassan was silent, which served as enough of an answer.

"Showing up at the Gala when you did, getting close to me, the assassination attempt of Killian and I. . ." the memories played out in my head, the sequence of perfectly timed events, my stomach sick again at the pressing thought, "all of it was an assignment from the Red Crows to infiltrate Valteria, wasn't it?" It wasn't as much of a question, as it was a statement. We both knew I was right, but I wanted to see if Hassan had the audacity to admit to it.

"The most unassuming plan is the drawn out one," Hassan shortly replied.

His answers made my blood hot with rage, with the deceitfulness he so proudly and cunning devised. "Why are you doing this?" I asked breathlessly.

Hassan's face became passionate and pained as his forehead crinkled in frustration at the question. "I am not a bad person, Allene. I am doing this for the equality of our people — the equality they deserve." His hands clenched at his sides, his zeal struggling to be contained. "Too many people in each kingdom feel the imbalance of power. There is too much of a divide! Peace is shortly achieved, only to be replaced again with vice. Power poisons hearts. You and I have witnessed it!" Hassan took a deep breath, his emotions spiraling out of control as he spoke. "You should understand. Your father betrayed you. All the kingdoms and their powers have only led to betrayal, not allegiances. If you take away the kingdoms, then unity is the only choice."

The treachery that had consumed me was replaced with burning rage. "My father was not a traitor!" I spat.

Hassan became stern, unrelenting in his cause. "He abdicated his throne for another."

My lip quivered as I stifled the urge to yell and argue. "So, what? You plan to rid all royalty and unite the kingdoms under the power of the Red Crows? Replace a few narcissists with one?" I scoffed, unable to contain the disgust of his pitiful logic.

Hassan growled. "If we don't cleanse the kingdoms of their royal lines, we won't ever be able to reform a way of order. We want diplomacy — not royalty. Out of anyone, you should understand how much having a divide of nations can hurt us. I know you felt despised due to your father's choice and consequences," he pointed out, trying to catch me in my own pains.

I clenched my fists in frustration as Hassan assumed he understood me. *Maybe he did.* But the thought of an enemy disguised as a friend — hidden as a love interest — who knew intimate parts of me and my life, left me severely unsettled.

Hassan and I became silent. I didn't know how to respond. As much as I hated to admit it, he was partially correct. Not in the solution to the problems, but the problems being there. I still despised the Red Crows and their entire mission, and I hated even more that Hassan was a part of it, but I understood their motives better as Hassan passionately defended their reasoning.

Hassan looked at me now and let out a sigh, his posture sinking and compromised. He bent over to help me off the ground and pulled out his pocket knife. I gasped, bracing myself for the pain I was about to meet when Hassan began to cut the rope. It unraveled from my wrists and fell to the ground, my hands free.

I blinked. "What are you doing?" I asked, deeply confused.

"I'm letting you go," he responded soberly.

"Why would you do that?" My mind was piecing together all the ways he would use, fool, or trick me once again, and although my hands were unbound, I didn't move my wrists, frozen in hesitation.

"I don't need my brother to hate me for hurting his best friend, and maybe Damien will offer me a bit of grace when I eventually see him again," he said, rubbing the back of his neck as he dodged my gaping stare. "Besides, even if I let you go, you can't avoid the inevitable, Allene. I know where you are going and what you have planned. It is impossible to win," Hassan began to walk away. "Don't follow me, and don't send anyone after me. I am helping you, but it will only happen once. If I see you again, there is no guarantee I can protect you."

I cringed at his last words and truly hoped for the same. I hoped I would never have to see him again. I hoped I would never have to see another friend walk away as an enemy. I hoped my heart would never have to hurt again like it was right then. But watching Hassan back away, and run like a coward to his true allegiance, I realized my hope only made me one thing. A helpless fool.

llene and Damien had been withdrawn all morning. Neither of them wanted to speak after Allene shared the news of Hassan's secret. I wish I could've said I saw it coming. I wish I could have predicted it — not just for the sake of being a step ahead of the Red Crows but also for the possibility of alleviating some of Allene's pain as she processed the disloyalty of someone she thought cared for her best interests and her kingdoms. And although I wasn't the fondest of Damien, he meant a lot to Allene, and knowing well the pain of betrayal from my own brother, my heart ached as he processed the mind-shattering truth.

Killian had cautiously stayed behind Allene, giving her space. He had maintained flawless composure as he watched her intently. Seeing his calm demeanor and ability to put her needs before his, to reign in the urge to approach her and fix her pain, it made me envy and despise him, as usual. It was a difficult gift to allow those you love to suffer alone, even if they needed it. I had been tempted all morning to confront Allene and try to ease some of her hurt, but deep down, I knew Killian's approach was the most appropriate, and I hated how easy he made it seem.

I despised him for two reasons. First, because he hadn't done what I wanted. He hadn't run to her, he hadn't insisted she speak to him, he hadn't demanded she pause and allow him to help her through it — he remained as Killian always had; composed as ever. Secondly, because I wasn't the man she needed right now. Killian was the man I knew she would want comfort from, and that hurt more than I thought it would.

I knew deep down Killian had achieved a piece of Allene's heart that I hadn't realized was available to capture, and I was afraid it was a part of her heart she wouldn't easily surrender for another to take over. I knew she'd given me pieces of her heart too, but I feared they were the parts she could live without — that she was realizing *I* could be someone she could live without, and it numbed my soul.

I hadn't been truly ready to let go of Allene. I still felt she was mine; she was just away for a little while. But the longer she was away, the more I realized the likelihood of her returning to me grew smaller and smaller.

I had been towards the back of our traveling group, deep in my thoughts and not wanting to take my eyes off

Allene, that I had been oblivious to the confrontation that had taken place at the front of our traveling party.

"Ambush!" a soldier shouted in alarm, my body tensing at the warning.

It wasn't yet clear to me who was attacking us — *my father, the Red Crows, bandits* — but it was clear from the sound of metal meeting metal that it wasn't a friendly encounter. Without fully understanding what was happening, I felt my world enter into slow motion as I ran towards Allene, pursuing my immediate concern — her safety.

Killian made his way in the same direction, barely making it to Allene's side a moment sooner than myself. He wrapped his arm around her shoulder and tucked her in close, using as much of his body as possible to shield her. I immediately wrapped my arm around Allene's other shoulder, Killian nodding in a short exchange of gratitude.

Allene's body shook underneath our arms, and her sobs broke through. I knew the last two ambushes she had experienced had not ended well, and Killian and I could both see the chaos had caused Allene to be thrown into an immediate panic attack.

"Take deep breaths, Allene, focus only on that. Breathe," I encouraged her, trying to distract her while Killian frantically observed our surroundings.

As Killian looked toward the fighting, he moved away for a moment. As soon as he let go of Allene, a group of men with their faces covered in sackcloth ran out from behind the trees — the tip of a sharp, cold sword pressing lightly into my back in a shocking greeting.

"Step back, arms up!" the voice behind me commanded.

Allene shut her eyes tightly and screamed as a man wrapped his arm around Allene's neck, holding a stout blade against her throat. His blue eyes peered cautiously through his mask.

"I said, step back!" the voice repeated, his tone imbued with the threat of hurting Allene.

I regretfully surrendered, knowing I couldn't reach for my sword in enough time, and I didn't want to risk Allene getting hurt by my stubbornness. I stepped back as Killian spun around, unsheathing his sword as he prepared to react.

"Name your allegiance, Praserians! Rebel or Crow?" the man yelled. *That voice. I knew it from somewhere.*

Killian's eyes had turned to a furious glare as he fixated on the blade pressing into Allene's delicate skin. Killian took a step forward, not considering a response of words but clearly a response of action.

"Wait! He's a f-friend!" Allene stammered on her words, her voice choked with tears.

We all froze. The solider behind me shifted his gaze to the man holding Allene, and Killian held steady as he studied Allene's face.

Allene's hand was shaking as she placed it on the man's forearm, patting it gently. Killian and I were speechless as we let Allene lead, shocked and confused at the sight we were watching as we all stood prepared for an attack.

"Trae?" Allene croaked.

I felt my stomach tangle in nerves as Trae's hand fell from Allene's neck, and he removed his mask, grumbling about how little he could see through the cloth, his eyes full of relief and surprise as he looked at us. My own eyes widened at the shock of seeing a familiar face. Even with the news, Killian didn't hesitate to grab Allene's arm when Trae let go, pulling her behind him.

"Amelia?" Trae's mouth gaped as he stared at her frantic expression. He squinted as he looked at me closer. "Wait, Aleron?" Trae laughed nervously, pulling back on the man with his sword still pointing at my back.

Trae ran his fingers through his hair, his hands sliding down his face as he shook his head in disbelief. Trae gawked as he came to touch my shoulder, gripping me firmly as if to confirm that what he was seeing was real.

Trae let out one more long laugh before he spoke again. "I'll be fooled. The dead, back among the living."

———————

Everyone was rightfully cautious and on edge as we all stood in a circle, our groups segregated, other than Allene, who was grinning for the first time today as she embraced Ezra and Noni on the other side.

I was still processing what my eyes beheld. People I never thought I would see again stood before me. I still couldn't believe that fate brought Ezra, Noni, and Trae to us out of everyone who could have crossed our path.

Trae stood next to Ezra, his tall stature towering over the rest of the group. Noni had been crying as she hugged Allene tightly, and Ezra seemed shocked by the sight as well, slowly observing Allene, and all the other people in our group.

The awkwardness of the attack hadn't quite dissipated, even after listening to the explanations. Trae had already profusely apologized for the misunderstanding. No one had been hurt in the ambush, but King Seger was not amused that those we would call friends would so carelessly attack our group.

Killian and I explained the relationship we had with each of them. Noni, the head seamstress at the castle in Praseria, and one of Allene's friends from her time there. Trae, one of Aleron's most trusted soldiers, and Ezra, the royal physician, but more importantly, Allene and Risa's grandfather.

Trae had done a fair job of calming King Seger's nerves. He explained that they had run into a small group of Red Crows the day prior, so when a scout in their group saw us from afar, they assumed the Red Crows sent us to find them.

Trae told us their group had been hiding since the attacks on Praseria and Valteria. He shared the rumors of the Hadway's and Amena's being assassinated, along with all the other kingdom's royal lines. They were one of many smaller groups that had been scattered during the attack on all the kingdoms. The Red Crows had quickly dubbed them "rebels" for abandoning the kingdoms and conspiring against the "rebuilding of order". Ezra's camp consisted mainly of Praserian's, with a handful of individuals from Lokali and Gree.

Everyone patiently listened as Ezra explained the kingdom's current situation. After the attacks on Valteria, Lokali, and Gree, many Praserians attempted to flee Praseria. The Praserian army had created a tight perimeter around the kingdom, allowing few escape points. Trae and Ezra had managed to be one of the first and only groups to leave successfully.

To our surprise, Valteria had been primarily abandoned, and many refugee groups from the kingdoms were uniting there. We were less than half a day's journey to Valteria. Ezra and Trae had ventured towards Veruje to see if any other refugee camps ventured further away to hide. Noni had been part of a separate group that had fled. Trae found them yesterday. They all agreed to follow Ezra and Trae back to the larger camp in Valteria, realizing the safety that would come in numbers.

All the refugees in Valteria were loyalists. They wanted the royal families to still rule the kingdoms. They were waiting for someone to ignite a fight against my father, King Vincent, but they feared no one would be strong enough without the royal family's presence. The Kings and Queens of Lokali, Gree, Gelva, and Valteria had been taken and reportedly killed. The only royals standing to everyone's knowledge were the four of us, King Seger, and possibly Queen Lidia. The status of Veruje was still unknown.

I could see the distress on Allene's face as Ezra recounted the news of Queen Laerina and the uncertainty of Queen Lidia. I wanted to be distracted by Allene's pain to help lure me from my own. The realization of the stranger — *the monster* — my father had become was overwhelming. He was the primary villain of this chaos. The displacement of families, the bloodshed, the towns and kingdoms in ruins, the attacks, and the betrayals, all flowed to one source. A source I thought I knew. A source I was embarrassed and ashamed to claim I was connected to. A source that had torn my family apart for his own selfish gain.

I struggled to comprehend how my own father could fathom doing what he had, and I feared how much further he would be willing to go for what he wanted. Peace, unity, and my family were clearly not on his list.

KILLIAN

While Allene, Ezra, and Risa were immersed in conversation, I spent time discussing a new plan with King Seger and Aleron.

Some of King Seger's men and Trae would scout out Veruje, hoping to gain more supporters, and secure Queen Lidia's army. If we had her army, King Seger's, and the rebels, we might have enough force to defeat my father and Nycolas. The rest of us would continue to Valteria, gather as many able-bodied men and weapons as possible, and wait for their return. We would then pursue Praseria, hoping to find the other royal families alive, especially our mothers, and the ultimate goal of defeating the Red Crows and my father.

It sounded straightforward, but we had many unknowns facing us. We already had Hassan, King Vincent, and Nycolas, who turned out to be part of the

Red Crows. I felt suspicious and uneasy, considering other enemies may lurk in our midst.

I couldn't let my guard down for the sake of Praseria but also for Allene. Her world was in shambles, her future uncertain. I desperately wanted to give her security and safety once again. I wanted to give her a home. I wanted her to belong. I wanted her to thrive. I wanted her to see the beauty and joy that her destiny as royalty could bring to her. I wanted to see the happiness she and I could have together. But in order to do that, I needed to reclaim what was ours from the beginning.

e had made camp for the night, everyone settling in among different burning fires as dinner began to be distributed. We all sat in a circle, picking at our meals as we attempted to chat about casual things.

I did my best to remain lighthearted, considering the stark contrast of yesterday and today. Today, a miracle occurred. Not only was I reunited with Ezra, but I had found Trae and Noni as well. For the first time in a while, I felt that luck may be on my side.

I enjoyed catching up with Ezra and finally introducing Risa to our grandfather. Their softhearted connection was immediate. I could see her processing every feature of his, comparing it to our father. We had so little family. Ezra was a comfort for Risa and me as we approached the future. Even if we lost in the upcoming battle to regain our kingdom, at least we knew we had more than just each other. We had Ezra too, and we hoped the rumors of our mother's death were truly only rumors, just as the rumors of our death had been fraudulent. The Red Crow's diligence in instilling fear in our people by erasing us from their hopes was effective, but lies they told could only thrive for so long before the truth would finally unravel.

As I finished the remainder of my meal, I could feel Noni's stare burning into me. I had been sitting between Risa and Ezra as we ate, and as soon as Ezra stood to clear his plate, her face became flustered as she rushed to come and sit next to me.

She sat down on the rock Ezra had occupied and gave a faint smile to Risa, who exchanged a short nod. "It is a pleasure to meet you, your Highness. I am Noni," Noni fumbled over her words, fidgeting with her hands in her lap.

Risa offered a sincere smile. "I am pleased to meet you, Noni. It has been a wonderful surprise to meet Allene's acquaintances while she was in Praseria," Risa's eyes flashed to mine in unspoken uncertainty, as if she was looking for permission to proceed. I gave her a single nod, encouraging her to continue. "Allene expressed the kindness you offered to her while she was there. I can better understand what made her want to stay now that I am getting to know you all."

Noni's lip quivered. "Your words are too generous, your Highness. I wish I could say they were entirely true."

Risa's brows furrowed in confusion as Noni nervously

tucked a loose piece of hair behind her ear. "Princess Allene—" Noni began.

"Noni, you don't need to address me as princess. Please, just call me Allene," I assured her, taking her shaking hand in mine as she nervously looked into my eyes.

Noni nodded, biting back on her lip to stop it from trembling. "Allene, I am undeserving of your good graces and thoughtful words. I was cold to you when you left Praseria. I was in shock when I discovered your identity and immediately regretted my reaction," Noni let out a rushed sigh, choking back on her emotions. "I wish I had dared to run to you, to stand by you as you stood alone. After the shock had settled, I realized I wasn't certain I would ever see you again. I told myself that if I ever did, I would apologize for mistreating you. As your friend, you deserved better. I hope you can forgive me," Noni rushed to apologize, her cheeks burning red and stained with tears as her head hung low.

My heart ached at the regret she had been holding on to. Risa looked towards me with concern and gently patted Noni's back. I gripped Noni's hand and helped her sit taller, insisting she look me in the eyes to understand what I felt.

"Noni, I have not held onto that. I have held onto all the moments you made me feel seen, important, and valued. The way you treated me in Praseria meant more to me than you realize," I took her round, plump cheeks in my hands, forcing her to look at me. "You are my friend. I placed you in a difficult position that day, and you had every right to be shocked. I should have told you." I meant every word, I hoped Noni could sense my sincerity.

Noni let out a sigh of relief, her hands covering mine as she leaned her cheek into my palm. "Thank you," she whispered tightly, squeezing my hands. Noni then looked to me cautiously, leaning in to whisper softly. "I know I haven't seen you in quite some time, and I may actually be going crazy after fleeing Praseria, but you and Aleron are — I mean *were* — grr, I don't know what I mean. What happened?" Noni's large blue eyes inquisitively begged for answers.

The mention of Aleron and the way things had been not so long ago left a hovering of guilt in my heart. Ezra, Noni, and Trae hadn't seen me since everything had happened, and the truth felt complicated to explain. "I'm still processing it all myself. . ." I admitted.

Risa cleared her throat, trying to distract the conversation from the turn it had taken. "Noni, did you know Allene's birthday is coming up?" Risa said, changing the subject.

Noni sat up in surprise and took a seat next to me. "It is? The timing of it is rather unfortunate. I am sorry the circumstances aren't lending to an ideal birthday celebration," Noni huffed.

I jumped in alarm as I felt hands clasp my shoulders and a voice shout from behind me.

"King Seger!" Damien's voice bellowed among the camp, making Noni and Risa jump as well.

King Seger sat up taller in surprise at Damien's outburst. In fact, everyone had. King Seger's eyes narrowed in on Damien as he stood firmly behind me, and he cautiously engaged with a silent stare.

"You are a man who enjoys a good celebration, am I correct?" Damien prodded.

"Are you suggesting we have a reason to celebrate?" King Seger heartedly laughed.

Damien patted my shoulders again, the camp's attention fully on us.

"We do. Princess Allene will be one year older, and slightly wiser too," Damien laughed out loud at his own joke, and King Seger's laughter followed quickly behind.

King Seger grinned ear to ear. "A celebration it is."

———————————

King Seger had unexpectedly packed many irrelevant supplies for traveling on foot to engage in battle. The fires that had been barely kindled to cook dinner had been stoked to full flames, as large tree branches had been placed against each other to give the fire more volume to reach. Musical instruments had been gathered, and songs were being played and sung. It seemed to get louder as the night went on, a clear correlation to the ruckus drawn by the consumption of King Seger's homemade drink that he had brought barrels of.

Although the scene before me wasn't exactly how I imagined celebrating my birthday, I appreciated Damien's acknowledgement and effort to do something special for me.

Risa and I laughed as Damien and Marshal graced everyone with a display of a dance chant they had learned in their knight training. The aggressive moves and obnoxious yelling of the performance were drowned out as I studied Killian's face as he sat across from me in the light of the fire.

The flames flickered against his sharp cheekbones and his defined chin, drawing my eyes to notice every angle of his perfectly proportioned face. The darkness of the woods behind him allowed the fire to illuminate every detail, and the orange flames gave him a soft, mellow glow.

Killian hadn't shared many words throughout the evening, primarily sitting back and observing others' conversations. He had seemed distant all day, and his expression remained stoic. As the night progressed, and his demeanor still unchanged through all the ruckus and laughter, I noticed a new type of worry and fear overcome me. The fear of the unknown when it came to Killian — the fear that if something seemed wrong, it might have to do with me. Seeing him in such a different mood left me apprehensive.

Killian cleared his throat and stood up, turning his back on the fire and walking into the woods. I felt my stomach twist with nerves as he left, the change abrupt. My heart raced as I observed Kijana follow Killian without an explanation.

Something was off. Watching Kijana pursue Killian without reason left me uneasy. I didn't take a moment to consider how it may appear if I followed too. I quietly stood up, Risa and Noni immersed in Damien's new dramatic performance, and slipped away, unnoticed as the others continued to loudly drink King Seger's dreadful concoction, and went in the direction of Killian — unknowingly sealing my fate in the process.

KILLIAN

I felt my stomach jump at the sound of branches cracking underfoot. I immediately reacted, spinning quickly on my feet, pinning the perpetrator against the nearest tree and pulling my fist back, ready to fight. My adrenaline was pumping as I stared at the aberrant eyes of Kijana. I had to force myself to take a breath as I realized I wasn't being ambushed.

Kijana studied me, her eyes untamed as she looked me up and down. I released her arm that I had pinned to her side and stepped back, creating distance between us. I focused on calming my breathing and the movements of my chest that were heaving overtime from the scare.

Although Kijana wasn't a threat, her presence and being alone together left me agitated. I hadn't spoken with Kijana, and an unexpected stalking in the late evening was off putting. I cautiously approached her as I tried to dissect the situation.

"Did you need something from me?" I carefully asked, doing my best to seem uninterested and bored, hoping she would go away.

Kijana nodded slowly, her eyes blinking at half the average speed. Whatever King Seger had shared tonight was causing some impairment to those who indulged in his offering, and he very publicly gave Kijana permission to have a night off before the impending battle ahead, which she clearly took too far.

"I know the stories and rumors about you, Killian. Your impact on so many ladies in the other kingdoms was a common report from our spies when they would check up on you. So, I have been dying to know how a fickle, dull, enemy princess secured a self-proclaimed, reputable bachelor?" Kijana's words slurred as she strung together her sentences, her breath repugnant as she got closer.

I raised my eyebrows, unamused. "Ah, you have heard rumors? Have you also heard rumors about my patience and my temper?" The question I hoped would raise the flags of warning, even through the dampening the drink had placed over her mind.

Kijana snorted as she laughed. "I have heard of your quick rage, which is why I don't understand how you married an uptight woman, with her only experience of a man being that of your brother," she drawled, taking a step towards me. "A man of your reputation and free lifestyle deserves to be entertained by someone that can clearly understand the appeal to let go, and enjoy what is in front of them." My body went rigid as Kijana placed her hands on my chest and slithered them up tightly around my neck, her breath reeking of the putrid drink that had extinguished her ability to filter her thoughts.

"Kijana, you are unwell, and I am afraid the rumors you have heard about me are just that — *rumors.*" I reached for her hands, which were constricting my neck, pulling away each of her fingers as I attempted to release her hold. "I will be gracious this one time. We can behave as if you did not approach me tonight. Heed my warning; I will not tolerate further ill-speaking of my wife," I cautioned as I narrowed my eyes at her. "I will be on my way now."

Kijana stepped in front of me, her small but robust and muscular figure solidly blocking my path. "Don't be hasty. I didn't mean to offend," Kijana's words came out rushed, her eyes wide with feigned innocence. "I can tell Allene hasn't been indulging you. I was simply offering a one-time exchange, and no one has to know," Kijana whispered as she rocked back and forth on her heels with false naivety. " You're angry at me for being thoughtful to your needs?" Kijana approached me again, her hand stroking my face.

"Do. Not. Touch. Me." My words escaped through gritted teeth. My tolerance for Kijana's behavior was nearly at its end. I had tried to calm the situation as best I could, afraid to ruin our alliance if I made a wrong move, but Kijana's resolve was more substantial than I thought.

"I don't prefer playing games of cat and mouse, but if

that is what intrigues you—" Kijana attempted to pull me in closer, her lips pining for mine.

I pushed her away, her feet fumbling beneath her. "This isn't a game, Kijana. You need to step out of my way."

"You are a prickly one, but I'm not deterred that easily." Before I could bark back, Kijana suddenly cried out as cold water rained down her face. Her feet began jumping in anger and shock as she searched for the source of her sudden shower.

Allene stood to the side, her face fierce and fuming as she threw an empty bucket at Kijana's feet.

ALLENE

After my outburst, I ran. The frustration, jealousy, embarrassment, and shock flooded my emotions so quickly that I couldn't sort through them. All I could do was run.

Killian pursued me, begging me to stop. I wanted to hide; I wanted to be left alone, but I knew in my effort to get away that I might get lost if I wasn't careful.

My running faded as I accepted that I couldn't outrun my embarrassment, or Killian. Killian's heavy footsteps neared me, his breathing ragged as he approached.

"Are you all right?" Killian huffed out, his hands falling to knees, his head to his chest as he tried to control his labored breaths.

"No," I snapped, my chest equally heaving from the exertion of fleeing. My body was beginning to shake. When I was angry, *really* angry, my body would shake. Now that I wasn't distracted by running, I was acutely aware of my reaction to the scene of Kijana throwing herself at Killian — I was enraged.

Killian's words were rushed as he fumbled to say everything he wanted to while he had my attention. "Allene, give me a chance to explain—"

"You don't need to explain; I know what happened, and I want Kijana punished." The words were like shards of ice, cutting through my gritted teeth.

"Allene, she's intoxicated," Killian stated dryly, but the explanation felt more like a defense and I spiraled further.

I threw my hands in the air, Killian's rational thoughts being the last thing I wanted to hear right now. "Even when she was sober, she made inappropriate comments about you! A brazen woman like that won't know her place if someone doesn't show her," I persisted.

Killian was perplexed, his eyebrows furrowing in confusion, his breath now evening as he spoke his next words. "Kijana said something to you about me?"

I grimaced and nodded. "I tolerated Kijana and her offensive comments for the sake of our alliance, but I cannot let this go. Moving on from it once was gracious enough." I folded my arms across my chest, trying to contain the muscles that were threatening to expose how deep my rage festered.

Killian's body tensed as he forced a sigh. "Allene, I understand your frustration entirely, I truly do, but we do need to consider what we risk by insisting on discipline for Kijana. I am sure after what happened tonight, and the shock she likely is processing after your visit and getting caught, she will reconsider approaching me again." Killian cautiously raised his hands as he approached me, like he was trying to tame a wild animal, my anger visibly radiating under the light of the moon. "I will be more on guard when Kijana is near me. I didn't realize she had feelings towards me. If we don't say anything, she will see us as doing her favor, and it would be a political advant—"

I threw my hands to my side that had turned into balled fists, cutting off his thought. "Killian, stop! Stop talking about how we should let it go, how it is in our best interest, and how it isn't a problem. It's not helping! All I want to do is go back and put her in her place!" I didn't mean to lose my temper with him as the words shouted from my lungs, but I didn't care about the repercussions. All I could see was red. I was livid.

"You want to put Kijana in her place?" Killian let out a brief chuckle as he attempted to suppress his urge to laugh, clearly not hurt by my outburst that he so graciously took the brunt of. "How would you do that?" He continued, his hand covering the smile that had spread to his lips. I was confident the glare in my eyes was enough to make him terrified, but he remained firm in place, his eyes challenging me.

"You don't think I can face her?" I pressed, folding my arms firmly across my chest.

Killian threw his hands up in the air, pleading his innocence. "I am not insulting you! I don't even think *I* could put Kijana in her place. She is stronger than both of us combined, and I am certain she has killed more people than I ever will. She is a terrifying individual."

I rolled my eyes and turned up my nose, unashamed by how childish I was behaving on the matter. At that moment, I didn't want to react the way a princess should. All I could think about was revenge.

"All the more reason to pursue justice," I insisted.

Killian let out a short sigh and placed a reassuring hand on my shoulder, my body shivering from his touch. "Allene, I am not trying to disregard or invalidate your feelings right now, but I am trying to understand. Nothing happened, and you caught her by surprise with the water debacle, so what is it? Why are you so angry right now?"

I unintentionally found myself biting my lip, the wrestle within myself was strong as I considered if I were to tell Killian the truth, or if I should lie. I felt my cheeks flush again with anger, knowing I couldn't suppress my feelings if I wanted peace of mind.

"It's wrong and it's disrespectful. Do I need more of a reason than that?" I couldn't hold myself back from raising my voice in frustration.

Killian motioned his hands downward, trying to get me to discuss the situation more calmly, but I didn't care.

"No, no, you're right — it was wrong and disrespectful. But we are royals; we have seen disrespect and been wronged more times than we can count. What is different this time?" Killian pressed, slowly approaching me as his eyes creased with worry.

My head snapped upright, my eyes pointedly set on

Killian's. "This time, it involves you," I stated in a hushed tone. I bite my lip again in hesitation as I spit out the words that followed. "You're mine."

Killian's eyebrows furrowed as he studied my face. His body was still, but not rigid. His blue eyes bore into my already over-heated face, making my body temperature rise even more. "Is this part of the act? No one is watching, Allene, we are alone," he reminded me, the words cutting me deeply as I debated if I should walk away or tell the truth. I had already embarrassed myself enough for a lifetime. Where was my pride? My thoughts raced back to Kijana, her hands on Killian's chest, her suggestions, and the mockery she had made of him and I. . .my heart raced with rage.

I inhaled sharply. "I know we are alone. I'm not acting." The truth felt freeing on my tongue, the sudden admission incriminating.

Killian still appeared confused as I moved in closer to better see his facial expression under the moon's dim light. "Did you mean it earlier when you said you would give me anything I asked for my birthday?" I inquired, treading the dangerous waters his selfless promise held.

Killian's face relaxed as his eyes communicated his sincerity. "I meant every word."

I nodded and bit my lip for the third time, and this time, I contemplated also biting my tongue. Killian had said exactly what I had hoped. Now, it was my turn to ask, and once I said the words, it would be wrong to take them back.

Is this really what I wanted? Is Killian who I wanted, forever? I may have been wrong, I may have been rash, I may have been out of my mind, but I couldn't stop myself from clinging to my feelings — I couldn't hold back the controlling, possibly sinful, but exhilarating desires of my heart. I chose to set my reservations completely free.

I looked into Killian's eyes, swallowing my fears of rejection and misunderstanding, and declared my birthday wish. "Will you Marry me, Killian? *Truly* marry me?"

Killian's eyes widened in pleasant surprise and followed with shock. He gripped my arms lightly, his touch offering an undeniable security.

"Allene, nothing would make me happier, but you don't need to rush your decision. I am not going anywhere." Killian tucked my hair behind my ear, his hand resting on my cheek. "I know you are still working through your feelings toward Aleron. I don't want you to decide hastily and later have regrets," Killian expressed his reservations.

"I don't need more time to consider my decision. I am certain of my feelings for you." I raised my hand to hold Killian's, pressing his cold fingertips into my warm cheeks. His touch left the feeling of my body melting into his. I smiled at the sensation. "I am consumed by you, Killian. I have never wanted to be tied to someone more than I do right now, and if you really mean it, if you feel for me the way you say that you feel, and if you want to give me everything I want, then marry me." The last words were a whispered plea, an eager proposal of my vulnerable heart being put on the line.

Killian's eyes devoured every inch of me, and the attention made me nervous.

"What I should say, and I want to say. . ." Killian's voice trailed off as he weighed the decision of how to answer.

"Can't what you should say, and what you want to say, be the same?" I shamelessly asked.

Killian gave a timid smile. "I wish it was that simple, but when it comes to you, it never has been. I have never deserved you, or the honor you give me by wanting to be by my side."

My eyes held his, the intensity in both our stares palpable. "Then make it simple. Tell me what you want."

As if it was the last prompt he needed, the final word to give himself permission, Killian leaned his body closer to me, and my eyes fell closed. His lips were only a breath away from mine, and I could taste his sweet words. One heartbeat. Two heartbeats. That was all it took for Killian to make up his mind, and to unravel me in the process. My eyes fluttered open at his hesitation.

"Love, marrying you, there isn't anything else I would rather do," his eyes eagerly searched my face, taking in every reaction and emotion they caused to flit across my features. "I'm yours," he breathed. Killian pressed himself against me, not holding back as he made his intentions clear, pressing a drawn out kiss on my quivering lips.

"I love you," I whispered, desperate to finally admit it

out loud, my breath escaping me as I hurried to communicate my feelings.

Killian's eyes glistened as he seemed choked up by my declaration. He smiled, the purest, unbridled smile I had ever witnessed him give. My heart raced at the sight. He was genuinely happy, and I felt a sense of pride and honor as I realized that unburdened, fulfilling happiness came from a relationship with me.

"I love you, Allene," Killian proclaimed back as he kissed me again, softly, sweetly, and leaving me in a puddle as he braced me in his arms when my strength gave out at his words.

My body felt untethered. Gravity couldn't hold my feet down any longer. My only hope of not floating into the night sky was clinging tightly to Killian's chest. Control was slipping through my fingers, and I couldn't hold on.

Kissing Killian was a different type of escape. My sense of risk was unrestrained. His touch was not wanted; it was needed. With each kiss, he unraveled the emotions I had bound up inside — the sensation rippling through my body like a flash flood of rain, bursting out and breaking free of all sanity. He was a pure, elegant form of torture.

I noticed Killian's hair was thick and soft as I twirled my fingers through it. I could hear a deep rumble in his throat and a new exhilaration translated through his lips. I felt a dull pain as he tugged at my lip with his teeth, taken back by his aggressive form of affection. It was utterly different from Aleron, and in that moment, I realized something completely different is precisely what I needed

— Killian had subconsciously been what I longed for. I hadn't realized it until he was directly in front of me, invading my thoughts every day, slowly finding his way into my heart — the tension and certainty it had created was unmatched.

Killian. I chose Killian.

ALERON

Something had happened last night, and my gut sank with the knowledge of it. Not only had Kijana been in a dreadful mood after coming back to the camp soaked to the bone, which none of us inquired of as she exchanged deathly glances of warning, but Killian and Allene had been different all morning with each other, their demeanor a stark opposite to Kijana's. The sincerity of their closeness and interactions was apparent, and it crushed me.

I assumed I had more time to change our fate. I believed Allene would allow her heart to remain open to me, but I was foolish to think it was something I could request or control at my will. If her feelings for Killian had solidified, it wasn't my place to intervene or tell her to feel differently. However, the reality of officially losing her forever was still unbearable to stomach.

My emotions were a mixture of anger and disappointment. Each time I glanced at them, snuggled side by side, it felt like it did the day I pushed her away, but this time, I couldn't numb the feelings by burying myself in solitude. Allene's continual presence was a vicious reminder of the never-ending pain of losing the woman I loved.

Each time Allene's eyes glimmered as she intently listened to Killian speak, any time he moved and she would move with him, the pain it caused me would deepen. The worst of it all was that Allene wouldn't pause to look at me, to consider my reaction — her entire attention was solely on Killian. I was not even a fleeting thought. I no longer held a place in her heart, and I knew she would eventually tell me the painful news herself. I had never wished so severely for a conversation never to happen.

As I sat among the small circle of our group, my heart felt like shattered glass, my emotions raw and exposed. Killian and Allene shared stolen glances, their eyes speaking a language only they understood, and it was like a blade twisting in my chest.

The ache was a constant presence, and the intensity of it was almost unbearable. Every time Allene's gaze sought out Killian's, I felt a pang of longing and loss. It was distracting, to say the least, as we gathered around the dimly lit campfire that night, the flickering flames casting eerie shadows on our faces.

Trae caught everyone's attention as he proudly stomped his way through the camp, holding up a trophy of fresh caught, pungent fish.

"Look what we caught in the river! What a feast!" Trae exclaimed as he threw down the large trout on a makeshift stone table and pulled out his carving knife. Then, he calmly began fileting the fish and offering the fresh catch to eager hands of the weary party.

Once the soldiers had eaten their fill, Trae approached the rest of us with a plate of the fresh, white fish.

"Eat up everyone, there is no guarantee when we will see another one of these again." Trae nudged the plate toward Risa and Marshal, then continued to Killian and Allene. Killian happily took a piece for himself and quietly took a piece for Allene. Before Allene could turn her nose up at the fish, Killian took the fish from her plate, and swapped it with his piece of bread. Allene smiled at his gesture, and my stomach sickened at the thoughtful scene playing out in front of me.

Ezra managed to gather my attention as he began a discussion about our plan moving forward. His voice, gravelly and authoritative, cut through my thoughts like a knife.

"Tomorrow, we will arrive at the outskirts of Valteria," he declared. "We have camps there of survivors that managed to evade the Red Crows. They're waiting for our direction."

Pulling me from the turmoil in my heart, Ezra's words attuned me to my royal purpose. This was what mattered now — the fight against the Red Crows, the group responsible for the devastation of Gelva, Lokali, Gree, Valteria and Praseria.

The plan proposed by Ezra was unanimous, and we rose from our makeshift meeting place to prepare for the journey.

Before I could hide away for the evening, Ezra's gaze shifted between Killian and me; his brow furrowed as he stopped us. "Prince Aleron, Prince Killian, I hoped to speak to you two in private."

Killian nodded and followed Ezra without a word, while I begrudgingly dragged my feet to follow.

Allene had patiently waited for me to return to my tent after my long conversation with Ezra and Aleron. Her eyes grew wide with empathy and concern as I entered and she read the stress displayed on my face.

I sat down next to her, letting my head fall into her lap. The serenity Allene evoked simply by being present and interested in my well being caused a reassurance inside of me that I hadn't experienced in years. She softly stroked a lock of my hair, the tugging sensation and the dropping temperature of the night both giving me chills.

I knew it likely wasn't tactful, but I was numb, tired and felt too heavy to engage in casual conversation when such a life changing matter had to be discussed with Allene. I didn't want to have the conversation at all, but I knew it had to happen.

I swallowed and cleared my throat, gaining the

courage to reveal the painful news that Ezra had shared with me.

"Ezra did some digging about my father's involvement with the Red Crows," I whispered softly, too exhausted to exert more energy than I had already given to the earlier conversation.

Allene remained composed, as if the news didn't surprise her. "What did he find?" she inquired.

I closed my eyes tightly. "Poison," I stated.

"Poison?" This time, her reaction was one of surprise, her body pulling back as she looked down at me.

I nodded in her lap, my eyes still tightly closed. "Vincent had inquired about opium. He made it appear like it was for medicinal purposes, but Ezra grew suspicious. Prior to fleeing the palace, Ezra managed to find an exchange of letters in Vincent's study, between him and Nycloas. They have been working together for months." My eyes fluttered open, settling on Allene's frozen figure that was backlit by the moonlight. I sought out Allene's hands, squeezing them tightly before I continued. "The timing of Vincent asking for the opium and the timing of your father's death align. Ezra confirmed in the letter exchanges that Nycolas obtained the poison from my father and had another member of the Red Crows disguised as a servant, slowly poison Faris."

Allene's eyes widened, and her lip quivered as she replied. "Vincent. . .killed my father?" Allene was silent as she tightly gripped my hands, her arms now shaking too. I pulled myself out of her lap and wrapped her into my chest. Allene sat motionless as her tears began to slowly seep through my shirt. She let out no sobs, but the tears continued as she wrapped her arms around my waist, clinging to me tightly.

I placed my chin on top of her head, and whispered the only words that felt right in that moment.

"I am so sorry, Allene. . . I am so sorry."

After a long while, Allene's cries eventually hushed as she drifted off to sleep. Seeing her in pain — so much of it in such a short amount of time — weighed heavily on my heart. We both were broken souls doing our best to cling to the few strands of hope and happiness we had left — and to my overwhelming surprise, that hope and happiness happened to be each other. And I would never let it go.

The next morning we set out, making our way to the outskirts of Valteria. As difficult as it had been to hear, I knew I had to share the discovery of our father's death with Risa. Pulling her ahead of the group, I opened up to her about the news. I couldn't anticipate how Risa would react, afterall, we were both physically, emotionally, and mentally exhausted more than we ever had been — the truth of our father's death felt like a breaking point to me, and I knew it wouldn't be any easier on Risa.

Risa had withdrawn immediately upon hearing the news. Retreating behind the rest of us, Marshal fell in line with Risa, matching her slow, methodical steps as she pressed on. No tears came, but I only think it was because she had none left to give.

I looked to my source of comfort. Killian's strides in pace with mine, the gentle squeeze of my hand a tethering reminder of the shred of hope and joy he had promised me on my birthday. I threaded my fingers through his, tracing the callouses on the tips of his fingers, letting myself memorize the feel of them as a distraction from going back to my home.

I looked over my shoulder and could see the trepidation in Risa's eyes, and realized it was likely reflected in my own as well. The princesses of Valteria, now reduced to weary, void travelers in their own land.

When we finally arrived, the sight was gut-wrenching. Valteria, once a kingdom of beauty and opulence, lay in ruins. Homes reduced to rubble, the laughter of children silenced, and the vibrant mountainside now a wasteland of despair. My heartbreak was palpable as tears welled in my eyes, already puffy and sore from the night before.

I knelt down beside a fallen violet flag, a symbol of Valteria's former glory. My fingers traced its tattered form with reverence. It was as if the weight of Valteria's destruction had settled upon me, and the burden was too much to bear alone.

Killian stepped forward, placing a gentle hand on my shoulder, and for a moment, I could share the sorrow. As we stood in the midst of the devastation, as my mind contemplated avenging my fathers fate, I couldn't help but hope that love, in all its complexities, would find a way to heal the wounds of our broken world.

Killian swiftly took my hand as Ezra led us to the group of refugees. Their weary and dirty faces lit up with smiles as Aleron, Killian, Risa and me approached the makeshift camp they had created. One by one, the refugees began to kneel as we walked by, each halting what they were doing to acknowledge our presence. The camp had become quiet, until one figure stood out from the crowd, shamelessly running to meet us.

I sighed with relief as I made out Sonora's face. Releasing Killian's hand, I ran to meet her, embracing her tightly as we laughed together — the only sound in the camp.

"My lady, you're alive!" Sonora clung to me, afraid to let me go.

"Sonora, you don't have any idea how much I have needed to see you," I replied, nuzzling deeper into her blonde hair to hide the tears of joy in my eyes at the sight of my lady's maid.

Sonora laughed again. "I believe I do, you clearly haven't been getting along without me, your highness. What on earth have you been doing to your hair?" She pulled my hair to the sides of my face, brushing it flat with her hands and shaking her head. "Let's get you looking like a proper princess again."

———————

Sonora, Noni, Modesta, Risa, and myself all gathered in one of the few buildings still standing in the village. The makeshift dressing room had a few salvaged dresses and beauty supplies strewn about on chairs and wobbly tables.

Noni seemed relaxed as soon as she picked up a rusty sewing needle to mend a seam in my tattered dress. Modesta, Risa's lady's maid, had been quiet as she softly brushed oil through Risa's tangled hair. Sonora couldn't stop smiling, the only one of us in the room who seemed able to muster any cheer.

Sonora cleared her throat in an attempt to break through the solemn mood.

"I know it isn't your usual pampering treatment, but I promise this is much better than your traveling beauty routine. The pine sap and dirt have left you both with a rather drab look." Noni offered a small laugh at Sonora's lighthearted attempt of softening our demeanor, but Risa wouldn't budge, which meant Modesta wouldn't give in either.

The awkward silence filled the dreary space quickly, and Noni became antsy under its pressure. Noni threw her hands into her lap and shook her head firmly. "Ladies, this won't do!"

"What has gotten into you?" Sonora replied, her hand hovering over her heart in surprise.

I couldn't help but chuckle seeing Sonora's appalled response to Noni's outburst. This was the Noni I had come to know — loud, obnoxious, and always perfectly out of line in her own peculiar way.

Noni sighed as she observed my laughter. "Now you laugh?"

I shrugged, and watched in the mirror as Sonora continued to work on my mess of hair. "I don't mean to laugh, I just know what you are going to say and I love that you are bold enough to say it," I answered.

Noni pouted as she went back to mending, her lips pursed together. "Well, if I am that predictable, I will leave it unsaid."

"Come now, Noni, don't be stubborn. I still want to hear it." I paused and looked at her. "I *need* to hear it." I meant it, and Noni could sense the sincerity in my voice. Her bluntness and her honesty were something I knew we all could benefit from hearing.

Noni shifted uneasily in her swaying chair, her eyes eager as she looked at me.

"I know your thoughts are heavy, but letting them weigh you down won't change our circumstances. Your people — everyone's people — are looking to you as beacons of hope. As hard as it may feel right now, you both need to be strong. Even if you don't feel that way, you need to at least look it."

Sonora raised her hand proudly. "I can promise you will look strong and rejuvenated, but it is in the delivery of your presence that will be the difference between seeming defeated or triumphant," Sonora added.

Modesta waited for Risa to respond before chiming in. Risa hadn't taken her eyes off of her tightly clasped hands, the pain she held inside evidently shown from the tenseness of her body. Risa didn't look up as she spoke.

"Strong?" Risa scoffed. "I feel numb. I have never been one to be able to act through my true emotions."

Noni's face lit up as she snapped her fingers together.

"Do you know what I do when I need to put on a face? As dreadful as it sounds, I focus on someone else's drama or pain. What you need is a dose of good gossip — something to bring temporary relief from your own sorrow. A distraction!" Noni exclaimed.

"That is dreadfully selfish," Sonora murmured.

"Call it what you will, it works," Noni quipped back.

The two of them exchanged heated glances. Sonora huffed and focused again on braiding my hair. "If it works, why don't you share your enticing gossip?"

"Mine? Unless you all want to hear about Trae's uncovered ability to flirt, or how my legs feel like they may fall off from all the walking the last few days, I don't have much else to offer," Noni admitted.

"Don't suggest a solution that you don't have the ability to deliver on," Sonora critiqued.

Noni's eyes were like daggers as she observed Sonora's smug face. I hadn't thought it possible for their two personalities to clash in this way, but the two were truly opposites.

"Good gossip?" I queried, trying to mend the situation. "I have something."

Everyone's ears and eyes perked up immediately, their attention burning into me.

"Don't keep it from us now!" Noni groaned.

I nervously laughed. "I suppose there isn't a great time to tell you all anyway, so it might as well be now." I paused, hesitant to say the words out loud, but the joy of them was stronger and I found them tumbling from my lips in eagerness. "I'm getting married."

Noni waved her hand and clicked her tongue in disappointment. "We don't want fake gossip, Allene."

I was quiet, my shoulders stiffening. "It's not fake gossip."

Risa finally turned to look at me and said each word cautiously. "What's not fake gossip?"

I swallowed hard and cleared my throat, ready to face her reaction. "I proposed to Killian."

"You. . .what?" Risa gawked, her mouth hanging open as she looked at me and the other three ladies in the room.

"Proposed?" Noni shrieked.

"To Killian?" Sonora staggered, her hands frozen mid-braid.

I nodded and everyone became silent.

Before anyone had the chance to divulge their thoughts, with impeccable timing, a familiar head with hair perfectly primped popped past the door frame. Queen Lidia pushed her way through the creaky, sticky archway and proudly commanded our attention.

"Cousins! Oh, my dear cousins, how have you been fair—"

"Allene proposed to Killian," Risa tattled before Lidia could even get her sentence out.

Lidia's face immediately dropped, her eyes blinking slowly as her face became more pale white than before. "What have I missed?"

ALERON

With the limited space for all of us to stay, Marshal, Damien, Trae, Ezra, a knight from Valteria named Ajax that Damien had a tense relationship with, Killian and myself had been forced to share the same tight quarters.

As Ajax, Marshal and Damien were previous acquaintances, they had taken to exclusive conversation in the corner of the room. Trae had tried inserting himself into the conversation a handful of times, but finally gave up and pursued talking with Ezra and me.

"Did you catch a glimpse of the Queen of Veruje?" Trae inquired, suggestively raising his eyebrows.

Queen Lidia had arrived, completing the last of our expected allies. Although I hadn't had the chance to meet her yet, rumors had already begun.

"I have seen her on one occasion over the past few years," Ezra replied curtly, snacking on an unripe pear.

Trae's dimpled smile grew wide. "Can you tell me if the rumors are true then? Is she unmarried?"

Killian had been staring out the single small window of the house, his gaze focused on the scale of the mountain nearby.

Killian laughed. "There is a reason she is unmarried. Don't waste your time, unless you want to be a memory like the many others."

Trae's eyes lit up. "I was raised to aim for the greatest result, but in this case, if being a memory is all I can get, then I am open to settling for it."

Ezra shook his head in disgust. "Trae, watch your comments. She is a queen, not an admirer. Why don't you meet her first before making such statements?"

"That is a valid point. . .I need to meet her!" Trae made his way to the door, skipping proudly with unchecked confidence.

Ezra quickly followed, muttering under his breath as he took another bite of his pear. "That boy may have left Praseria behind, but he certainly didn't have to leave his manners."

It didn't take long for Marshal, Damien and Ajax to follow suit and exit the house, leaving Killian and me alone. The room was already stuffy, and the added silence brought extra discomfort. I arose from the hard chair I had planted myself in, ready to get out for the fresh air.

"Aleron, I need to speak with you."

Killian's words made my body tense. I regretted not taking my chance to escape with the rest of the group.

Killian leaned back against the window, his shoulders square and tall as he calmly looked at me.

I felt my jaw tighten as I replied to his statement. "What if I don't want to speak with you?"

Killian slowly nodded, masking well any pain the comment may have elicited. "I would understand why you feel that way, but you don't have to say a word, I only need you to listen. As your brother, it is something you need to hear from me."

My stomach dropped. "I don't want to hear it."

Killain sighed. "I honestly don't want to say it. . ."

"Then don't," I snapped. "This is the first time you have asked to talk to me in years, so if you feel you owe me an explanation or apology for anything, I can assure you, I haven't ever expected one. As it stands, you still have no reason to talk to me, so let's leave it that way — we've gotten good at it after all." The words came out sharper than I intended, but when it came to Killian, I had never been good at reeling in my emotions.

Killian moved forward now, his face uneasy — an expression I hadn't seen him wear, ever. The pit in my stomach grew.

"That's precisely why it's important we have this conversation. I regret not being honest with you. I regret disappearing without giving you an explanation. I'm ready to give you the answers you deserved before I left," Killian proceeded.

I scoffed. "Your sincerity is hard to get behind considering you and I are only in the same room because of a forced circumstance. If this situation hadn't occurred with the Red Crows, things wouldn't have changed. *You* wouldn't have changed," I pointed out.

"That's not true, my return to Praseria was supposed to be the turning point," Killian defended his claims.

"You came back to Praseria for your own gain," I bit back.

Killian clenched his fists, and slowly uncurled each finger as he let out a patient exhale, his eyes tightly shut. "No, Aleron, I came back for you. I had left, for *you*. Everything rotten and selfish I have done, has been for you." Killian shook his head, his hands combing through his hair. "If you would allow me to explain, you would finally see that I am not the person — the monster — you've made me out to be."

"Stop, please, just stop," I spoke through gritted teeth, throwing up my hands. "I know how rotten our father is. I know the story and reasoning for you leaving is likely valid and understandable. I've seen parts of you the last few weeks that I thought I would never see again. The brother I used to know has returned, and it should be comforting, but it isn't. I see you mending one part of my trust while I watch you break it in another." The words felt like a sinking stone in my stomach.

"What do you mean?" Killian clarified, his eyes squinting in confusion.

"Allene," I blurted out the words I had been holding back, the anger rushing too quickly to stop. "I'm talking about you falling in love with Allene, and manipulating her into falling in love with you."

Killian seemed cautious as he considered what he would say now that the accusation was being addressed. "I don't want to keep anything from you anymore, little brother. You're right, I am in love with Allene. I won't lie to you or pretend otherwise," he confessed.

My frustration was boiling over, my words hurrying out all at once. "Why? Why did you do it? Was winning over Allene some twisted form of satisfaction for you? Knowing that you took one of the few remaining people that meant anything to me?"

Killian's eyes became like fire as he got closer to me, his jaw clenched in irritation. "You don't think I tried dissuading her? I know that I am not the better choice, and Allene knows it too. Allene and I were not something I sought after. Our paths coming together as they did shouldn't have happened."

I scoffed at his admission. "Fine, let's call it fate that brought you two together. If you could go back, would you change it? Would you have removed yourself as an option?" I pressured him on.

"No," Killian quickly replied without hesitation.

"No?" I gawked, the muscle in my jaw feathering in frustration.

"No, I wouldn't change it," he reiterated.

My hands raised in defeat. "Thank you for proving to me that giving you the benefit of the doubt and allowing myself to think you had changed would have been a massive regret," I spat, hoping each word would hurt as much as he had hurt me.

Killian's despondent stare warned of a frightful reality I would soon be faced with. I began to make my way to the door, downcasting my eyes in an attempt to avoid his next sentence altogether.

"She proposed to me, Aleron."

My feet immediately cemented into place as Killian's dreadful words mocked me by repeating in my head.

"Excuse me?" I whispered in disbelief, more to myself than to Killian, but Killian didn't pause to reply.

There was no sense of joy as Killian broke the news to me again, no sadistic pleasure that I expected to hear in the words that he spoke, but the weight of his words left me drowning. "Allene. She proposed to me on her birthday, and I said yes."

I thought I would be prepared for that moment, considering Killian had already put me through betrayal, I thought it would feel similar to before, but this time, this news, this duplicity was reaching a proportion I hadn't ever imagined. My hands balled into fists, my body tensing in outrage. Killian's disheartened and sobered expression wasn't enough to mend the wrong I felt.

I had lost. I had lost the fight for Allene's affection. *But I still hadn't heard it from her.* I wouldn't completely close off my hopes until Allene had told me herself. But the suspicion of the truthfulness to Killian's statement was stronger than I thought it would be. I immutably knew the validity of his story, and that made it worse.

I couldn't stop my voice from turning into a growl as I responded to Killian. "You may have Allene fooled, and you may have even convinced yourself of your repentant heart, but let me assure you, there is no possibility of your redemption in my eyes, brother."

Killian's jaw clenched, his teeth grinding together as he stood uncomfortably still.

"I am not seeking redemption or reformation of our relationship, but I hoped you would at least settle on liberality," Killian put forward.

I opened the door, unable to endure another moment in the same room as Killian. I needed the fresh air, I needed the space, and I needed time to process the reality of what Killian had said.

I slowly shook my head back and forth, not even considering his offer. "I won't do that. I grieved the loss of the brother I knew long ago. I suggest you do the same."

KILLIAN

The day had passed by painstakingly slow. After the argument with Aleron, and reconciliation now further away than ever before, the sorrow of the situation weighed me down. With the arrival of Queen Lidia, I hadn't seen Allene — their conversation enduring for hours. Without Allene to distract me and while waiting for somewhere to go, I began to feel restless.

I had anticipated the confession of my true engagement to Allene to not be well received by my brother, and I couldn't be angry or upset at him for his reaction. I knew it had been unexpected and I also knew it would hurt him. I *hated* hurting him. And I hated even more that over the years I had managed to convince him that I wasn't affected by it at all — that watching Aleron be in pain and suffer at my expense was a selfish tendency of mine that would surely never pass. I hated that in his eyes, I had no chance of changing. I would permanently be the egotistical older brother who's only agenda was to be irresponsible and self-seeking.

I knew the truth to my actions, but it didn't make me feel better. The pain was there because the care was there — I truly cared about Aleron's opinion of me, and I desperately wanted him to understand my desire to restore our brotherhood to what it once used to be. If I had any chance of gaining back the brother I had lost, it would have to be done in honesty.

Aleron needed to know the full story from when I left, up until now. But I couldn't share that if he wouldn't listen — and as angry and defensive as it made me feel, I understood his hesitation. I would be disappointed if he eagerly and easily trusted someone again that had hurt him so deeply. I loathed *I* was the person who had caused him so much pain.

As I walked outside to get some air, my foot met Damien's back.

"Hey! Watch where you're going!" Damien shouted, rubbing his muscles where he took the hit.

I blinked, feigning boredom. "You're in the way," I growled.

Damien's head snapped back to shoot me a glare. "No, I was *patiently* waiting for you to finish brooding in solitude."

My eyes narrowed with impatience from his attack. "Are you expecting me to thank you?"

"Well, I was being polite, wasn't I?" Damien exclaimed.

I rolled my eyes. "I wouldn't consider our interactions polite."

"I wouldn't consider it either," Damien snipped.

"Then why the sudden urge to be polite?" I shot back, my eyebrows raising to my forehead.

"Because you matter to Allene. And if you matter to Allene, I have to try my best to have you matter to me too," Damien muttered, clearly annoyed.

I exhaled and took a seat next to Damien, who cautiously slid as far away from me as he could on the narrow stairs.

"You are a better person than I am," I stated, unable to restrain my thoughts from staying put in my mind.

Maybe it had been the fight with Aleron, or my horrible fatigue from the long journey, but I felt my guard fall as I sat next to a dumbfounded Damien. Protecting myself by being brusque was tiring. I was ready to put aside my contentious personality to those that made an effort with me. I was ready for a change — I was ready to be myself again.

"I don't think I have had a chance to say this, but I am grateful Allene has you, Damien. You're a devoted friend. You continue to exceed my expectations with your grace and patience. I apologize if I have made our relationship difficult before it had a chance to begin."

Damien was silent for a long time as he watched me fumble with my hands. He cautiously spoke. "I may be a supportive friend, but that doesn't mean I am easily swayed. Is this a ploy? Are you seeking temporary approval from me with kindness and compliments?" His eyes narrowed at me, the emotion in them wild and clear.

I couldn't help but laugh at his suspicion. "No, it's honesty. I plan to do better. I want to be the man I used to be, for Allene, but also for myself." I let out a long sigh, leaning back casually on my elbows. "I may not be able to return to my honorable name or redeem myself from the opinions of people, but I can do my best for Allene. She's put her faith in me, and I refuse to break her confidence." My lips went in a hard, straight line as I reflected on the trust she had placed in me, and the vulnerability of choosing to be tied to someone with as stained of a reputation as mine.

Damien snapped his fingers enthusiastically at my response, like he had set up a trap for me to fall into and he was excited I took the bait. "That is why I have given you the grace I have. If Allene see's goodness in you, I trust that it's there." Damien shrugged, picking at a frayed hem on his dirtied pant leg. "I may not know your story, but I know we all go through our own journeys, and I'm sure she's based her judgment of you on that. Your heart has merits that others can't see yet."

I stared back at Damien in awe and wonder as he offered a slap happy grin. "You don't know my story, yet are you so willing to believe that?" I asked in confusion.

Damien nodded. "You forget I am going through my own story right now. I am facing a betrayal from my older brother, but I *know* Hassan. I can't help but hold out hope that there is something to be redeemed. . .that there is a logical explanation for what he has done." Damien shoulders sagged from the weight of his worry, his eyebrows creasing. "This version of him I am currently faced with, it isn't him. I am fighting for that, for the return of the brother I know him to be." Damien stood up and brushed off his pants, letting out a short sigh before placing a firm hand on my shoulder. "And although Aleron might not see or admit it, I am certain he has been fighting for you too. Give him time. If you're as good as person as Allene seems to think you are, you can find your redemption."

With a turn of his heel and a shut of the door, Damien had managed to do something no one had ever done. His words brought tears of hope to my eyes.

My heart sank like a stone in my chest. I had hoped to avoid it — to shield Lidia from the painful truth, but there was no escaping it now. In the hours of talking, everything had come out, and Lidia was doing her best to absorb the information. Sonora, Modesta and Noni had politely left, allowing privacy for our conversation.

I met Lidia's gaze, my eyes filled with sorrow. "Lidia," I began, my voice trembling with regret, "I am terribly sorry."

Lidia's face paled, and her hand went instinctively to her chest, as if to steady the sudden ache within. Her shoulders sagged, and for a moment, she seemed to age before my eyes.

"Hassan," she whispered, her voice barely above a breath. "I never thought. . ."

"He fooled us all," I said softly, reaching out to place a

comforting hand on her arm. Although their interactions were short, and it was Lidia pursuing any level of flirtation during our visit in Veruje, I could understand her devastation of misjudging someone's character you had come to care for.

Lidia stood, clearly stunned as she took a few visible steps back like the news had been a physical blow. "I thought our reality couldn't get more shocking, Allene, but I leave you alone for a few weeks and the entire world turns upside down!" Lidia threw her hands up in the air.

Risa grimaced at Lidia's reaction as she stumbled away to steady herself against the wall.

"Lidia, we must focus on the battle ahead. The Red Crows must be stopped, and our kingdoms restored. That is our priority right now, we can't allow ourselves distractions," Risa interjected.

Lidia's eyes grew wide and her arms threw up in a temper. That was the first time I had ever seen Lidia frustrated. "Distractions?" Lidia scoffed in disbelief. "Girls, I love you like my own daughters, you know this, but for all that is good in the world, what have you been doing? You have allowed every possible distraction to take over your responsibilities! You are princesses! You have duties and obligations that cannot be overlooked. You have people relying on you!" Lidia raised her hand up and lifted a finger to go along with each reason we were in the wrong.

"Your mother has been missing for weeks, your kingdom is in ruins, you have had to call upon the help of every other kingdom in an attempt to save your own, you discover your father had been poisoned to death, and an ally and confidant was a traitor right in your midst! Have you both been so distracted by your hearts and focused on love that your resolve faltered? Could you not have remained strong, to be responsible and noble until this disaster had passed?" The onslaught of insults and rage from Lidia came fast and hard, each one digging deeper into my heart than the first.

Risa immediately looked down in shame, tears spilling over the corners of her eyes. Lidia's words had stung. She had already given her opinion of my engagement, but the added discouragement only festered my hurt. I didn't want our first conversation back together again to be driven by such vice, but Lidia's temper could only be matched by being met with my own.

I stood behind Risa, rubbing her shoulders as she buried her head in her hands.

"Our actions have been only noble and responsible," I began, my defensiveness taking over. "This journey has been horrendous, I nearly died on more than one occasion in an attempt to gather all the kingdoms I could to help get our mothers back. My father died only months ago, and that grief is something I have been living with every day. The marriage proposal was a political advantage at a time when we desperately needed one, and the Hassan situation took all of us by surprise, even his own brother!" I shut my eyes, taking a shaky breath as I was reminded of it.

"Say what you will, but we have been doing the best we

can, and I will not be shamed into feeling irresponsible for allowing myself to still find a little bit of joy in my mess of a life right now. It is especially ironic coming from the woman who makes challenging responsibility her life's work!"

Lidia's eyes widened in disbelief and embarrassment. She stood rigidly, brushing out her bright pink dress and fixing the placement of her hair before proudly straightening her shoulders. Lidia made her way to the door and turned to look at our dispirited faces.

"Tensions and circumstances are heightened right now, and we all are weary from our travels. Let us retire for the night, and speak when we are refreshed and calm in the morning."

———————

Time had proven to me its strength in metamorphosing our reality more quickly than we could imagine possible. Even with almost every facet of my life diverging, one thing found a way to stand firm and constant. The mountains. The mountains hadn't changed; their magnificence had remained.

Staring at the interlacing gray rock and greenery that scaled its way to the sky, I nervously held my breath, worried if I blinked or breathed that they may disappear. I dared to close my eyes, deeply inhaling the crisp air that transported me home. It carried me to happier memories, happier days. Days of trail rides with my father, days of writing melodies to follow the song of the birds that echoed in the canyons, days of easy innocence as Damien and I stuffed our faces with dessert inspired picnics, with no worries to tear us down.

I rubbed my ruby ring, my mind still dreaming on with false hopes and unreachable pasts. I felt my chest burning as I held back my cries. The reality of my situation hit me. I was terrified, and I desperately wanted my father. *Why did you have to leave me when I needed you the most?*

I wanted to scream the words, but I held them in as I attempted to bury my sobs. I often wondered if my father could hear my prayers, pleas and lamentations. Did it hurt him as much as it did us to have him gone? Was he peacefully living on? Was he watching us in the eyes of the birds or the breeze of the wind? Did he even know the pain I bore? I had so many questions that didn't have answers, and the unknown left a deeper grief.

A warm arm wrapped around my shoulders, followed by another tangling itself at my waist. Before opening my eyes, I caught the scent of leather, and melted into the strong embrace timed perfectly to gather the pieces of my broken heart.

Killian pressed his lips against the crown of my head. "I found you," he whispered.

Killian's three words pierced my soul. He may not have intended them in such a way, but the words felt like an answer to my pleadings. *My father had heard me. He knew me. He was there.* He had used Killian to speak to my worries.

My heart raced as I felt an overwhelming rush of

comfort and warmth at the realization. My father wasn't physically there, but he hadn't left me.

I turned into Killian, eagerly returning his embrace. He held me softly, letting me take in all the relief and energy I needed from his presence.

"You had me worried, love," Killian's voice hummed.

"I'm sorry I worried you, I needed a moment to escape," I confessed, sinking deeper into his chest.

Killian sighed, remaining firm as he rubbed circles up my back. "So did I. Do you mind if I join you?"

"What happened? Are you alright?" I asked, pulling away to see his expression; to make sure he was all right.

Killian leaned his forehead into mine. "I had an argument with Aleron."

The corners of my mouth turned down. "I had an argument with Lidia."

Killian chuckled in annoyed amusement. "I'm assuming our arguments were rooted in the same cause."

I knew he was likely correct in that assumption, and based on Killian not expounding further on his discussion with Aleron, I wasn't going to probe him to tell me more of how it went.

"Are you OK?" I inquired.

Killian shrugged, still reserved at the topic. "It'll blow over. I'm more curious about you. Are *you* alright?"

I offered a smile. "I'm better now. That's what matters."

We held each other quietly for many moments, taking in the sun as it slowly began to set, illuminating all the trees in a deep orange hue. "How did you find me anyways?" I asked. This part of the mountain was a place of refuge and solitude I had found years ago, and it wasn't easy to find.

"Damien hinted that I may find you here," Killian simply replied.

"Damien?" I couldn't contain the surprise in my eyes, and Killian let out a deep chuckle.

Killian nodded. "We are friends now."

"Friends?" I scoffed in disbelief at what I had just heard.

Killian cocked his head to the side, biting back an amused grin. "Don't sound so surprised, you're the one that claims I am so lovable, remember?"

I laughed. "You are, and I am relieved to hear you two are friends now. If Damien can come around, I'm sure everyone else will too. We just need to give them time."

Killian's curly hair fell into his eyes as he dropped his head. "Time may repair some opinions, but not all. I don't have much confidence in Aleron changing his mind about me."

I could feel the immediate loss of hope in Killian at the mention of his brother, and I hugged him closer. "Did you tell Aleron the truth, about the real reasons why you left?"

Killian's long eyelashes fluttered closed as he took in a deep breath before answering my question. "I attempted to, but Aleron isn't ready to entertain it. I don't blame him. I've only let him down time and time again, and to add to it, the love of his life is marrying his low-life brother."

I brushed back Killian's curls, placing my hand on his warm cheek. "Will you let me talk to him? He might listen to me."

Killian offered a grim smile. "I appreciate the sentiment, but I won't let you fight my battles, love. With all the rumors he has heard about me, I'm certain he can't tell the truth from the lies, and it can be exhausting untangling it. I caused the mess in the first place, so I have accepted that I will need to live with the consequences."

I felt a pit begin to form in my stomach as I dared to approach the topic. "I've actually been meaning to ask you something. Since you mentioned it — the rumors — how many of them are true?"

"Can you clarify what rumors you are curious about?" Killian queried.

I began to feel flustered, but I did my best not to show it. *This is perfectly reasonable to ask, Allene, you are marrying him after all. You should know these things.*

"I've heard about *the bachelor* prince Killian. I suppose I am curious where I stand in the line of your past loves," I shied away at the last few words as they uncomfortably left my tongue.

"Past loves?" Killian let out a fast laugh as his amused, blue eyes searched mine. "Allene, those rumors are exactly that — rumors. Nothing went past strategic one time flirtations to allow news to travel back to Praseria about my reckless personality. I wanted to convince my father that I was too distracted and enthralled with women to plot anything against him. Have you been worried about this for a while?"

I cleared my throat. "No, I wasn't worried, but after the incident with Kijana, I may have found myself. . ."

"Jealous?" He smirked at the thought.

"Curious," I corrected abruptly.

Killian held back a smirk. "You were jealous. *Unfairly* jealous."

"Why is that unfair?" I quipped.

"Because if anyone should be jealous, it should be me. When it comes to past love, you have more history than myself." My face burned red. "And since we are having this conversation, I have been wanting to ask you something too." Killian's smile grew coy. "How many times have you kissed my brother?"

I stuttered in reply, completely shocked by the question. "Excuse me?"

"How many times have you kissed Aleron?" Killian firmly reiterated, pressuring me to give him some formative answer.

"I don't recall," I gulped.

Killian's piercing eyes sparkled as if he was hoping that would be my reply. "If you can't recall, then I better be cautious. I can't permit Aleron bettering me in that regard."

Killian's strong hands cupped my face as his warm lips met mine. I felt his curls brushing against my cheeks, his tender urgency in each kiss sending tingles down my spine. Time passed differently in those moments — the world spun a bit slower, and my heart felt lifted.

Killian pulled away, after moments or many minutes, I couldn't tell, but he held a look of satisfaction as it flashed across his beautiful face. "Now I hope we are at least even."

ALERON

The sun was down, and I was still waiting. I hoped the delay would allow me to gather my thoughts, but time was not proving to benefit me. My anxiety climbed whenever someone walked past, my body on high alert for her arrival. The temporary homes and shelters gave a source of dim light as I continued waiting in patience, realizing she would have to arrive at any moment. I rehearsed what felt like a hundred different scenarios and conversations, none of them ending in the result I hoped for.

I hated that I could hear them before I could see them. Allene's hushed laugh and whispers reached my ears. The sound would usually send me into a state of joy, until my bitter eyes took in the sight of the source of her laughter.

Killian saw me before Allene could. His face became dark and rigid as he abruptly stopped walking, turning Allene away from me. He bent down to whisper something in her ear, then casually kissed her forehead before bidding her goodnight. The sight gutted me.

Allene came my way, still oblivious to my presence, and stepped back in embarrassment as she noticed me standing outside her temporary home.

"I didn't mean to startle you," I approached Allene slowly, trying not to alarm her more than I already had. "I was hoping I could speak with you privately."

Allene offered a tight half-hearted smile and motioned in her direction. "Follow me."

We quietly walked past the silent homes, making our way to a clearing. Allene stopped underneath a large oak tree, hidden from any prying eyes. Allene stared through the trees on the other side. Her face became like stone, motionless and hard as she quietly spoke.

"Do you remember this place?" she asked.

I was quiet as I tried to recall the significance. I scanned the area, trying to piece together what I was missing. I tried to picture the dim clearing with more light, and it suddenly came to my mind — an image of a fight that I couldn't ever forget.

"This is where it all began," Allene answered before I had the chance to reply. She approached a large boulder that lay to the side of the clearing, placing her hand on the weapon my people had launched at her own.

"I hadn't experienced fright like I had that day. I didn't see an ending where I made it out of that battle alive. Then waking up the next day, although a shocking and pleasant surprise, being greeted in a kingdom I had been indoctrinated to fear, I thought I wouldn't survive the week." Allene turned to look at me as she continued to recall the memories. "But then I met you, and you proved me wrong in every regard. You cleared up every misconception and worry I had about you, your kingdom, and for the hope of our people. You have brought people into my life I never would have known had we not met on that day. Noni, Ezra. . .my own grandfather, I wouldn't have met had it not been for you." Allene choked up at her last words, holding back the emotions that were surfacing. I wanted to reach out to her, but I held myself back, patiently waiting for her to steady her thoughts.

Allene nervously rang her long hair in her dainty hands, biting her lip as it quivered.

"I can never fully repay you. How does one pay a debt of giving someone a chance at a new life? For giving someone a better future then they could have ever imagined? Had you not shown me grace and mercy that day, I wouldn't be standing here right now. You saved me, Aleron." Allene's gaze held mine, unwavering through her tears. "And despite all your kindness towards me, I've hurt you." Allene's voice cracked on her last words, her guilt breaking through the surface.

I couldn't hold myself back any longer. I swiftly moved to Allene's side, gently placing my hand on her trembling shoulder.

"Please don't say that," I begged.

Allene shook her head, her hair falling in front of her face and tingling my arm as it brushed against my skin.

"It's the truth, I won't be a coward and ignore what I have done to you. I *hate* what I've done to you," Allene reiterated. She was adamant in taking responsibility.

I felt my hands begin to shake with anxiety and frustration as I swallowed my pride to muster my response. I reached out to lightly pull Allene's chin upward to look at me — I needed to convey the sincerity of my words, and I knew she wouldn't believe it if she couldn't see my face. Once she gave in and let her eyes settle on mine, I took a deep breath, and continued.

"If we are admitting blame and faults then let me focus on mine. I've hurt you as well. My actions were the catalyst to all of it. You almost died that day *because* of me, not in spite of me. Your heart became vulnerable to others because I pushed you away first. The results of these circumstances are not yours alone to claim responsibility for." It caused me immense pain to say it, but it was the truth. The savior Allene had graciously portrayed me to be did not include my own shortcomings. I had let her down too.

I sighed deeply as I stepped away, placing distance between us. "Allene, I don't want you to harbor regret or remorse about the outcomes of your choices. I want you to be free of guilt, and I don't want your heart to be pulled in different directions any longer." My voice was steady, but we could both hear it laced with sadness as I spoke. "I am letting you go."

The words were surreal. They stung. They were not

what I had rehearsed. Deep down they were not what I wanted, but they were right.

The words hung in the air like a bittersweet melody, and tears welled in my eyes. Allene's accountability had only affirmed her kindness, and it only deepened my respect for her.

Allene had fallen quiet again, but I still had one more message to convey to her. I refused to feel shame, and continued to speak as her soft blue eyes cautiously and curiously observed me.

"This isn't how I imagined it ending. I never presumed that it wouldn't be me. But you deserve happiness, and if that happiness is being with Killian, then I won't intervene any longer." My words made it out in a faint whisper.

Allene's expression was difficult to discern in the shadow of the night, but I could sense her stunned surprise.

"Aleron. . .I don't know what to say."

I understood her being speechless. If we had come to this point, what else was there to say? I asked for one final promise before parting our separate ways and concluding our pursuits of one another.

"Allene, promise me you won't regret your decision? If I know that, then I can let you go without regrets of my own." I had to know she was certain of her choice. To have any chance of putting her behind me, I had to know there was no chance of hope for our relationship.

Allene nodded, her voice choked with emotion. "I won't. I hope you find the happiness you deserve, Aleron."

The offer of her good sentiments should have brought me peace, but as I walked away I realized how devastating it truly was — that the happiness I had found in being with her, couldn't be reciprocated — that I couldn't be her happiness too.

ALLENE

The morning brought a different demeanor to Lidia's presence. A mutual exchange of apologies mended the cordiality between the three of us. Lidia had returned to her regular self, and with that she brought a sense of authority, excitement, and grace to the chaotic assembly of haphazard rebel troops from Praseria, Valteria, Cenan, Veruje, Gelva, Lokali, and Gree.

Along with amends being made with Lidia, amends had also been made with Aleron. I still felt in a state of shock of how our conversation concluded the night before. I finally felt at peace to love Killian how I should — unbridled and unmitigated. Ii sighed, knowing the relief would be short lived.

The air was thick with tension and anxiety as we gathered in the war tent. It was a room where decisions of life and death were to be made, a room where we would decide the fate of kingdoms.

I glanced around at the faces of those assembled, each one a key player in the battle that lay ahead. It was a diverse group, united by a common purpose—to defeat King Vincent and the Red Crows, to reclaim our kingdoms, to save the queens, and to put an end to the reign of terror that had plagued our lands.

Lidia's silver dress resembled armor — a fitting for the environment — that gleamed in the feeble sunlight, and her dark eyes held a determination that matched the severity of the situation. Her arrival was a beacon of hope in our darkest hour.

Damien stood near the large map of the battlefield, his sharp eyes focused on the strategic markings where the Red Crow's had been spotted by King Seger's spies. His spies had tracked King Vincent and Nycolas's movements, as well as the queens' locations since their kidnappings. King Vincent had them right by his side the entire time, ready to use them as bait to lure us in.

Damien's presence was commanding, and his confidence unwavering. How had he changed so much in such a short amount of time? What happened to the young boy I grew up with? Life the last several months had been harsh to us, forcing Damien into a man sooner than I would have expected. Without knowing how his family had fared in Selvet, he was more eager than the rest of us to put this all behind, to find his family, and begin to repair the damage Hassan had done to their name. My thoughts flitted to Feira, so full of life and blind trust, and my heart ached at the burden she would soon bear of her eldest brother's betrayal.

I silently hoped that the fervor in Damien's eyes would be enough to bring Hassan back from his choices when they next met, that he might be able to make his family whole again before they even realized they had been shattered.

Gorgeous Risa was well rested for the first time in days, and her countenance was notably brighter as she appeared to be her more positive self — being the sunshine we needed as she delicately stroked the single bracelet adorning her arm, using it as a distraction from the reality in front of us.

Marshal, his expression stoic as always, was a silent pillar of strength. He had earned our trust on the journey, and my sister's heart, and now he stood with us, ready to protect those he had come to care for. His loyalty was unquestionable, and his skills in battle were unmatched.

Aleron stood with a solemn expression, his gaze fixated on the map. He had proved himself as a skilled diplomat and was well-received by everyone. He was well received by everyone, evidenced by his uncanny ability to forge alliances.

King Seger exuded confidence and authority, while maintaining his unpredictable rambunctious personality. Despite the ups and downs with his acceptance of our alliance, his dedication to our cause had shown to be unwavering.

Trae leaned casually against the wall, his mischievous

smile never leaving his face as his doe-like eyes gawked at Lidia, both of them exchanging playful glances with one another.

Ezra, taking things much more seriously, stood in the shadows, concealing most of his features, his presence reassuring. It felt like the closest thing to having my own father there at such a vulnerable time.

Killian stood beside me. His eyes, usually filled with mischief, were now filled with determination. He had a score to settle with his father for the destruction of his kingdom, and for imprisoning his mother. He was more than just a formidable warrior and a prince — he had become the man I had come to care most for.

As we discussed our battle strategy, our conversation conveyed a mutual sense of purpose. Each one of us had a role to play, a part to contribute to the greater whole. We were united by our determination to rid our kingdoms of the Red Crows, to bring justice to those who had suffered, and to ensure that peace would once again reign.

If there was anything that this war had reminded us, it was how much we hated having enemies. We were all hurt from everything that we had lost, and we had nothing to show for it. The one thing that lent us hope was we were connected in a deeper way than we ever had been. That alone may be the key to undoing the past and paving a brighter future; one without war and without hate.

As the hours passed and our plans were finalized, a sense of resolve settled over us. We were ready for the battle that lay ahead. We were ready to face the Red Crows and King Vincent. We were a formidable alliance, a force to be reckoned with, and we would conquer our enemies.

As I looked around at the faces of my family and companions, I felt a deep sense of gratitude and pride. We were not just a group of individuals; we were bound by a common purpose and a shared determination. Together, we would face the Red Crows, and together, we would emerge victorious.

Chapter 35 -Killian

After the strategy meeting, we left to act immediately upon our assignments. The battle would take place tomorrow, and swift preparations were required if we were to execute our plan accordingly.

Allene and I diligently instructed the survivors that remained in Valteria of our plan to attack. The crowd mumbled to themselves as we spoke, and we felt nervous that there may be some push back from the people. However, at the conclusion of our words we were relieved to hear claps, shouts of excitement, and praise for the plan we were pursuing. Having the support of the people was critical as we moved forward.

As the armies assembled for the impending battle, Allene and I found ourselves hand in hand, drifting through the crowd, our thoughts consumed by the weight of the imminent fight. Allene let out a long sigh, her expression filled with a solemn determination that mirrored my own.

"Killian, do you believe we can truly put an end to all of this?" As much as she tried to disguise it, I could see the small bit of uncertainty in Allene's eyes.

The reach my father had accomplished astonished even myself. He had achieved more than I would have credited him for. He had been deliberate, cunning and wise in his planning. Nearly all the kingdoms had fallen. In his eyes, I am sure he had indefinitely won. I knew he was likely waiting for us to make our next move — eager to prove his point that he, and only he, could be the greatest of us all. I knew he felt unmatched, and I knew that would be the reason he could falter. His arrogance was his worst enemy, and taking advantage of it would prove to be my strongest weapon.

"I don't believe it, I know it. The Red Crows' and my father's greed and vision for the future of the kingdoms — it ends tomorrow," I answered reassuringly.

All the pain my father had caused me personally flooded into my mind. For years I had harbored resentment. I had worked to process the damage my father had emotionally and physically inflicted upon me. Being in a headspace to trust anyone was a victory to me, and being in a place to love someone, and have someone love *me* — that had been nearly incomprehensible.

I tugged Allene's arm, spinning her into my chest as I held her closely — clinging to every moment with her before the dread of tomorrow. Allene hugged me tightly, her breathing warm and steady against my chest. I stroked Allene's hair, and her body melted deeper into mine with each caress.

"I want our kingdoms restored to peace. Seeing the people today, the children. . .all those families displaced and scared — my heart breaks that we couldn't do more to prevent this in the first place," Allene whispered in a disheartened voice.

"I will admit the current state of our kingdoms are bleak, but I don't have any doubts that our future will be entirely different," I encouraged, attempting to soothe her worry.

"How can you be so certain of it?" I could hear the doubt creeping into her voice, her shoulders slumping in my arms at the premonition of defeat.

I paused, heavily considering my answer. "I have waited years for this day, and I won't let it slip through my fingers." I pressed a soft kiss on Allene's forehead. "I won't let you down, love. You have my word."

I was determined that by this time tomorrow we would be reunited with our mothers. Our kingdoms and people would be restored to the safety and comfort they once knew. My father and all the Red Crows would be apprehended and surrender. Allene and I would forge new connections between all the kingdoms. The piles of rubble and disaster would be repaired and stand in even greater magnificence and glory. Once all was made right again, our wedding would officially take place.

It all sounded too good to be true — it also sounded

like too much to ask. But if so much of my life could surprise me, then so could our odds of winning the battle ahead, and all the other aspirations that followed. I hoped my recently found good fortune could carry with me just a bit longer; long enough to put an end to all the pain; long enough to finally have a fresh start. A new beginning.

ALERON

Upon entering the city, we assumed we would be greeted by the Red Crows' army. I had an expectation in my mind for how this would unfold. I was wrong. I considered myself prepared for the sights I may see upon returning to Praseria, but I was shocked at the scene before us. Given all that had already happened, I shouldn't have been surprised that my father wanted to leave a memorable impression, but even for him, this escapade felt low.

Seeing the Red Crows' flag waving proudly in the air upon entering my home left a pit in my stomach. The crimson red flag, with its embroidered gold crow, was a symbol of greed and bloodlust. It felt like an illusion. I was unfathomable how we had gotten to this point.

The gates to Praseria were flung proudly open, not a guard in sight. Where there would regularly be soldiers standing to watch the gates, a red, silk cloth had been wrapped around something laying in the dirt beneath the gates' archway. Killian and I exchanged hesitant glances as I approached the stand alone gift.

I bent down, picking up the delicate fabric and the heavy item it had been wrapped in. I unfolded the silk to reveal a crown — a crown that I had seen many times before. My mother's crown.

I delicately held her crown in my hands, as Killian approached me from behind, picking up a note that had fallen out as I undid the wrapping.

My Sons,
Welcome home.
Leave your armies at the gate.
We should settle this like true Hadway men.
You know where to find me.

Killian and I looked at each other, our faces pale as we contemplated our next decision.

"What does it say?" King Seger's voice boomed amongst the soldiers, causing everyone to stir with unease.

Killian and I turned around to face our concerned friends. Killian silently handed off the letter to King Seger to read, while Damien, Trae, and Marshal scrambled to read over his shoulder.

King Seger cleared his throat, his demeanor reposed as he spoke to us. "I may have spies with more intel than all the other kingdoms combined, but you two have an advantage the rest of us do not. You know your father better than any of us do. This decision is yours to make." The weight of King Seger's words was heavy because they were true.

"Keep the army here. Aleron and I will approach our father alone." Killian didn't hesitate as he offered us both for self-sacrifice, not even allowing me the option to give another opinion.

"We came here ready to fight. There is no reason for you two to go in alone. What if something goes wrong?" Damien chimed in, his eyes sorrowful and filled with pity as he looked at us.

"You mean what if our father kills us?" I stated the real question bluntly.

Killian didn't even flinch at my words. "I know my father won't hurt Aleron. If something goes wrong, Aleron will signal for your assistance. Be alert and be ready to attack at a moment's notice," Killian commanded.

King Seger gave a firm, curt nod, the fire in his eyes from the excitement of battle still burning as he shook Killian's hand. "May good fortune be with you."

Killian turned to Damien, placing a firm hand on his shoulder

"Don't let Allene follow after us. Promise me you'll keep her safe," Killian pressured.

Damien gave a dejected nod. "I promise. In return, promise me I won't have to tell her bad news. You better return in one piece, and with the Red Crows' surrender. Understood?" Damien challenged Killian's stare, his eyes alight from his request.

Killian's hand didn't move, his grip on Damien's shoulder tightening as he sighed out his next words. "I promise to do what is best for everyone, but especially for Allene."

Damien understood the gravity of Killian not being willing to confidently keep the requested promise. For someone as self-assured as Killian, it was a sign of the severity of the situation.

Killian nodded farewell to the rest of the group and motioned for me to follow behind him. I was tempted to hesitate, to give another option, but I knew his approach was right. I caught up to my brother, both of us walking with determination as we approached what used to be our home.

I muttered a question to Killian under my breath, trying to distract myself from the eerie silence. "What makes you think father won't hurt me?"

Through this, our father had shown sides of himself I had never seen before, being the leader of the Red Crows, the largest of them all. I didn't have any expectation of his grace to be extended to me now.

Killian's eyes dimmed as he looked toward our home,

his face a harsh, cold mask. "No matter how far our father has fallen, and how narcissistic he may be, he is a man of pride, and fears disappointing his queen." His gaze shifted to my feet, then flitted back to the castle ahead. "Bringing any harm to you would be crossing the line."

The dispiritment in Killian's voice was subtle, and I likely wouldn't have caught it had I not noticed the quick down turn at the corners of his mouth. All these years I had honestly believed the detachment from my father was voluntary and facile on Killian's part. That was the first time I thought my assumption may have been wrong.

With no delay, Killian took a few strides past the palace doors, and sealed our fates in the process.

ALLENE

I knew something went wrong. As soon as we stopped, the urgency in my stomach propelled my feet to the front of the group. The halted soldiers were not a sign of victory, it was a sign of wavering, and I was frightened to discover the reason why.

The crowd of soldiers parted and I was greeted by familiar faces. King Seger, Trae, Marshal, Damien, and. . .my heart stopped.

The words flew out of my mouth in an accelerated, fiery flurry. "Where are they?" I snapped, my eyes immediately settled on Damien to divulge everything.

"King Vincent requested to meet with them alone," Damien replied soberly.

My mind was racing, but I did my best to hold onto my senses, to cling to the few wits about me that I felt slipping away. "How could you let them go to be slaughtered?" I accused.

"Killian is convinced King Vincent would not let any harm come to Aleron," Damien defended.

"To Aleron? What of Killian?" I scoffed, catching the distinct word choice Damien conveyed. "You don't have any idea the cruelties Vincent is capable of, even to his own sons. How could you let them make such a foolish decision?" I stepped away, motioning drastically with my arm to the men spread out below us. "We have an entire army! Isn't it clear King Vincent's request likely stemmed from his intimidation of the forces we bring with us? We have a true chance to stand and fight against him! How could you let them risk their lives after all we have done to defeat the Red Crows?" My reaction was flustered and fierce, any patience inside of me had left days ago. The situation was too intense to muster any false appearances.

"What of the lives of the selfless soldiers? As terrifying as it is, Killian is trying to spare the innocent," King Seger interjected. "They made the right choice, Princess Amena, and we are ready and waiting if they need our assistance."

"We won't be of any assistance to them if they're dead." The words slid coldly off my tongue.

"Patience is a virtue. The wisest choice we can make is to wait," King Seger replied pragmatically.

Though it took every ounce of my will, I refrained from interfering. With King Seger and the others, I waited. Painfully, silently, apprehensively. I wanted for the nightmare to end.

KILLIAN

The castle was eerily quiet. There were no soldiers waiting to ambush us or servants eager to escort; it was as if the entire palace had been vacated. Our footsteps echoed against the marble floors, emphasizing the fact that we still hadn't seen another soul.

For how much had changed outside of the castle walls, much of the inside remained untouched. It felt just like home.

Aleron and I slowed our pace as we approached our destination. The door to our father's parlor was cracked, sunlight seeping through into the hall, yet the sight was anything but inviting.

Aleron and I exchanged concerned glances as I took the lead to cautiously nudge open the door.

The parlor was as I remembered. Father's prized boar head was proudly hanging high on the central wall, while his other trophy kills lined both sides of the room. Short bookshelves adorned the lower portion of the walls, and his favorite elaborately decorated rug covered most of the marble floor. Father's oversized blue velvet chair was turned to face the large window that had a perfect view of the distant ocean shore, and in the chair sat Vincent, collectedly focused on the view in front of him.

Aleron and I stopped by the doors. We knew our father had heard us enter. He had been anticipating our arrival, even put on quite the show for it, but he hadn't even flinched at the sound.

Vincent let out a long, drawn out sigh, his head falling slightly to his chest before he brought it back up again. He stood from his chair, and slowly pivoted to face us.

Vincent's black and silver peppered hair framed his face, his dark blue eyes cold as ice, while his deep red attire brought a different intensity to his strongly built frame. The crow insignia placed on the breast portion of his cape grabbed our attention. The ease in his expression left an unsettling pit in my stomach, his sinister smile a traumatic reminder of haunting past days I had wished to bury.

"Sons, you have returned," Vincent proudly declared, his announcement concealed for only us to hear, as there was not another visible soul in the room.

Aleron and I remained still and rigid at the entrance of the study. We both cautiously waited to see the way Vincent would dictate the direction of the conversation.

Although I hadn't admitted it to King Seger, my father's note had left me perturbed. His request for in person, one-on-one negotiations meant only one thing — he thought he could best his sons, and more importantly, it seemed like he *wanted* to. He needed this fight to be personal. He didn't want only victory over the kingdoms, he wanted victory over u*s*.

"No one is with you?" Vincent cocked an eyebrow in suspicion as he looked out in the direction of the door.

I shook my head once, my eyes not leaving the view of my father. "We followed your request. Only Aleron and I carried on past the gate," I placidly assured him.

Aleron's lips pressed into a firm line, his hand resting on the hilt of his sword, his eyes appearing like a rabbit caught in a snare. "Your additional *"gift"* didn't go unnoticed either. Laerina and Eveline, the queens, where are they?" Aleron pressed, courageously taking a step towards the ghost of our father.

"We are all together at last, and that is the first thing you ask me?" Vincent's voice hissed, dripping with bitterness. He shook his head as he casually leaned against his chair. "Your first instinct isn't to challenge, negotiate, or interrogate me?"

Aleron puffed up, his bright doe eyes proud as they glared at our father. "You may have forgotten this along the way, but honor is one of the greatest virtues. Protecting my family, especially my own mother, is a way of fulfilling that virtue. You may have been willing to easily let that go, but I refuse to place *anything* above my honor," Aleron proclaimed.

Vincent's eyes squinted in frustration as he let out an

exasperated groan. "Aleron, you were always the weak one. I had hoped time and challenges would allow you to open your heart to the vision, but I fear you will continue in blindness to the necessity of our rebellion and remain oblivious in your breadth of view," Vincent drawled.

"Necessity?" I retorted for Aleron, my hand now also gripping my sword in frustration. "You have destroyed everything, father, for nothing more than your foolish ambition and power." My eyes narrowed on Vincent's glowering smirk. "You murdered King Faris."

Vincent's eyebrows shot up at me in humored surprise at the statement. "You've been more resourceful than I thought." Vincent laughed. "I have been actively obtaining information too. Hassan informed me of the unexpected relationship between you and the princess of Valteria," Vincent said, his lips pressing into a thin line, his nose scrunched, like he had eaten something sour.

Vincent focused on Aleron, as my brother shifted uncomfortably in place from the heat of our father's mocking stare. "I wasn't surprised by your brother's ignorant fancies for the girl, but you Killian," Vincent's indifferent gaze flickered back to me. "I was taken back by your foolishness."

"On the contrary, these last few months have helped me finally come to my senses. I suppose that is one thing I can thank you for, showing me the qualities and characteristics that I will never aspire to emulate."

Vincent cocked his neck to the side, his posture and

expression unimpressed as he bit his lip, snorting out an annoyed chuckle as his eyes burned with loathing.

I did my best to maintain a blank expression as I asked the question that I had wanted to ask for months. The question I desperately hoped would merit a dignified, humane response from Vincent.

"Do you regret it? The rebellions, the disorder, the destruction, tearing apart our family, the hurt you have personally inflicted, the killing — do you feel penitent for any of it?" I sucked in a breath, truly fearing his response.

Vincent scoffed, rolling his eyes as he shook his head. "Are you indicating that I could be so weak as to feel remorse?"

Aleron flinched beside me at Vincent's reply. "It isn't weakness; anyone in a sound state of mind would acknowledge the hurt they have inflicted on others."

Vincent spoke through clenched teeth as his eyes glared at Aleron. "I am not anyone. You, my sons, are not *anyone*. We are royalty, although you both are too short sighted to see the power that presents to you," he spat. "I am willing to do what is necessary to ensure our family an unprecedented legacy. I don't care who it hurts, what it destroys, or who may die from standing in my way." Vincent flashed a coy smile. "That includes even you, my sons. And your precious princess, and every other royal that does not bear our family name."

Vincent's last words rang as a threat, and a deadly promise — one that involved Allene, and the mention of her on his vicious lips was my undoing. The rage that had slowly been building up inside of me throughout the insufferable conversation with my father had now hit a peak. My body was beginning to shake, and all I could see was the color red — red like the blood my father had spilt in his cruel game for more power, and the blood he was still willing to shed to officially secure it.

I didn't want Vincent to see just how much the mention of Allene had shook me. I wouldn't give him the satisfaction of having riled me. I did my best to channel all the anger flowing through me into my clenched fists, now tucked at my sides, and my sharp words.

"This ends now," I declared, removing the option for negotiations on the matter.

Vincent's wicked smile appeared on his lips, my reaction amusing to him. "Killian, always so quick to defend the helpless. I see some things don't change, even after all these years." Vincent shook his head, a *tsk* sound rolling off his tongue. "I raised you both better than this. Where is your respect for your elder? For your father? For your *king*?" Vincent's voice bellowed across the room, the fire and heat in his eyes threatening to have us shrink away.

With Aleron by my side, seeing the true nature of our father, I somehow felt braver than I had before. As horrible as it was to watch, and endure, I felt a twisted sense of relief that for once, I wasn't facing it alone.

"You can attempt to claim as many titles as you please, but you do not deserve our respect," Aleron spat bitterly.

Vincent's eyes became hard and fierce as he passed a hard glance at Aleron. I knew that glare too well. Vincent slowly rocked back and forth on his feet as he approached Aleron and I. Vincent stopped in front of us, his large frame shadowing us both as he gripped his knuckles. "Is that so?" Vincent scoffed. I knew that tone too; the alarm bells sounding.

Vincent's body shuddered as he cocked his neck to the side, his fiery anger pulsating through his veins. "I. Don't. Deserve. Your. Respect?" Vincent spoke harshly and distinctly, the hiss and burn of each word being branded into both of us.

Aleron remained firm, not flinching at Vincent's attempt of intimidation. "No. Not now, and not ever again."

As soon as the last word left Aleron's mouth, I knew it couldn't be held back anymore. Vincent's fist pulled back and released, with Aleron's face as the target recipient, and I immediately reacted. I shoved my shoulder into Vincent's chest and pushed with all my strength, causing his punch to go off balance and miss Aleron's face, while instead I received a misdelivered blow to my left shoulder blade.

Vincent gripped my shoulders in resistance, and we stood with our arms locked against one another, our foreheads now colliding with force.

"Aleron, leave! Find Laerina and mother, and get them safely to the others!" I yelled under strained breath as I fought against my fathers strength.

Aleron ignored my command, and instead ran to my side, his eyes worried and wide as he tried to free my father's grip from me. Vincent's grip tightened more fiercely against my arms in response, and I groaned under the pain as he attempted to twist me into a headlock.

"Aleron! I won't say it again! Leave, *now*!" I demanded with urgency in my voice.

Aleron seemed flustered as he looked between my face and Vincent's, who's anger was so hyper-focused on me that he had complete disregard for anything Aleron was doing. Aleron shuffled in hesitation but he seemed to understand — this may be the only chance that one of us had to escape to search for the queens, and it did them no good if we were both tied up against our father.

Aleron ran out of the room, the sound of his footsteps disappeared in an instant. I hoped he would find them. If I didn't make it back to Allene, I at least hoped that stalling my father would be enough to return her mother to safety.

Drawing my attention from Aleron's retreat, I focused on my father. Vincent had always bettered me in strength, and even with my own personal attempts of training to fight against my father, he still was stronger than me, even after all these years. Within moments of Aleron disappearing, Vincent had successfully twisted my arm behind my back, abruptly pulling it up as I cried out in pain. He pulled me in closer, his other arm gripping around my chest as his scruffy cheek brushed against mine.

My first instinct was to react, to maneuver out of his grip, but I knew if I wanted to best him, I had to pretend to be the boy he remembered long ago. The son he remembered would never fight back, and he especially didn't have enough skill to better his father. I would allow him to think that for a bit longer, letting it play into my strategy of catching Vincent by surprise at the right time. I gritted my teeth, forcing myself to patiently take the abuse once again, and to play ignorant and helpless.

"Killian, my eldest son, my *prodigy*," Vincent's words rang with aspiration as his hand pinched my jaw, his firm grip forcing my face to look at his as he spoke. My body cringed as he continued in a proud tone, his rough forcefulness for my attention a distant memory I had buried and hope to never experience again. "Your potential is not lost to me. I created this for *us*." Vincent abruptly shoved my body forward and to the ground, the back of his heel digging into my shoulder blades as his weight pressed me against the floor.

"Take this chance of redemption while it is still offered. Surrender alongside me this ridiculous ideal that our forebears created." Another blow was felt as Vincent's foot made contact with the lower part of my skull. I cringed in defense and rolled to my side now, my arms circling to the back of my head for protection.

Vincent was unfazed by my attempt to defend myself, as he stood above me, his eyes glazed over in passion and rage. I took the gap as an opportunity to rise back to my feet, disregarding the sharp, pulsing sensation vibrating in my head. My father still seemed unfazed as he continued his speech.

"You have an opportunity to not just be a prince, you

could be *the* prince. You do not have to be limited to only this kingdom, you can have jurisdiction and glory over them all!" Vincent's voice was almost hysterical now as he held out his hand in an eager attempt for me to shake it in agreement. "All you have to do is join me, son. Stand *with* your father, not against me."

The wildness in his eyes was beyond my reach. My heart was heavy, burdened by the weight of betrayal, but also fueled by a resolve to end this madness once and for all. My gaze reflected no sympathy or understanding, only fires of vengeance.

I steadied my voice, making it resolute, as I faced the man who had become an even greater enemy to me than before. "Father, I have learned a lot from you," I started, trying to garner his attention and focus. "I have learned to be selfish and indifferent. I have learned to be disagreeable and tactful. I have learned to be stubborn and self-aware. Because you have taught me all of these things, my answer is simple," I said, smiling coyly. "I will not join you."

Vincent's eyebrows furrowed in confusion as I continued. "I am *not* your prodigy, I am your sufferer. You may have hoped all those years of abuse and forced cooperation would have enslaved me in fear to serve your agendas, but I am only loyal to myself, and I still have people to fight for." I let out a fast, irritated laugh as I looked at the pitiful man before me, the man who I was ashamed to admit had terrified me for far too long; a mistake I wouldn't be repeating.

"I will not step aside and watch you hurt those I love any longer. This is your opportunity to surrender peacefully." I gave Vincent my offering of peace as I drew my sword, the tip of it only inches from my fathers neck.

Vincent cracked a calm smile and followed it with a disappointed scowl. "I am truly sorry that is how you feel, my son. I was hoping I could change your mind."

With a roar and not a second more to contemplate my words or continue our conversation, Vincent lunged at me, his sword unsheathed as I met his attack with a fluid grace, our blades clashing in a symphony of steel. Each collision and strike carried the weight of countless lives lost to his rebellion.

The world around us faded into a blur as we moved in a dance of betrayal and attempts at redemption. I saw flashes of our past, the moments of supposed fatherly love and guidance, now more deeply shadowed by the darkness that had consumed him. There was no turning back.

With every fiber of my being, I fought with a determination that came from the love for my people, my kingdom, my family that remained, and the woman who captured my heart. The ground beneath us quaked with intensity, the air carrying our cries of defiance and anguish through the sandstone castle walls.

I had dedicated myself to practicing combat when I left Praseria. I had anticipated this day would come in some way, and I had wanted to be prepared. Enduring my father's years of abuse had shown me every side of him. I knew his habits and patterns when he was angry, and they were simple for me to predict. Each swing of a sword was followed with a frustrated groan as I foiled his attempts.

With each block, Vincent's anger intensified and his efforts had become more drastic. He had underestimated me. I had an advantage he hadn't predicted — he had never seen *me* angry. He had never seen me fight back. He had never seen what I was truly capable of.

With the next swing of his sword, I dodged the blade and managed to fumble the hilt out of my father's hand. With both swords now in my grasp, I whipped around to place them at the base of of his thick neck, his awed expression and gaping mouth indicative of how little skill he had expected from me.

Vincent stumbled back, trying to escape. Defeated and broken, he slowly lowered his head.

"It's over, father," I said, my voice heavy with regret for not stopping him sooner. "Surrender, and let us find a way to rebuild what you have destroyed."

I did my best to mask the pleasure and equal pain in my eyes at witnessing my father knelt before me. "Yield," I pressed, closing in on my father once again, his back now against the wall. He had nowhere to run to, and no weapons to counter with.

Vincent scoffed in amusement, barking out a bitter laugh. "I won't yield," he hissed under his breath, my fathers arrogance persistent to the very end. One of his eyebrows shot up as more *tsk* sounds slid off his tongue. "I am disappointed. You have forgotten some of the important rules of combat, son."

Before he could finish delivering his words, a sharp sensation penetrated my shoulder. The shock of the excruciating pain doubled my body over, the reality of what was happening only slowly being processed as I breathed through the urge to scream.

"Even I know the basics. Never approach your enemy alone, never trust the enemy, and never turn your back in enemy territory." The familiar voice almost pierced more than the dagger that caused blood to trickle down to the edge of my sleeve.

"You're right," I coughed through gritted teeth, the muscles in my jaws feathering from the pain. "I was foolish to assume any of you would fight with dignity and honor. After all, you both were far too eager to turn on your own families. The level of trust I should have placed in your fairness should have been non-existent." The words were more of a reprimand to myself than to them.

I didn't allow myself to lose the grip on the sword, but I struggled to stand upright as I faced Hassan's proud face. My father now stood to his feet, snatching his sword from my limp hand.

"As heartless as you may deem me to be, I have no intention to stay to watch how this ends. Hassan, I will see you in Valteria and my son," Vincent placed his hand on my shoulder, slowly pulling out the dagger, making me fall forward again in pain. His hand squeezed the wound, bringing tears to my eyes as I held back the cries. "I will see you in a time beyond our own."

With a cold brushing of his shoulder, my father left

Hassan to finish the deed that he didn't have the courage to do himself. I don't know how he made it seem so easy. Earlier, I had the chance to take his life, but I couldn't. Despite the type of man I knew him to be, it didn't make me feel justified in seeing him dead. He was my father after all.

I thought of my mother and Aleron, and how difficult it would be to wake up every day with the knowledge that I had killed someone who was dear to all of us, even if it was in odd ways. Yet the same man I held compassion for, had none for me. Leaving his own son to die, and having no regrets follow the decision. Any shred of redeemable hope for my father was gone — and I feared I soon would be gone too.

ALERON

$\mathcal{I}$ rushed the halls, starting my search for the queens in the dungeon. My efforts came back unfulfilled — every room and corridor was deserted. I had searched two floors, when I decided to try the obvious choice. I made my way to the top floor. This was my mother's room, and I held onto the hope that she would be inside.

When I came upon the familiar closed door, I took a deep breath as I noticed the lock on the outside of the handles. This was the first door that had something out of place. She had to be inside.

I hurriedly knocked on the door, waiting to hear her voice. I could hear shuffling in the room. I knocked again. This time, my knock brought forth a faint whisper.

"Hello?" It was Laerina's voice.

"Queen Amena, is my mother with you? Are you alright?" I asked.

"Aleron?" Eveline's voice was choked with emotion. Her footsteps ran to the door, her hand firmly falling upon the wooden frame, shaking the door from the other side. "My sweet boy! You are alive! Are you all alive? We are fine, we are fine," my mother began to cry through her words, overcome by my unexpected arrival.

"Killian, Allene and Risa are safe. We are all here, and I am here to take you back with us," I assured them. "There is a lock, give me a moment while I work on getting the door open."

I pulled out the small knife that was attached to my side. As I worked on picking the lock, Eveline quietly sobbed through repeated apologies.

"Aleron, I am so sorry. I was horridly foolish and oblivious to the plans unfolding around us. I was ignorant to your father's actions, with the Red Crows and to you and your brother. I am so sorry." My mother continued to blubber behind the door. I tried to hush and reassure her as I worked, but my concentration was hyper-focused as I had almost picked the lock for a second time. Laerina tried to soothe her as well, offering words of comfort and hope.

"He is here now, that is what matters. We will be reunited with our children. We will survive this. We can make it right," Laerina consoled her.

I finally heard a click, and the lock gave way. I threw the lock to the ground and my mother had already pushed the door open, her arms immediately embracing me.

I held my mother tightly, instantly relieved as I took in

the sight of her. Laerina and Eveline were both untouched and assured me they had only been in strict confinement, no physical harm had been inflicted. Eveline's thick, dark hair was in a floppy mess around her face, where it was usually neat and clean. I patted her head against my shoulder, her cries slowly suppressed as I held her.

"We have to go, mother. Follow me," I motioned for them both to fall into stride behind me as we made our way out of the castle. We made it to the last set of doors, ready to make our final exit to Praseria's gates, until our path was blocked by a familiar figure.

Nycolas stood in front of the doors, holding his sword at his side, the weight of it propped against the floor.

"Did you think it would be that easy?" Nycolas asked, his eyes gleaming with sinister intent.

I felt my mother become rigid as I smoothly pushed her behind me, distancing myself from her and Laerina, to create whatever barrier I could between them and the man before us.

I drew my sword and observed the distance between Nycolas and I, carefully observing his firmly planted feet, and readying myself to strike at the first sign of motion they may show.

"This is my home. I assumed coming and going as I pleased would always be easy," I replied smugly.

Nycolas huffed. "This kingdom is no longer under your control. I have been given clear instructions to ensure you don't cause any problems, and apprehending your sword seems like a wise place to begin." Nycolas held out his hand, motioning for me to hand over my weapon.

I made my way forward, ready to return his request with a fight, until I heard footsteps behind me and felt a snag at my side. Before I could react, the next sound I heard was Nycolas's breath catch in his throat.

Laerina stood next to me, her face merciless as the dagger that had been securely at my hip was suddenly lodged deeply in Nycolas's neck. My mother let out a scream at the sight, and I immediately shielded her view with my body, turning her into my chest as I prevented her from observing the scene.

Nycolas fell on a knee, his stunned eyes leaking out a few droplets of tears as his body slowly slouched to the ground. No words escaped his lips, only heavy breaths. Laerina held a grave expression, her hands shaking slightly. She didn't say a word, but I could tell her actions were not decided lightly. I'm not certain she had killed anyone before, and I worried for her as she fixated on Nycolas's body that was twitching slightly on the marble floor.

Laerina finally let out a whisper. "That — that was for my husband."

Laerina brushed out her wrinkled green dress, and straightened her shoulders, stepping around Nycolas's body like it was a dirty puddle on the floor, and made her way out the door. My mother and I had no choice but to follow suit, leaving behind Nycolas and the castle, and Killian.

I wanted to turn back around, to go back for Killian, but I knew I had to see the queens to safety. I wouldn't allow his individual sacrifice to be in vain. He asked me to find them, and I needed to deliver on that command.

However right my decision was to continue back, I dreaded that I would have to face Allene. She likely knew by now what we had done, that we had approached our father on our own. The small victory of retrieving the queens would be a short lived celebration when it was noted the person I lacked. I wish I could have approached the group with all of us in tow, and I cringed realizing I had failed in the whole scheme of it.

Immediately upon approaching the group, I spotted Damien and King Seger, their expressions eager. Eveline had not let go of my hand, clinging to me tightly as she came to see the unfamiliar faces.

I spotted Allene, nervously pacing behind the first row of soldiers. Her eyes flickered from the ground and grew wide in remission as she observed her mother. Moving past the soldiers, she ran to Laerina's side, embracing her tightly.

"You're alive!" Allene exclaimed.

Allene held back tears as Laerina hugged her. Laerina's shaking slowly subsided as she held her daughter. Allene's gaze fell to me, and then to my mother.

Allene let go of Laerina and came to softly hug Eveline. "I am so relieved you are both alright. We have been desperately worried about you."

Laerina came back to Allene's side, placing a hand on her shoulder. "We were worried for all of *you*. Is Risa OK?"

Allene gave a curt nod. "She is healthy and well. She is with cousin Lidia at the back of the group."

Laerina exhaled in relief and turned to face Aleron. "Thank you for coming for us," Laerina said quietly.

"I couldn't have done it alone, and you helped just as much with your escape," I added.

Allene raised an eyebrow. "Helped? Did you fall into trouble? What happened?"

Laerina seemed shy at the question. "We ran into Nycolas, but it wasn't a hindrance. Aleron and I handled it quickly," Laerina simply stated, being humble at the part she played in their successful escape, or possibly not wanting to relive the surreal moment.

Eveline shuddered at the mention of it and Allene seemed to pick up on the discomfort we had run into. Allene didn't press for further explanation, understanding Laerina didn't want to go into details.

Allene did her best to mask the anxiety she was feeling as she looked towards me. "What about Killian? Was he with you?" I could see the mixture of confusion and gratitude in her blue eyes as she addressed her question. She tucked her hair to one side, as she casually peered behind my shoulder to see if she could spot movement in the distance — to see if she could spot *him*.

"Killian insisted I leave him in order to search for the Queens," I admitted.

Allene did her best to remain composed at my answer, but my mother couldn't.

"Killian is inside the castle, alone? With your father?" she interrogated.

"I told him I would stay but Killian seemed to have it handled and insisted that I leave to find you," I defended myself again.

Eveline's eyes raced with panic, her hand clasping her throat as she seemed to struggle to breathe in the air. "Your father is not alone in that castle, and Nycolas was not the only soldier there. Your brother is vulnerable being alone. The manipulation of your father terrifies me, Aleron. He is in serious danger," my mother warned.

Allene began to fidget with her ruby ring, her eyes fixated on the castle and her legs inadvertently began moving towards the gates.

"We need to help him before something happens!" she exclaimed.

I caught her wrist, dragging her back. "We cannot act impulsively. The note insisted we go alone. If we make any decisions to send in additional soldiers, we need to all be in agreement. We need to talk to King Se—"

"Your Majesties!" a panting voice interrupted, the messenger winded and in a hurry. The young man from Lokali held a hand to his hip to assist in holding himself up as he huffed out the rest of his message. "We have been sent a declaration from King Vincent, and we need your immediate response."

"Vincent?" Aleron repeated the question a second time.

"I spoke to him myself, your majesty," the messenger said again, his voice even more frantic than before.

My heart sank. The group of us went rigid. No one had the courage to say it outloud, but we all knew what it meant. *If Vincent was alive, and Killian hasn't returned, what happened?*

The possibilities and fears flooded my mind, and the correspondence between the messenger and Aleron was only a numb buzzing in my ears. Risa came to my side, her arm rubbing mine as she tried to return me from my stunned state. I felt cold as my body was shaking in frustration and anxiety.

How could this be happening? How much danger was he in? I had already lost my father and Hassan to Vincent, would I really lose Killian too?

"Hostage?" I caught Aleron clarify, my thoughts now eager to catch all the information I could in hopes it would be useful in locating Killian.

"Yes, your majesty. The Red Crows have taken all the women and children in the survivor camps as hostages. Vincent said we have one hour to surrender all members of the royal families. If we do, the Red Crows will spare their lives." The messenger's darting gaze watched each of us with unease.

"And if we don't?" Risa withered.

"Then we get the battle we came here for," Lidia grimly interrupted, not allowing the young man to give an alternate answer.

Lidia's statement was correct. This is what we had expected. We had planned for a war. We knew the forces we had gathered, and we knew we had a chance at defeating the Red Crows. What we hadn't planned were innocent hostages.

The weight of our decisions were already heavy as we fought to protect our people and restore order in our kingdoms. None of us had thought to leave extra protection with those in the temporary camps. None of us thought the Red Crows would be focused on our citizens if the royal families and their armies were headed in their direction. The Red Crows thought a step ahead and considered our people to be a chink in our armor, and they were accurate in the assumption that it would make it difficult to move forward without a consequence — one way or another.

"I refuse to put our people in harm's way," Laerina interjected.

"I understand your hesitation, cousin, but if we sit back the Red Crows will still have control over your kingdoms, which isn't an option either if you are wanting to let your people return to their homes and live in peace once again," Lidia argued.

Laerina sighed, her shoulders remaining upright and strong despite the weight she felt. "I don't see an easy way to decide this."

"I suggest we take a vote," King Seger proposed. "All the royals present, with soldiers' and civilians' lives on the line, raise your hand if you want to proceed with battle."

King Seger, Queen Lidia, and Aleron raised their hands immediately upon King Seger's invitation. That left Risa, Eveline, and Laerina against it, the three of them looking uncertain as they turned their attention to me. I was the only one left to make a decision.

"What's it going to be, princess?" King Seger prodded, a look of boredom on his face as he awaited my answer.

I looked back at the castle, anxious to see Killian walk through the gates to give us the good news — that maybe somehow his father had been defeated, that he had actually been victorious, but there remained no sign of him.

I took a deep breath, weighing heavily on my choice. I reflected on what my father would have done, and what Killian would do, when suddenly the prompt came to me. *Do what you know is best; don't doubt your discernment.*

Without any hesitation in my voice I gave King Seger my reply. "We fight, and we restore what is ours."

The pain in my shoulder was throbbing, but what was irritating me more was Hassan's smug stare. I don't know how long he had been looking forward to literally stabbing me in the back, but his growing pleasure was sadistic.

"Enjoying seeing me in pain?" I questioned bluntly, masking in place an expression of indifference.

Hassan chuckled as his nostrils delicately flared. "I wouldn't say I am enjoying it, but you were quite the thorn in my side. Seeing you in this manner makes me feel satisfied and hopeful that life can be fair," he drawled.

I raised an eyebrow at his comment, trying to hide my ragged breathing. "Is that why you are doing all of this, fighting alongside the Red Crows? To make things fair?"

Hassan seemed offended by the question. He knelt down, his elbows on his knees, his steely eyes level with mine as he answered me. "I would attempt to explain it to you, but you can't possibly understand. We have lived such different lives. We can't all wait to be handed opportunities in life, your *highness*," Hassan hissed.

I made a weak effort to stand up, leaning lightly against the wall for support. I balanced my sword in my arm that was uninjured. It was my right arm, and I was left-handed. I had trained in dual-handed combat, but fighting with my right was not my strength, especially against a large, unharmed, and perfectly healthy soldier. "That is sound advice. In the spirit of opportunity, I won't hesitate any longer," I crooned.

Hassan's eyes became excited to see my willingness to still challenge him. He posed ready, his sword drawn. Hassan arced his sword toward me, and with a swift movement, I countered his blow, his blade finding its mark with embedding accuracy as it met the stone wall I had been leaning on seconds before.

Hassan stumbled back from the impact and regained his footing. I pressed on for an advantage, focused on keeping my movements fluid despite the pain that coursed through my body. With each strike back and forth, we began to wear each other down. We both drove back at one another with relentless determination.

I waited patiently for a decisive blow, and captured an opportunity when Hassan attempted to strike with his opposite hand. I ignored the pain as I moved my sword to my dominant hand, and delivered a successful strike to Hassan's side.

Hassan fell to his knees, his sword slipping from his

grasp and clanking onto the floor. Hassan grimaced as he held his side tightly, crimson blood slowly staining through his shirt.

I had the advantage now. I could eliminate him as a threat, but staring into his frustrated and defeated eyes, all I could think about was Damien. Our odd and new friendship had only just begun, and I didn't have the heart or strength to end his brother's life, even if he had attempted to take my own.

Between ragged breaths, I left Hassan with my final thoughts, hoping mercy would be enough for him to reconsider his allegiance. "Vengeance is never satiated with blood. Forbearance is the only true way to reformation. For your own sake, I hope you can see that now."

I turned on my heels and left Hassan to fend for himself. I hoped his anger and lust for retribution would subside. I hoped he would see the error of his ways.

Despite the odds, I emerged victorious, and I needed that luck to extend to me one final time, as I took care of my father, once and for all.

No one opposed Allene's deciding vote. After a short time to organize ourselves according to our new plan of action, we were ready to depart. A handful of skilled soldiers were assigned to extract the survivors as we distracted the Red Crows with our other forces. The soldiers marched out in eagerness, ready to answer the message sent to us by meeting the Red Crows in battle.

"Aleron!" my mother shouted out as she ran to meet me before I left with the rest of the soldiers. She didn't attempt to hide the distress she was feeling as she shakily placed a caressing hand against my cheek. "Please be safe. I only just got you back." Eveline's lips quivered as she rushed to deliver her next words. "I am so sorry, my son. I am so sorry you have been put in this position. I feel responsible for being blind in all of this." My mothers head fell to her chest in defeat.

I pulled back my mothers hand and placed it softly in mine, giving her fingers a gentle squeeze. "You cannot blame yourself, mother. You are not accountable for father's actions. I too could have made a greater effort of being aware," I exhaled, the truth of it forming a lump in my throat that I swallowed back down. "All we can do now is try our best to make things right."

Eveline stifled her sobs as she wiped away a free tear with her other hand. "I plan to do just that — to make things right. But in order to do so, I need both you and your brother to return to me." Her eyes were full of devastation, her face crumbling as she looked at me. "Promise you both will come back to me? Promise me you won't leave each other again?" The last sentence caught in my mothers throat. The anguish at the thought of one of her sons not returning to her shattering her heart.

What my mother wasn't aware of, was the guilt and gratitude I had felt for Killian as he aided my escape to find Eveline and Laerina. His willingness of self-sacrifice had shown a side to Killian I knew deep down existed, but I had tried hard to dismiss. For whatever reason, hating Killian had been easier than forgiving him. Forcing him to be the villain in all of this was easier than him being the secret hero — but how wrong and petty I had been in my thinking. Watching the image of my father crumble before me made me see Killian in an entirely new light. I forgave him, and I sought restitution with my brother.

What my mother didn't realize is I had already made up my mind. I wouldn't abandon my brother. If we were to lose, we would lose together — but I had always been fond of happy endings, and that is what I was determined to have in the end.

My heart hadn't stopped racing since they had left. Damien, Marshal, King Seger, and Aleron, along with the largest portion of our makeshift army.

Laerina, Risa, Eveline, and myself had been moved out of sight of the battle. The fighting that started shortly after they left had become a low hum in the distance, the sounds a dull echo consumed by the vast forest that absorbed every shout or cry, shrouding them into a whispered secret from our prying ears.

Lidia stood afar off from us, her armor glinting wildly in the light, while commanding a small group of her soldiers with a fierce elegance as she gave them their next directions. After they gave their queen a respectful nod and bow, the soldiers turned on their heels and headed in the direction of the refugee camps.

Lidia strode over, her eyes filled with sorrow and pity

as she looked upon us, then back in the direction of her departed soldiers.

"You're leaving us, aren't you?" Laerina said solemnly.

Lidia winced, then smiled with her eyes. "I will always fight alongside my soldiers." Lidia placed a comforting hand on Laerina's arm, patting it gently. "I promise I will return when the victory is won."

"*Our* victory, I hope," Laerina added.

Lidia's smile grew as she challenged her cousin. "Laerina, where is your faith? You know I never lose."

Laerina huffed out a labored laugh. "You're right, I should know that better than anyone considering all the times I have been a victim to your various games. You and your ego. . ." Laerina shook her head, chuckling as she and Lidia silently reminisced memories they shared.

Lidia looked at Risa, giving her a comforting smile and then turned to me, her features a mix of emotions. Instinctively my hand shot out to capture Lidia's, tugging her back. "Take me with you," I pleaded.

Lidia's eyes grew sad as she looked between Laerina, Risa and me. "You're not a soldier, Allene," she whispered, as if afraid to offend me with the hurtful truth that I had already known.

"I can't just sit here and helplessly wait for news," I objected.

"Allene, you have done your part. You recruited the help of Lidia, and of King Seger," Risa interjected, her tone drenched in compassion that I wasn't willing to accept.

"It's true, you have been crucial in successful negotiations and alliances. You helped secure forces of strength we wouldn't have had otherwise," Laerina added.

My knuckles turned white as my hands clenched into fists, my anxiety and lack of control causing my emotions to slip. "It isn't enough. There must be more I can do," I said through a frustrated groan.

Lidia took my hand, clasping it firmly. "You have given us a true chance at winning the battle. You have served not only Valteria, but all the other oppressed kingdoms as well. You have done well, Allene."

I wished I had found comfort in Risa, Laerina and Lidia's words, but despite the truth to them, I still felt useless. The love of my life had yet to be seen, since being left alone with his father. With only the knowledge of Vincent being alive to deliver a message, it left me consumed in the possibilities of what happened to Killian — what went wrong? I was desperate for the answer, and I needed to know he was alive.

Deciding to not delay Lidia further, we let her leave, but the air had been heavy since her departure. The time that had passed had felt like hours. The silence from all of us was somber and eerie. We had no ability to distinguish who was winning. We had nothing to distract us or keep us occupied, aside from our intrusive thoughts that painted hundreds of devastating pictures that tormented each of us.

The sun was high in the sky as the evening rolled into place, its warmth softly melting into our skin as the rays beamed on our faces. The cheerful and temperate weather was a stark contrast to the scene just a mile away. The outcome of all of this would determine if the weather was a sign of good fortune or of a cruel twist of fate. In that moment, with no answers to cling to, it only felt like a half-hearted blessing to ease our troubled hearts — it wasn't enough.

I fell on my knees, shut my eyes tightly, and pushed aside all the painful possibilities of our destiny. I clutched my ruby ring and broke the silence of us all as I prayed out loud. I could feel the stares of our small group burning into me as I spoke.

I prayed so fervently and desperately that I knew it would fall on someone's ears — whether that be God's, a higher power, or my father, I didn't care — I only needed a small miracle, and if prayer was all I could do, I would pray and plead until we received the outcome that we all needed.

I heard rustling and could smell Risa's lilac scent as she kneeled beside me, her presence and closeness a comfort I clung to as she joined her hands with mine to offer her own silent prayers. Not soon after, Laerina joined, falling to the opposite side of me, and then Eveline. The four of us formed a friendly circle, hand in hand, as I pleaded my hopes, and emptied my fears to the universe to receive as it would.

In the focus of my laments, I had just barely heard the sound — a bristle in the trees — my reflexes slow as my eyes opened to the scene in front of me.

It all happened too quickly. Just beyond the clearing, I

spotted a grizzly looking soldier, his beast like stature impossible to dismiss as he tried to conceal his imposing frame behind a jutting tree. I watched as he stealthily knocked an arrow into his bow with ease aiming at his targeted recipient: Risa.

My eyes widened in shock, my mind trying to catch up to sight before me, my instincts driving me to scream a word of warning and shove my sister to the ground. But before my reaction could be delivered, I watched as the soldier's eyes bulged, a shock of his own spreading across his features.

Appearing behind the man, Kijana's form came into view, her face covered in black warrior paint, the color matching the inked tattoos on her skull, making her braided blonde hair stand out.

Glowering at the Red Crow soldier, Kijana held him firmly against her body, shifting her position to bear his weight, her eyes wild and fierce as she observed the blood beginning to stain the man's chest where her dagger had met its mark.

My delayed scream finally escaped my throat, and commotion ensued. Laerina and Eveline shot to their feet, their eyes widened in horror as they witnessed the dying man displayed in front of them, and despite the fear and panic threatening to overtake me, I shoved Risa to the ground, diverting her eyes from something she would never be able to unsee.

With a thud and grunt, I watched as Kijana threw the soldier to the side of her like a sack of potatoes. She took a step over him, not even flinching as her foot pressed against his fallen body like he was a rug and not a man, and my throat went dry.

There was a reason Kijana was King Seger's second in command, and why we had called her *blondie bear*, and why even Killian had insinuated he wouldn't be able to fight her — she was built differently than any woman I had met. She was ruthless, and absolutely horrifying.

I shuddered to remember that this was the same frightening woman I had dared throw an entire bucket of water on. My anxiety however was followed by a quick sigh of relief as Kijana stopped in front of us, each of us trembling in shock.

Kijana held out her left hand to me — the only one that didn't have a display of wet blood coating her skin. A silent peace offering it seemed to be as she lifted me off the ground with ease.

"Thank you," I muttered to Kijana in meager appreciation, my breath rapid and fast, my body still processing the close call of it all. If Kijana hadn't been there. . . I shook my head. I didn't even want to consider what the outcome would have been.

Realizing the oddity of our rescue, my eyebrows furrowed in confusion. "Why are you here? How did you know we were being targeted?"

As grateful as I was to have Kijana on our side, I had no knowledge that she would be so close by. The area we were set to wait had been far from the battle, we had not expected to be confronted by anyone, especially as we had sat in silent stillness for hours prior. If Kijana had been waiting in the shadows the entire time, she had done an incredible job remaining unseen.

Kijana's shoulders became tense as she looked to me, her eyes flitting to the trees beyond the clearing. "You are the Princess of Valteria and Praseria, and according to my King, you are my ally. King Seger and Prince Killian wanted to ensure you would be protected. They sent me and some of my men to quietly watch over you while you waited out the battle."

"I'm glad you're on our side, Kijana," I admitted, the truth of my words readily felt by us all.

Kijana cleared her throat, her posture shrinking against the other three women nodding in unison as they balked at our savior. Risa, Laerina and Eveline each mumbled a version of gratitude or thanks to Kijana for her brave, life-saving actions.

Kijana gave us a curt nod as two of her soldiers suddenly appeared, both of them dragging the body away from the scene and deeper into the woods, as if nothing had happened at all.

Kijana sighed and looked at me once more, her eyes masked in embarrassment and suffering. "Princess Allene, I am not one to normally apologize. . ." Kijana stated simply, as if it should be enough to fill in the remaining words she refused to say out loud.

I was still angered at Kijana's actions, the events of that night still fresh and raw. But I couldn't deny that animosity could briefly be lifted, that her actions rectified a small piece of the ill-will I felt towards her. Kijana had saved Risa's life, and in retrospect, saved mine. To many, that would warrant me being in Kijana's debt, but that was something I was not willing to be.

Realizing we were at an impasse with neither of us breaching the long stretch of silence, Risa spoke up.

"Please, promise you won't go far," she pleaded through teary eyes, like a child desperately clinging to her mother.

Kijana held a stern expression as she gave a grave nod. "I assure you this is almost over, your majesty. Then we can all go back home."

KILLIAN

When I arrived at the scene of the battle, it was difficult to distinguish the progress through the chaos. I wasn't certain how long the battle had been raging, but I could see the men were beginning to weary on both sides as the cause for their fighting flickered in their hearts. Without a burning reason for the mayhem, resolve began to falter. King Seger had buoyed the spirits of our side as his war cries echoed through the battlefield. He had proudly placed himself at the front of the fight, his example a motivation for the men to continue.

In the distance, I spotted the flag of the Red Crows waving proudly in the wind. Underneath its traitor insignia, I caught sight of my father, notably comfortable as he reserved himself in the back of the battlefield, letting his soldiers deliver forth the efforts of his plans. *I won't allow him to be a coward any longer.*

"Killian!" A voice carried through the crowd of soldiers. My eyes searched for the source and fell to Aleron's exasperated face as he ran towards me. Gripping my shoulder for some stability of the pain from my earlier injury, I jogged to meet him, grimacing with every step.

"You're injured?" Aleron frantically observed the blood that had stained through my clothing. "Did father do this to you?" Aleron's face dropped at the reasonable accusation.

I dodged the question, my shoulders tense from the pain. "Did you find mother? Is Allene safe? Are we gaining the upper hand? What have I missed?" My thoughts rushed out all at once.

Aleron didn't hesitate to answer, smoothing on a face of indifference as he gave a curt nod. "I found Eveline and Laerina. I ran into a bit of an obstacle on the way out with Nycolas, but we took care of it. Allene is in a safe location with Risa, Laerina, and mother. King Seger and Damien are pushing the armies forward. Marshal, Lidia, and her group of soldiers went to retrieve the hostages back at the refugee camps." Aleron breathed out a shaky, drawn out sigh. "The Red Crows are putting up quite the fight, but they weren't expecting our numbers. Our plan is working," Aleron confirmed, the good news still shrouded in the darkness of what we faced.

I nodded with satisfaction to hear all that I had hoped I would hear, trying to focus on all the positives Aleron had mentioned. "There is only one last thing to do then." I looked in the direction of our father, and Aleron's eyes followed, immediately understanding my implications.

"Killian, you're hurt," Aleron stated, his jaw clenching as he weathered over if it was the right decision to continue voicing his thoughts. His eyes were grim and stern as he chose to proceed. " You don't need to be focused on this right now. You need to get to safety until this is over. Go be with Allene and protect the queens, we can handle this," Aleron reached for my uninjured arm, attempting to drag me away.

I shrugged off his grip, unyielding to his suggestion. "Since when are you soft towards me?" I interrogated.

"Since I thought you wouldn't come back," Aleron snapped. He let out a sigh, his quick reaction of anger subsiding as he attempted to explain. "You didn't see the panic on mother's face like I did when she heard you stayed behind. I can't face her again and tell her that I was the last one to see you alive." Aleron's eyes fell closed. "The guilt would be too much," he said dryly.

"That's the only reason?" I pressed.

Aleron hesitated, his expression turning grim. "Is it enough of an answer that I don't want to lose my brother?"

Something in Aleron's answer sent a shot of intense understanding through me, making me cognizant of every sensation and feeling, the dominating emotion being one of fear. "It is, and I hope you can see why I can't let you fight this battle alone. If something happened to you, I wouldn't be able to forgive myself either," I admitted.

We both fell silent for a moment as we analyzed the stalemate we had been placed in.

I cleared my throat. "It seems we only have one option."

"What is that?" Aleron inquired, his eyes narrowing expectantly in my direction.

I extended out my good hand, waiting for Aleron to take it. "We fight together."

Aleron gave a rare smug smile, accepting the invitation and firmly shaking my hand. "Let's win together too."

————————

We tactfully went around the fighting in pursuit of Vincent, making it to the other side of the field with ease. Guard posts had been sparsely placed, and we only ran into a handful of soldiers as we made our way to the opposite side. It was as if our father had been hoping we would try to engage in a fight, leaving as little resistance to us as possible.

We watched from behind the trees as we observed Vincent being approached by one of his soldiers. The soldier bent down and whispered something in Vincent's ear. Vincent smiled at the exchange and slowly stood up from his chair.

"He knows we are here," Aleron stated and anxiously shifted in place.

"I knew he would be waiting for us. Getting here was too easy," I observed, stating the obvious.

Acting as if he could hear us even hundred of yards

away, Vincent's eyes moved immediately to our direction as he clutched his sword at his side, and made his way to meet his sons — one last time.

"You both took longer than I expected," Vincent shouted as he approached Killian and I, his sword dragging behind him as he slowly made his way up the hill. "Your strategy so far has been far from noteworthy, my sons." Vincent laughed to himself. "I would admit to failing in properly educating and training you both to account for your sloppiness, but that wouldn't be truthful. I taught you both everything you needed to know, but you failed in application and deliverance of the lessons you have been taught." Vincent stopped, and casually leaned against the gold hilt of his sword, a sneer spreading across his face.

"For claiming to be a fighting man, you sure have a lot of words to say," Killian pointed out with irritation.

Vincent offered a vicious smile, his nostrils flaring. "I figured you would appreciate my delay considering your injury," Vincent said, pointing his sword in the direction of Killian's shoulder.

Killian didn't recoil, a mask of solemnity plastered in place as he stared at the stranger in front of us. "How generous of you, I thought your stalling was due to the intimidation of fighting both your sons. I am relieved to hear it's actually from your concern for me," Killian replied sarcastically.

Vincent let out a biting laugh. "If I had been intimidated by the threat of you two, would I have even dared to ignite such a rebellion? You are far from being a worry, you are only a small annoyance to the process. Your self-confidence is humorous," he glowered.

Each word my father spoke felt like a shard of glass grinding into my skin; hearing him was physically painful to endure. I had enough. The conceited, boastful, deceitful, harmful man that my father had become would no longer be tolerated by either of us.

I didn't wait for another response from Killian. As the sun cast its warm glow upon the forest clearing atop the hill, I drew my sword. My heart was heavy with determination.

Vincent strode forward with a malevolent grin curling at his lips. His sword gleamed ominously in the sunlight, a fitting symbol of his tyranny and oppression.

"You two are the greatest disappointments of my reign, but that ends today," he sneered, his voice dripping with contempt as he raised his blade.

Killian and I exchanged a silent nod, our resolve unyielding. We knew this was our last chance to end our father's reign of terror, to reclaim our freedom and honor, and we wouldn't let it slip from our grasp.

With a primal roar, our battle began. The clash of steel echoed through the forest as our swords met in a deadly dance. Despite his injury, Killian fought with a ferocity born of desperation, his every strike fueled by the need to protect his pride and his people.

Vincent was a formidable adversary, his skill matched only by his cruelty. With each blow, he pushed us back, driving us closer to the edge of defeat as our battle had moved deeper into the thick forest.

Vincent swept one of my legs from underneath me, the unexpected maneuver tripping me to the ground. Killian immediately reacted to our fathers short-lived victory. Killian's sword caught the edge of Vincent's arm, and red blood immediately seeped from the flesh wound, following Vincent's cries of frustration and pain.

In a desperate gambit to secure the upperhand, I leaped from the ground and lunged forward, my sword flashing in a blur of silver. Even with the distraction of his injury, Vincent was faster, parrying the blow and seizing me by the throat, his eyes gleaming with triumph.

My father dropped his sword to his side, and whipped out a small dagger from under his sleeve, pressing firmly the cool metal blade against my throat.

"Drop your sword, or it will be the last breath your

brother takes," Vincent threatened to Killian, who had his sword pressing into our fathers back. Our father tightened his grip around my neck, cutting off my airway as I desperately tried to pry off his secure hand. His foreboding glare, the hatred shining in his eyes, making me wither in his grip.

Killian's eyes frantically flashed between Vincent and I as he wrestled with what he was going to do. I was so focused on trying to breathe that I couldn't communicate my wishes to Killian. He finally had the chance to end this, and I hoped he would have the courage to not put me first.

Killian staggered backwards, dropping his sword, along with our opportunity to settle things once and for all.

"Release him," Killian begged, dropping to one knee in submission to our fathers request.

Vincent's grip didn't loosen. I began to see specks of black as I heard him mutter. "You're a pitiful fool." With all the force he could, Vincent threw my body to the ground. I felt myself gasping for air as I heard something crack in my chest. The air I had so desperately needed was still not coming, and all I could focus on was the excruciating pain.

Vincent stepped on my chest, placing all his weight on the ribs I was certain were broken. I screamed out in pain. Vincent's face beamed with victory as he thrusted his hands in the air, the dagger gleaming as he narrowed its intended target to my racing heart.

Killian lunged forward, grappling with our fathers hand, and taking him to the ground. It all happened so suddenly that I was uncertain if either of them had been hurt. Vincent and Killian fell next to me, Killian's body on top of our father. Killian was panting as he stood up, and then I saw it — our fathers blade, thrust into his own stomach. His eyes were bulging and wide as his head fell to the side, his glazed over, unsettling stare set on me.

Vincent's hand hovered over the stab wound, his mouth trembling as he let out a haggard gasp. The color was draining from his face as he looked at Killian, his eyes brimmed with tears.

"I won," Vincent pitifully exclaimed.

"You haven't, it's over, father," I groaned under my breath.

Vincent gave a shuddered breath, his willy stare unsettling to see. "Losing to my own blood. . .is that really losing after all?"

His voice became weaker with each word, but he continued on anyway, eager to get out his final thoughts. "*I* raised you into the men you are. In the end, you mustered up the courage, Killian, to do what had to be done," Vincent whispered, an oddly curved smile appearing on his face as he grimaced in pain. "Maybe you are my son after all."

Killian's expression was hard as stone as he witnessed our father struggle to take his last breaths. A single tear escaped the corner of Killian's eye, leaving a trail down his cheek.

It was finally finished.

————————————

King Seger, Ajax, Marshal, and Damien had found us shortly after. Ajax sent word of King Vincent's defeat, and in response, the Red Crow's immediately began to surrender. Ajax and Marshal set off to organize and confine the large group of prisoners that would each be given fair trials before determining their fate.

King Seger went to assess our soldiers, counting the dead and assisting the injured. Damien stayed with Killian and I, as we made our way to personally give the news of victory to Queen Laerina, Queen Eveline, Risa, and Allene.

The walk to the clearing was far, and the evening was falling upon us, the temperature dropping rapidly. Thankfully, Damien had commandeered two horses to accelerate the travel and cut the distance. Killian insisted on riding on his own, while Damien and I shared a horse, the silence between us all harsh and chilling.

Although I couldn't speak for Killian and Damien, I suspected they were as numb as I was. Damien was still likely processing Hassan's betrayal, with the additional knowledge that he attempted to murder Killian, to which news his face had distorted into clear revulsion. Killian and I were still accepting the death of our father from our own hands, and the kingdoms that were left in shambles for us to piece back together.

This dreaded battle had previously seemed to be our most daunting task, but now considering all that would be required of us to rebuild and repair, the war suddenly seemed miniscule in comparison to all that was ahead.

As we approached the clearing, the sun was starting to set, casting a warm glow against the backdrop of trees ahead. Damien lowered his voice, his demeanor one of reverence. "This journey hasn't been kind to any of us. None of us have made it out unscathed in some way, but I want thank you both for the sacrifices you made along the way to ensure we were victorious today, and for proving me wrong about you both," Damien said, his head turning to now look at Killian, who I barely caught wincing in pain from each jostle of his horse, and I held my tongue that was tempted to point out his condition. Damien continued, unaware of what I had seen flash across Killian's face as he continued his sentiments.

"Thank you for making it out alive. I don't know what I would have done if I had to tell Allene. . ." Damien's eyes grew dark as he looked now to the clearing, shaking his head of the intruding thought. "Thank you," he concluded, leaving the rest of his thoughts unsaid.

Killian nodded his head, offering only a low grunt in reply, as his glossy eyes suddenly lit up for the first time since leaving the scene of the battle. Through the trees, Allene appeared, and her reaction to spotting us in the distance was a full sprint in our direction.

Killian kicked his horse ahead, a sudden burst of

energy surging through him as he was eager to greet her. Damien and I followed behind, and in only a few moments, we were all reunited.

Allene's light blue dress was covered in dirt, her eyes puffy and red, her hair whipping in the wind as her unbridled smile screamed Killian's name with glee. Killian rushed to dismount his horse and the beast barely halted before his feet landed on the ground to capture Allene in his arms. His entire body was covered in blood, grime, and sweat, but Allene didn't even hesitate as she embraced him closely, tears of relief and joy overcoming her.

"You're alive, you're alive, thank the heavens, you are alive." Allene's rushed words repeated over and over again for everyone to hear, while Killian stroked her long hair and hushed her cries, his own face displaying relief as he rested his exhausted chin on top of Allene's head.

Eveline burst into tears at the sight of us as well, rushing to meet me, similarly pulling me in for a hug that seemed I would never escape. Eveline's shaking hands looked me over from head to toe, observing the blood that also coated me, and a sigh of relief when she realized it wasn't my own.

Laerina and Risa joined the rest of us, both of them greeting Damien with overjoyed smiles.

"Is it finished?" Eveline asked, desperation and fear heavy in her voice.

I gave a solemn nod, and Eveline's features flashed with a moment of heartache, and quickly replaced with dejected acceptance. The words didn't have to be said; if the battle was over, it also meant her husband had been killed. She was a widow. Killian and I were without a father. The reality didn't need to be addressed out loud, for it to be felt by us all.

Allene finally pulled away from Killian's embrace, her eyes taking in the full sight of him, her lip quivering as she observed every evidence of the battle he endured. Her eyes widened in horror as she noticed the warm blood that was still pooling at Killian's shoulder.

"You're wounded," Allene declared, while Killian did his best to appear surprised, his eyebrows raised at the observation.

"It's a small flesh wound," he insisted, while Allene's face turned to panic.

"We need to get you to a physician. Ezra. . . he isn't far, he had to help one of Kijana's injured men. Damien, go with Risa, she can show you the way. Bring him here at once." Allene's demands were on the verge of spiraling as her short-lived relief was replaced with earnestness for Killian's well-being.

Killian took a step forward, his arm hanging casually over Allene's shoulder. "Love, I'm fine. I am capable of walking to Ezra myself," Killian insisted.

Allene bit her lip, not allowing herself to argue with him, as she motioned for Damien to assist her in helping Killian walk to the clearing. Damien hesitantly lifted Killian's arm over his shoulder, and the two of them began walking, while Risa ran ahead to bring Ezra back to meet them.

"You'll be fine," Allene muttered, more to herself than to Killian, doing her best to draw comfort from her own words.

As I walked behind them, wincing in pain from my own injuries, although none as grave as Killian's, I noticed the blood seeping from his wound had accelerated, and it seemed Allene and Damien had noticed too.

We all watched the color drain from Killian's face, and his steps began to turn sluggish. Allene and Damien both stopped, Damien shifting Killian's weight onto him as he lowered Killian to the ground.

"Killian!" Allene's desperate scream echoed around us, as her hands shot to his wound, her weight pressing against his shoulder to stop the bleeding. His warm blood began coating her fingers, his eyelids fighting to stay open, the life in them starting to dim as exhaustion overtook him.

Eveline sunk into the ground, her hands caressing Killian's face as she laid his head on her lap.

"My son!" she yelled through rapid sobs.

Allene was shaking, her eyes locked on Killian's pained face.

"Killian! Do not shut your eyes, don't you dare fall asleep! You can't leave me like this. I can't lose you too!" Allene shouted at him, the rest of us stunned into silence at the lack of what we could do.

Allene clenched her eyes closed as she took a deep

breath, her arms trembling from what seemed to be the smell and feel of his blood on her hands.

"Ezra! I see Ezra! He's coming!" Damien shouted, patting Allene's shoulder as he gave his friend a shred of hope.

Allene's head fell into Killian's chest, her cries raw and pleading as she stroked his sweat stricken face.

I felt nauseated, the sight of it felt too much to bear. My own chest felt like it may cave in as I watched the scene before me.

My mother, who had already lost her husband, was now desperately clinging to her eldest son. The woman I once loved, the woman I cared the most for was breaking in a way I never wanted to witness. My brother that I had accepted that I was getting back, that I was finally ready to repair all that had gone wrong between us, was slipping from my life once again.

"Don't leave me, please. Hold on just a bit longer. Just a bit longer," Allene mumbled over and over again.

Watching Allene and Eveline caused something to break inside of me. Tears streamed from my eyes as I watched Ezra step into view, peeling Allene off of Killian's unresponsive body, handing her to Risa who clung to her sister tightly. Ezra's training helped him remain level-headed and composed as he assessed the situation.

If Ezra was worried, he did a skillful job of hiding it, and I envied his ability to master his emotions, then a part of me felt pity for the man realizing how much he would have had to have witnessed to learn to compose himself so.

The sun had finally set, Ezra working tirelessly to seal off Killian's wound with the light of torches and the full moon, Killian still yet to regain consciousness, his breathing labored and heavy.

We all waited in eager anticipation to know if this war really would conclude with our own happy endings.

ALLENE

Two grueling days had passed. My chest felt like it was caving in on my weak heart, beating faster than it was ever intended to for far too long, and I could feel its overuse beginning to have side effects. As weary and dizzy as I felt, my head pounding in a splitting headache that brought illusions to my eyes, my worry for Killian's physical state overrode all my other functions and needs. I could feel myself becoming hollow from within, withering away as time felt frozen, forcing me to rigidly endure this prolonged nightmare.

I hated that I understood Killian's pain of watching me slip into unconsciousness while in Cenan. The roles being reversed was torturous.

I hadn't cared to change out of my ragged clothes, and only did so when Risa and Sonora had literally forced the dress over my head like I was a toddler who couldn't be bothered with such frivolous things.

I couldn't stomach a meal, not when Killian had still not woken up, but Noni had still tried to force feed me, managing to get me to nibble on a few bites of bread or fruit if it didn't require me to put in any effort other than opening my mouth to chew. My focus was needed elsewhere.

My sore eyes focused intently on timing the rise and fall of Killian's chest, ensuring his low breaths were still occurring. When my eyes became too heavy to remain open, I would settle for resting my hand over his heart, letting the subtle movements of life flow through my fingertips, letting the rhythm of it steady my mind.

Ezra had assured me this was a normal reaction to Killian's wound. The fever, although keeping him in a dazed state, was a good sign. It showed his body was still working to fight off any infection, and that although slow, it was healing. And even though I believed every word given Ezra's extensive experience as a physician, it still left me sick to my stomach and impatient.

Being back in Praseria's castle, sitting in Killian's old room for the first time, had been different than I had envisioned. Killian being able to show me his home, to confront the ghosts of his past together in this place, was what I had looked forward to when the war was over.

The circumstance of Killian, fevering and asleep for forty-eight hours, was not something I had accounted for.

Sitting on the plush ivory bed, my head began to fall forward as the stars began to grace the sky. I heard a low moan, and assumed I must be dreaming, or that it had been my own drowsiness that had stirred such a sound. Until I heard it again, and felt a subtle shift in weight on the bed.

My eyes, suddenly alert and aware, flashed to Killian's face, that was wincing. And although it wasn't an expression I wanted to see, it was an expression nonetheless — an expression that meant Killian was alive, and for the first time in two days, I could truly breathe.

Allene's frigid cold hands had been enough to jar me awake, the startling sensation of her frozen fingertips sending a shiver through my body and I could feel myself wince in reply.

I could hear Allene let out a sigh, followed by laughter as I opened my eyes to behold her angelic face.

Allene's soothing presence was only a breath away, her hands cradling my cheeks as her piercing blue eyes devoured every inch of me. Her satin locks fell across my cheekbones, tickling against my chin, the smell of her lavender scent distracting me from the pungent smell of myself.

I felt my nose crinkle in disgust that Allene could even stomach being so near to me when I smelled so putrid, and I realized, if I smelled this bad, that it meant I probably looked even worse.

As tempted as I was to flush in embarrassment at the

ghastly state I was in, Allene's gleaming smile made all my insecurities melt away, as she looked at me like she had never seen a more striking human in her life.

"Killian." Allene's delicate whisper of my name tugged me even further into consciousness, and my surroundings became vibrant in my view.

I knew immediately where I was as soon as I observed the maroon paint that coated the ceiling above me, and the crystal chandelier that hung in the center of my vaulted room. My aching muscles had been cushioned by my ivory, feather bedding, and my body sunk deeper into their comfort as the pain began to radiate to every nerve-ending. I was aware of every scratch and bruise, and I couldn't help the groan that escaped my lips.

I immediately regretted letting the pain win as Allene's relieved face had flitted with concern.

"Where does it hurt?" she inquired, her ice blue eyes eagerly searching for the source.

My throat felt like it had been filled with sand as I rasped out my first word in what felt like days. "Allene," I croaked, a smile twitching on my lips as I watched her posture soften at hearing her name in return.

Allene's eyes brimmed with tears as she grasped my hand, squeezing it tightly. "Yes?" she replied softly.

I did my best to raise an eyebrow, my eyes swallowed up in hers. "We only just made it out of a war, and you're already sneaking into my bedroom?"

Allene sniffled against a chuckle, her shoulders shaking in laughter. "You can jest at a time like this? Do you know how agonizing my life has been the last two days while I waited for you to wake?" Allene's eyes became grave, her voice low and grieved. "Killian, I thought I had lost you, more than once."

I nodded, understanding her suffering more than I would care to admit. I too had watched and waited for her to wake up, and those few hours of waiting had felt like weeks. Every minute was a throbbing memory that clung to the fears laid to rest deep in my subconscious — the dreadful fear of losing what was most dear to me — of losing her.

I squeezed Allene's fingers that had become warm now under my feverish touch.

"I'm sorry I had you worried, love. I won't let it happen again," I promised, and was rewarded with a tender smiling gracing Allene's soft pink lips.

Allene nodded quietly, wiping away her tears. "I need to get Ezra right away, he told me to fetch him as soon as you were awake."

Allene stood up, the side of my bed suddenly vacant and cold, and I instinctively reached out to grab her hand, not wanting to let her go.

"Thank you for staying with me," I said, the words of gratitude a scratchy whisper.

Allene held a tight smile as she leaned down to place a light kiss on my sweat stricken forehead.

"There is no place I would rather be."

The moon cast a chilling glow against the backdrop of the ocean. The crashing waves in the distance played their usual song, as a handful of stars flickered in the sky. I could taste the salt on my tongue as I took a deep breath.

It had been such a long time since I had experienced these sensations. I hadn't imagined I would be standing here four weeks ago. The speed of change was still surreal to process, but every bit of it was real.

In the crucible of conflict of the Red Crows, the inevitable denouement unfolded as the last vestiges of resistance crumbled. Faced with overwhelming opposition and the grim reality of their circumstances, the Red Crows had laid down their arms and surrendered.

Laerina and Eveline had taken it upon themselves to see to every traitor's trial, determining their varying fates.

However, it seemed Eveline and Laerina had aired on the side of mercy, and we all had been grateful for it. The worst of the punishments was mandated labor to repair the damage caused by the resistance. By showcasing minimal punishment, Laerina and Eveline hoped to undo any ill-will that may have lingered in the hearts of the people by handling things in the opposite way of the Red Crows — displaying what a monarchy offered as defenders of their people.

King Seger and cousin Lidia had made their way back to their kingdoms a few days after the battle had ended. The remaining survivors among the kingdoms of Praseria, Valteria, Gelva, Lokali and Gree, found themselves adrift in a sea of uncertainty. With their homes ravaged and futures unknown, they all sought refuge in the relative stability of the kingdom of Praseria, which had the most remaining infrastructure of them all. The Hadways had welcomed everyone eagerly, assuring room for anyone who had a desire to stay. Here, amidst the ruins of their former lives, we all began the arduous task of rebuilding our shattered kingdoms from the ground up.

The Valteria I knew was gone. The prospect of it was harrowing and also liberating. My father's hopes had come to fruition in the end. The unity of everyone's struggles was more bonding than we had ever imagined it to be. United by a shared determination to reclaim what was lost, the survivors of the kingdoms were forging bonds of solidarity that transcended the boundaries of their former allegiances. Together, we toiled ceaselessly, laying the foundations for a brighter tomorrow even as the specter of past conflicts loomed large over our collective consciousness.

Seeds of reconciliation began to take root. Old wounds were healed, and bridges of empathy were built between former foes. It was something I never thought I would witness. In the shared struggle for survival and renewal, enemy kingdoms had become allies, and the disparate threads of fate were woven together into a tapestry of resilience and hope.

As the kingdoms stood, though the road ahead was fraught with challenges and uncertainty, we marched forward undaunted, guided by the flickering flame of hope that burned bright within our hearts.

The kingdom of Praseria, amidst the ruins of the past and the promise of the future, would begin anew.

Snapping me from my thoughts, a single arm wrapped around my waist, pulling me tightly into an embrace. I could feel Killian's steady heartbeat as he held me close, the sensation of it the single most comforting thing.

His shoulder, which was still healing, had been placed into a sling. Although time had helped Killian's injury improve significantly, he was still undergoing treatment. I gently patted his arm, selfishly grateful he had gotten up to come see me.

After what happened with his father, and from nearly losing his own life, Killian had isolated himself from almost everyone to heal and recover. He wasn't ready to talk about the events that had unfolded that had led to our final victory, and I wanted to allow him the time and distance to process how and what he needed to.

I knew the pain of losing a father, but our circumstances couldn't have been more different. The relationship with Killian's father was previously complicated, and I knew he likely carried much regret and remorse for how things ended. Any closure Killian had wanted or needed would likely be unattainable without Vincent here.

Part of me hoped Killian would feel comfortable and ready to talk about it, while another part of me was grateful he hadn't broached the conversation yet. Even after a month, it still felt raw.

I felt some relief that Vincent was no longer a threat — after all, he had poisoned and killed my father, but it also made the situation even more unbearable. Vincent had caused the people I loved the most an unimaginable amount of pain.

I didn't know if Killian came to visit me to discuss the subject of his father, but I hated to admit that I wasn't ready to have the conversation yet. However, if that were his intention for coming here, I would give him that opportunity to talk about it.

"You should be in bed," I stated, not pushing for it or suggesting it, but simply stating the obvious.

Killian placed his lips right next to my ear, his curls brushing the side of my face. His soft touch on my hip sent chills down my spine as his delicate fingers traced patterns against my dress, the lightweight fabric allowing the heat of his touch to penetrate every nerve, the sensation pleasantly distracting me.

"According to who?" Killian whispered in a deep, husky tone.

"Your doctor," I rebutted through the haze his voice had left my thoughts in.

Killian slowly grazed his lips against the shell of my ear now, and placed a soft kiss at the top of my jaw bone. "What if coming here was part of the doctor's orders?"

I turned to look at him, doing my best to gain the courage to dissuade his behavior. "I know your doctor very well — he wouldn't have said such a thing."

"Ezra said that fresh air would be good for me," Killian defended.

"On the balcony in my room?" My eyebrows shot up in a suspicious side glance.

Killian's look of innocence disappeared. "Well, Ezra didn't specify the location, but I can imagine being with you while *also* getting fresh air would increase its efficacy tenfold." Killian pressed another gentle kiss against my forehead, and this time I noticed the exceptional warmth from his lips.

I placed the back of my hand against his forehead, observing that his skin was slightly hot to the touch.

"Killian, you are starting to get a fever again. You need to lay down." I pulled Killian to my bed, softly pushing him to lay against the pillows while I soaked a towel in the water basin on my desk. I carefully sat next to Killian on the bed and dabbed the wet rag against his face, a practice we had become too familiar with the last several weeks. Killian seemed at peace as he settled deeper into the pillows of my bed, letting out a long sigh.

"Can't you be the one to take care of me?" Killian inquired.

"I am hardly qualified," I reminded him while firmly placing the rag on his forehead.

"I don't think a qualified medical professional is what would be best for me right now."

"I would absolutely argue that to be false," I chuckled at his attempts to evade Ezra's expertise.

Killian caught my hand, his eyes fervently searching mine. "But I can prove it. I am feeling significantly better already. Being near you is its own kind of medicine for me," Killian winked, sending a shiver down my spine and turning my stomach into knots.

"Such flattery. . . you're right, you must be feeling better," I teased.

Killian tugged my hand to place it against his chest. My heart raced as he moved onto his side, smiling as he propped himself up on his uninjured arm, his body leaning into mine.

"Allene, my love," Killian taunted in a low, quiet voice, "please let me stay. I promise, it is what's best for me."

In the soft glow of candlelight, I chose to savor the moment of peace. Killian's eyes were alight with admiration as he earnestly looked at me. Despite the exhaustion etched on his features, there was a spark of mischief in his gaze.

A soft blush tinged my cheeks as I reached out to gently caress Killian's uninjured arm. "If that's truly what will make you feel better, then of course you can stay," I conceded, not having it in me to fight or argue after all we had endured. It would be a long while until I was ready for any sort of fight.

Killian's lips curved into a knowing smile, his eyes twinkling with affection. With a tender gentleness, he lowered himself back onto the bed beside me, being mindful of his injured shoulder. My heart swelled as he watched me, my fingers itching to soothe his pain. I ran a hand back and forth on his good arm, and Killian moaned softly at the pleasure of my touch, his eyes falling closed.

"Allene?"

"Hmm?" I hummed.

"I need you to say it again."

"Say what?" I asked perplexed at what he was implying.

Leaning closer, Killian brushed his lips against mine, a feather-light touch that sent shivers down my spine. It was a sweet, lingering kiss, filled with unspoken promises.

"That you are truly mine forever; that you want to be my wife — that you'll be my queen." Killian's brow furrowed as he realized how his words may be received, and he immediately added a clarification. "It's not to boost my confidence, it's simply that I love to hear it. It's surreal to me that I found you, and that you chose me." His gleaming white smile graced his handsome face, and the simple action left me in a jumbled mess as I pondered his words.

I couldn't help but smile, my heart overflowing with love for the man beside me. "I love you, Killian," I whispered, my voice barely above a breath. "I choose you. Always."

A fire seemed to lit up in Killian's eyes as he let out a sigh of relief. "I will never tire of hearing that," Killian replied, his gaze never leaving mine.

"That's good, because you'll be hearing it for a *very* long time," I chuckled. "But before that, we have a few things we need to set in order first."

Killian seemed concerned at any presumption of delay. "What is it?"

"The finite, *obnoxious* details," I teased, shaking my head.

Killian's expression fell flat, stern, and serious. "Nothing involving you is obnoxious, Allene."

I raised up my fingers as I listed out the discussions we still had to have. "Wedding planning, deciding how to best merge our kingdoms, what the dynamic will be with our families, working out continued alliances," I hesitated and held back the additional item that came to my mind. *Addressing a funeral for your father.* I shook my head, redirecting the conversation to cover up the almost spoken thought. "All of that isn't obnoxious to you?"

Killian paused and took a moment to sincerely consider my question before giving his perfect answer. "Not at all; all of that is a means of starting a life together

— a life I am figuring out with you. It sounds like quite the exciting list of conversations to me."

Killian drew in closer once more, placing a final gentle kiss tenderly on my lips. In that moment, amidst the whispers of victory, I knew that together, we could conquer anything that stood in our way.

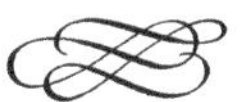

The crisp, still morning air stirred an awareness inside of me that I hadn't wanted to face. The events of yesterday were still at the surface of my thoughts, the mixed feelings spiraling my mind even further into wonder.

It had been six weeks since the battle, and finally, a small memorial service had been held the day prior for my father. With so many having been hurt by his actions, it felt wrong to hold a grand funeral for the man who held a complicated space in all of our hearts.

The hurt from his wrongdoings were still potent and real to all of us, but even still, after much discussion, we knew his death needed to be acknowledged in some way. The memorial service had been limited to myself, Aleron, Eveline, and Allene. It had provided me more closure than I had realized, almost like a part of my life had still been frozen in the past, but with the recognition of Vincent —

in all his good, and his bad — that painful part of my life felt like it could officially come to a close; like peace could be made with the wrongs I had been dealt by his hand.

I suppose that is what made today feel so odd; so different, and light. Like a part of my past had been made free. Without the fear of my father looming over me, I was able to live fully in happiness like I never had before.

My mother's laughter snapped me from my thoughts. I turned to see Eveline's hands full of peonies as she bent down and attempted to pick a zinnia to add to her growing bouquet.

I bent down for her, picking the yellow one, her favorite color. She offered a soft smile as I handed the blossom to her to place in her delicate hands. Aleron approached us from behind, carrying baby's breath to add to the pile.

"Watching you two tending to my garden alongside me brings back memories of when you were young boys," Eveline's eyes lit up as she seemed to be reliving the memory. "Killian used to get so frustrated because Aleron, you would want to plant seeds in his portion of the garden. Killian, you were always so worried Aleron would ruin the hard work you had put into your area. Until the seeds Aleron planted had bloomed, and you saw that he had chosen dahlia's. He had picked your favorite flower, and he had planted them in abundance. He had put your wants first all along, and from then on, you let him share your side of the garden," Eveline sighed, placing her flowers in a nearby bucket.

She reached a hand out to both of us, patting our arms. "I have hoped for this day for a long time," she confessed, looking at each of us fondly. "I didn't know what means would bring us all back together but I had always prayed it would happen eventually," Eveline's voice choked at the end as she tried to restrain her tears.

Aleron and I exchanged a quick glance with one another. The memory she recalled had come back to my mind quickly, and the feelings of the past flooded with it. Aleron and I had been much different back then. It was something I had also hoped for us — to return to that brotherly state. I could feel us getting there — slowly but surely, with time, our friendship could be repaired and reignited once again.

"We are grateful for it too, mother," I assured her.

Eveline gave a short smile and nod until her face became much more serious. "You boys have to promise me something," she let out a shaken breath before continuing. "I have already lost your father, and I thought I had already lost you too, Killian. I have had to bear much heartache. If I experience anymore, I don't know if I will be able to survive it. Promise me you both will stay? And not just stay, but be the brothers you could have been if things hadn't occurred as they did?" Her plea was a mere whisper, her eyes darting between the two of us as she eagerly awaited our answer.

The desperation of her requested promise could be felt by us both. I couldn't speak for Aleron, but I knew I had already been feeling that exact desire anyways.

"We aren't going anywhere mother," I assured her, quieting her worries.

Aleron's face was difficult to interpret; I couldn't tell how he was feeling. With a short pause, he smiled at Eveline. "Yes, we aren't, and you aren't going anywhere either, mother. You put us through quite a lot as well, remember? Now that we are back together, things will be much different now," Aleron replied.

Mother displayed an unbridled grin. "My heart is full. I have one more sincere but difficult question to ask of you both," Eveline ambiguously alluded. Aleron and I both raised our eyebrows in confusion.

"What is it?" I probed.

Eveline seemed uncertain as her gaze roamed over us both, her nose scrunching in discomfort as she began. "Allene. Will you be able to repair your relationship if Allene is here?" Eveline boldly asked.

I immediately felt my blood start to simmer at the mention of my fiance being a barrier to our friendship, but before I could think of my defense, Aleron had already replied.

"Allene and I have already settled things between us. I have always valued her happiness above anything else. Killian is the answer to that, and although I may have originally been apprehensive to accept it, I can honestly say I am happy for you both," Aleron assured me, the scowl I had been expecting replaced by a look of under-standing and empathy that I struggled to comprehend. "It won't be an impact to our friendship, I promise," Aleron concluded, a short nod extended to me as he watched me process his forgiveness. Forgiveness I never thought I would receive. Acceptance I never thought I would see.

"Even with the ongoing discussions of merging our kingdoms? Do you understand what that would mean for you, Aleron?" Eveline pressed, her eyebrows furrowed in worry.

Aleron gave a solemn nod. "That Allene would be the queen of our kingdom? That I would remain as the prince of a kingdom that Killian and Allene would rule over?" The clarification hung heavy in the air. Aleron offered a fast smile. "Yes, I am aware. I truly think it is the best thing for all of us. Our kingdoms would be much stronger together than apart, and with Killian and Allene's marriage, it only makes sense. Besides, I have my own hopes for when that happens," Aleron added.

Mother raised her eyebrows in intrigue at Aleron's statement. "You do? And what is that?"

"A new name for the kingdom," Aleron declared. "With all the change, the merging of the kingdoms, the lands, and the people, we need a new name. We will still be divided if we identify as Praserian's and Valterian's," Aleron explained.

I nodded my head, slowly processing Aleron's suggestion. "That is a considerable thought. What name did you have in mind?" I asked.

Aleron smiled, the name smoothly falling from his lips like he had rehearsed it a hundred times before that moment. "Elveria."

Mother and I nodded together, repeating the name over and over again softly as we processed the sound of it.

"Elveria. So we would all be called. . .?" Mother inquired.

"Elverian's," Aleron clarified.

Mother and I smiled. "Elveria it is," I said.

————

Aleron was right about the effects choosing a new name for the kingdom would have on unifying the people. We had a new sense of purpose; a renewed sense of identity.

So much had been solidified in just a few short weeks. All the refugees had been placed into stable living conditions, and their integration back to their daily roles and professions had gotten the economy of the kingdom moving again. This was a feat the queens had taken upon themselves, acting as diplomats together. With the announcement of my marriage to Allene, and the passing of both the King's, Eveline and Laerina saw themselves in a new position in court. They wanted to be the voice of people, the liaison for royalty, with the hopes of avoiding the frustration the people had previously felt that had caused so many to side with the Red Crow's. They would ensure every side was heard and represented for our new kingdom.

Risa and Marshal were engaged, their wedding set to take place during the autumn season. The two of them had been nearly inseparable since the announcement.

Damien had been chosen as the leader of the Elverian

armies. With his new position and title, his family's name had been restored after the adverse effects of Hassan's involvement with the Red Crows. His father, mother, and sister were devastated over the news of Hassan, but they had focused on the positives, clinging to the hope of restoring their family. Damien visited Hassan regularly in his confinement at home, still trying to reach the brother he once knew. Hassan had fallen into a grave depression since the end of the war, his actions causing severe remorse and regret, but Freria was seeing a change in Hassan, slowly, day by day, back to who he once was before the Red Crow's had possessed his heart.

Trae had been recruited by Lidia to go to Veruje to assist her battle horses with training, and he gladly obliged the request, hoping to form another kind of relationship with Lidia in the process, or at least gather a new experience by being in Veruje, or so he claimed.

King Seger had returned to his kingdom, and had promised to come visit Elveria before winter. Kijana hadn't said anything prior to departing, keeping a safe distance at the back of the group as King Seger said his last goodbyes before leaving.

Laerina and Ezra had buried any animosity between them regarding Faris and everything that happened in the past. Allene had been overjoyed seeing Ezra become so well integrated into the family. A piece of her heart had been returned to her by having him in it.

Aleron had been assigned as the new leader of outside trade and diplomacy. The position required him to travel outside of the kingdom, but he had been thriving in developing the relationships with the other kingdoms and maintaining peaceful relations and alliances between us all. It was a role he fulfilled well, and the love he had for the travel aspect had surprised him. It made me overjoyed to see him happy in the capacity he chose.

Allene and I had set the date for our wedding. August 8th. Eight, the number of infinity. It made me happy to realize that it would finally be coming to fruition.

I knew even with all the victories and progress that the path ahead was fraught with challenges, but also filled with hope. Together with Allene by my side, we would rebuild our kingdoms and forge a future where love would conquer the darkness that had once threatened to consume us all.

llene's finger traced haphazard designs in the sand, quietly humming as her hand would erase each creation and begin a new one. I sat with my legs folded into my chest, my eyes set on the jutting rocks in the distance as Killian and Damien climbed to the top to jump off.

Memories came flooding back into my mind as quickly as the tide came in. It was surreal to think that a little over a year ago, Allene and I were at this exact beach, in a much different circumstance. Neither of us knew the relationship we would develop after our fate of meeting. Those same rocks resulted in a much different outcome when it was me cliff jumping.

"It's as peaceful as it always was," Allene whispered to herself. "I missed the taste of the salt and the dewiness the air leaves on my skin. There is nothing else like it."

I nodded in agreement. "I wondered if I would ever

enjoy this view again. I never imagined I would, especially with you and Killian here," I admitted my honest thoughts.

Allene stopped tracing her hands in the sand, her eyes shying away from mine. "I am sorry if this is odd for you," she apologized.

"It was me that asked to come along with you guys, remember? I wouldn't have asked if it made me uncomfortable," I pointed out.

Allene was hesitant but eventually nodded. "I am relieved you feel that way."

"Visiting this beach before, it was always a lonely experience. I can truly say that I am glad I am with all of you right now." The words came out light, easy, like the memories between us were no longer something to avoid, or to fear. That a comfortable peace could be exchanged between us once again.

In the distance we could hear Damien shriek as Killian pushed him off the rocks. We watched as Killian confidently followed suit, his entrance into the water much more graceful than Damien's. Allene and I laughed as we heard Damien's excited yells from the rush of the adrenaline.

"One day when I get enough courage, I will try it too," Allene declared, a twinkle of determination glimmering in her blue eyes.

"We've got lots of time, and besides, you are no longer a visitor here. This is your home," I reminded her.

"Our home," Allene clarified.

I nodded in agreement. I knew one day this would be our home. Although I didn't envision it to happen in this way, as the brother-in-law and not the husband, it had settled with feeling right. Elveria was the answer we all didn't realize we needed. Elveria was home.

My dearest friends circled about me, bustling to add all the finishing touches to my hair, face, and dress. Risa straightened out my veil, Noni added extra blush to my cheeks, while Sonora placed pearls in my hair. They each stepped away when their role was finished, squealing with excitement and pleasure to see the results of their labor.

"You can't wait a minute more, come, come! You have to see for yourself!" Risa exclaimed, pulling me to the large mirror by the balcony. Risa hung on my shoulder as she watched me take it all in.

Sonora had elegantly crafted my hair into a masterpiece of overlapping braids, layering over one another to create one large braid that trailed down my right side. The pearls had been perfectly placed into each weaved section.

Risa had put together the perfect color palette of varying shades of plum and pink hues to dot my eyelids, cheeks and lips, giving my skin a smooth appearance and making my eyes an even brighter shade of blue.

Noni had dedicated all her time the last three weeks to crafting a one-of-a-kind wedding dress. The floral lace that lay over the cream fabric bundled into a bustle at my side, leaving the lace to drape down my body in beautiful waves. Along the middle of my stomach was a pristine satin pearl colored bow that was tied perfectly in the center. The sleeves for the dress were capped short, considering the heat and humidity that August brought.

With finishing touches, Sonora clipped some pearl and gold drop earrings to my ears, their length hitting below my jawline. Looking at everything all together, I could say it was the only time I had felt like a work of art.

"I can't thank you all enough for all the work, time, and thought you have put into all of this. Every detail has exceeded my expectations," I told them, sincerely taken aback by the woman staring at me in the mirror.

They all beamed at my satisfaction and I couldn't help but hug each of them.

"Don't you dare ruin your hair!" Sonora shouted at my embrace.

"Or wrinkle your dress!" Noni huffed.

I laughed as I gave Risa a hug, the only one of them to not offer a form of protest. Risa hugged me back tightly.

"I am so happy for you, Allene. You deserve this day more than anyone I know. I truly hope you will have a life of joy with Killian by your side." Risa's sentiments meant the world to me, but I couldn't linger on them long after hearing a familiar dramatic sigh from the corner of the room.

Damien had patiently waited for us to be finished, clearing his throat for the attention of his presence. He was ready to pass along a bouquet of flowers for me to hold.

"Oh, yes! We almost forgot about the bouquet!" Noni said, pushing Damien over to me. Damien seemed emotional as he gripped my hand, his joy for me sincere and palpable.

"I knew you'd grow up one day, I just didn't think it would be so soon," Damien said softly.

I shoved his arm with my bouquet. "I don't know how that is possible, I was always taller than you, remember?"

"No — no you weren't," Damien wagged a finger of disapproval.

"It's alright, you can claim that you are the taller one now, and the more grown up of us if you need to," I winked at him.

Damien offered a tender smile. "I won't be far behind you with growing up. You watch, next year, I will have found someone for me too," Damien promised.

I smiled, hoping my dear friend was right. Seeing Damien marry and start a family would be a surreal moment to witness. I know how deeply he hoped for it now, and I hoped that for him too.

The door to the room creaked open as Laerina, Eveline, and Ezra entered my room, smiles spread widely across their faces.

"Allene, you are breathtaking," Laerina immediately said, her eyes swelling with tears.

Eveline nodded. "I can't imagine a more beautiful bride, and a more fitting woman to be the new queen."

Laerina and Eveline looked at each other, exchanging a small smile. Laerina took something from behind her back, handling it delicately as she removed the fine, white cloth that had wrapped the item, and held it for me to see. It was a tiara, lined with small rubies, pearls, and diamonds, with a large ruby placed in the very center.

"This was meant to be given to you by your father. It was his gift to you, to complete your ruby ring." Laerina let out a shaky breath as she stared at the heirloom in her hands. "The ring he gave you was to remind you of your potential and your destiny. The tiara was meant to be given to you when you blossomed into the role that you were meant for. I can say he would have beamed with pride today to give this to you."

My fingers lightly followed the ridges of the tiara, feeling each groove and piece of it, taking in every detail my father had crafted just for me. "It is beautiful," I whispered to myself. Laerina took a step forward and smoothly placed the tiara on my head, firmly pressing it down to secure it into place.

Ezra didn't even attempt to hold back his tears as he placed his soft hand against my cheek. "It suits you perfectly." He choked back another flow of tears and lightly coughed, suppressing his emotions as best he could. "This is a day I always prayed I would see and get to be a part of. Thank you for making this old man's wishes come true."

I gave Ezra a tight embrace, wanting to cling to this moment forever. Pulling back, I took in each of the friendly faces that surrounded me in the room. Faces I hadn't imagined being here, friendships I only dreamed of, a wedding I hadn't thought would take place. My body hummed with anticipation and excitement, and my heart swelled with love and appreciation for my guardian angel — my father — orchestrating a life for me that was greater than I could have ever imagined.

KILLIAN

*E*ven if I had tried, I couldn't have envisioned a more perfect day. Being arm in arm with Allene as we walked through the crowd of our people was the greatest moment of my life.

Allene clung to my arm as she steadied herself with each step, gracefully dragging the long train of her dress behind her in pure magnificence as we made our way to the altar. I watched her in awe at the display of her grace as we approached Ezra, who had gladly taken the role of sealing our marriage.

Allene and I bent down on our knees at the altar, taking one another's hands as we looked at each other. I recognized the faces of our family and friends, I appreciated the presence of our people, but Allene had my sole attention. I couldn't take my eyes away from her glowing face.

Ezra had given the required pleasantries, and gave his

additional well wishes to us. Allene and I looked at each other eagerly, anxious to come to the part of the ceremony we had been longing for over the last few weeks.

Ezra smiled, taking our joint hands and lifting them for everyone to see.

"Let it be written and sealed that upon this day, the 8th day of August in the first year of the Elverain calendar, history is made as Killian Hadway and Allene Amena are declared husband and wife, helpmeets and companions, eternal partners, with all the blessings of the heavens invoked upon them to fulfill their duties as King and Queen of Elveria. May the heavens and your ancestors protect and magnify your newly appointed roles and callings. All arise! And honor your new King and Queen! King and Queen Hadway of Elveria!"

Cheers erupted from the crowd as I pulled Allene to stand by my side, each of us taking in what this moment meant.

Allene leaned in close to my ear, her voice distinct from the roars around me.

"I love you, Killian." The words were simple, but the meaning was everything.

I pulled Allene in close, and placed a gentle kiss on her lips. The noises of the crowd grew in reaction, but there was only one reaction I was focused on.

Allene's eyes had closed and a smile grew on her beautiful, breathtaking face. The face of the woman I was lucky enough to call mine, forever.

"I love you, Allene," I whispered back, reiterating the hold she would always have on my heart.

We walked back down the aisle together, hand in hand. Our future had been sealed, and together it would be made.

THE END

ACKNOWLEDGMENTS

I want to thank my sister once again and her contributions in helping formulate my ideas. I want to thank my husband and my family members that have been there every step of the way, sharing in my excitement as each book progressed. I want to thank my beta-readers and all the readers that took a chance on my first book and have stuck with me to the end. It means everything to me to know others have read the world I've created — that it could be more than just for me. Thank you for making that dream a reality.

Kaydrie grew up in Mapleton, Utah and currently lives in Utah with her husband and two little boys. She loves baking, traveling, all things Disney, and spending time with family and friends. She has had a love for literature since she was a little girl. Some of her fondest memories are bonding over books with her father and mother. She has been writing since she was 12 years old. Her books are creations of what she wanted to read as a teenager. These books that were once exclusively hers to enjoy are now available for the teen and young adults across the nation.